ATRAVESAR
To Get Across

C.E. Ostra

Amapolaris Press

Lyrics on page 60-61 adapted from "The Cowboy's Lament," pp. 41-44,
Songs of the Cowboys by N. Howard Thorpe © 1921. Public domain.

Lyrics on pages 186 adapted from "Wildwood Flower (I'll Twine 'Mid
the Ringlets)," by Maud Irving and Joseph Philbrick Webster, 1860.
Public domain.

All other lyrics were written by the author.

This is a work of fiction. Names, characters, places and incidents either
are products of the author's imagination or are used fictitiously. Any
resemblance to actual events or locales or persons, living or dead, is
entirely coincidental.

ISBN 978-0-9895477-0-3

Typeset by Amapolaris Press
Cover design by J.K. McGann

Printed in the United States of America

The Savior who wants to turn men into angels is as much a hater of human nature as the totalitarian despot who wants to turn them into puppets.

Eric Hoffer, *Reflections on the Human Condition*

I don't do drugs. I am drugs.

Salvador Dalí

1

Celan, cross-legged under the crackling blue sky, tugs the pail of water closer and readies herself for the transfiguration. Her nut-brown cap of hair shines in the sun as she positions her hands on the rough wood and breathes deeply, as she has been taught, letting prana flow. A shiver runs down her spine as a wave of shimmering stars shoots across the surface and a ripple of sound fills her mind before slackening back into silence. It's safe now, to drink.

She dips a small hand in and cups it, raising it to her lips and savoring the coolness in her throat like a river cutting through long-parched ground. Transing water is a child's job and she relishes it. It's something to do, a way to feel useful, and good practice on days when she isn't at 'scuela.

Scrambling up, she grabs the handle of the pail with a well-bronzed hand, dusty skirts brushing her slim calves. Shoulders squared she hefts the ungainly load and steps carefully up the rutted dirt track toward a squat adobe. Inside, her mother lies in the narrow bed as she has done for months; her hair is dead white and she seldom speaks.

'Those who walk out into the snow can come back with great knowledge,' the elders say, 'but mostly, they don't come back.'

Celan doesn't think her mother is coming back. Still, she loves her.

Crossing the thick threshold of the house her arms prickle with a sudden chill. The door has been open all day with her comings and goings, checking on Mair and then slipping out into the yard to play strange solitary games – making up stories and singing bits of songs. Tia Jillyanne left some lunch and will return in the evening with dinner if Celan's sister hasn't shown up. Cyrinda is seventeen and often takes off for parts unknown. When she's here, though, she makes her presence known. There's no ignoring Cyrinda.

Celan sloshes the bucket into the makeshift kitchen and, with a grunt, heaves it up onto an ancient table. She dips in a cup and fills it, then gingerly carries it into the her mother's bedroom. It is dark and cool, a safe little cave, and she tiptoes over to the bed where Mair's hair spreads like a white sheet over the rough brown pillow. The eyes on her smooth, youthful face are closed and her thin chest rises and falls rhythmically but otherwise she is utterly still. Only a fly buzzes fitfully in a corner.

Balancing the cup on top of a rickety crate, Celan slips off a sandal and stealthily advances on the annoyance. Thwack! The fly zips off unharmed to bumble against the ceiling for a few confused moments before alighting on a corner of the crate. Holding her breath, she inches forward, all concentration on the tiny insect. A little closer and...*Got him!* The dead fly drops to the floor as the cup teeters and she lunges for it, managing to keep it upright but splashing some water onto a small, silvery vial resting on the splintered wood. From the bed, her mother makes a weak noise.

Celan stands frozen for an infinite moment before Mair resumes her shallow breathing. *Children don't touch transfers!* She knows this, but she doesn't want to leave it sitting there in a puddle. So, steeling herself, she reaches for it with trembling fingers.

Nothing happens; no sudden jolt on contact. The transfer sits neatly in the palm of her hand like any other thing and she wipes it off on the hem of her skirt, taking care not to dirty it. The elders can be so silly sometimes. It's not like she'd ever open it. She's just a kid; she can trans well enough without transferon. Dabbing at the last of the spill, she replaces the vial on the crate. Then she taps Mair's shoulder.

"Mom," she says. "Are you thirsty?"

No answer.

"Mom." She grasps more firmly and shakes.

Mair's eyes fly open, revealing deep brown pools like shady autumn springs. It takes a few moments for her to fully focus, when she does she turns her head minutely toward Celan.

"Are you thirsty?" Celan repeats.

"Yes," her mother murmurs.

"Do you want to sit up?"

"Por favor."

Celan leans in to assist. "You have to push yourself. Use your hands, there you go."

Once she is propped up and resting against the wall, Celan fluffs the pillow behind her mother's back and picks up the cup.

"Can you hold it?"

Her mother nods and reaches for it, raising it shakily to her lips. Water is about the only thing she will take anymore and she drinks greedily. When she has drained the cup she exhales.

"This is good. Very clean. You transed it, Celan?"

"Uh-huh."

"Bueno." Mair sighs and closes her eyes again. "Who knew of all my daughters you'd have the best touch?" She says this with obvious pride and Celan beams.

"You want me to trans *you*?" she says eagerly. "I've been practicing. Jada said I was the best in her class last week!"

But her mother's mouth turns down then and Celan

wonders if she's thinking of Nola, her eldest sister, who barely ever learned to trans at all. Nola passed on six months ago; she and her man Dex were racing rollers with a bunch of their friends out on the mesa, Dex was driving, and somehow they flipped over. Neither one survived.

Some said Dex did it on purpose. Not of his own free will but because the techs put their bots in his brain. Celan doesn't know what to think. She only met Dex once. He was slim and pale, with a shy smile peeking out from under the brim of a big hat. He didn't seem crazy, bots or no. He'd barely said a word.

Nola first ran off seven years ago, when Celan was almost three, to go live on Transway where she'd been born and raised an expro – one of those who subsisted on the old strip outside the city. 'Tramway,' they called it in the old world. 'Expropriada,' they called her.

Nola hated it here in the ranchos. The other kids had been at Pranascuela together for years and could do all kinds of things she couldn't. They thought she was stupid; she thought they were 'sheltered little pricks.'

Celan knows all this because Cyrinda has told her. She barely remembers her eldest sister from before she left, only the Nola that came to visit with bright white hair and an angry stare. Mair had cried, seeing her then, but Nola didn't care. All she cared about was the techs and how they weren't fair.

'They barely even think we're human!' she'd fume.

The elders were no better, in her opinion. 'They left the expros to die!'

All of this seemed a bit much to Celan, who thought the elders were nice (for the most part) and who'd never even met a tech. Sometimes a few kids would climb all the way up to the peak and look over into Albakirk, the tech city. Celan has done this. The hunched dun buildings and shining pyramids were so neatly arranged, so clean and exact. She wondered what people did in there all day, and why they were so scared to come out. Sure, a lot of things got poisoned, but that was a long time ago. It was better now. And besides, anything you transed was perfectly safe.

A sudden cough from Mair shakes her out of her thoughts. "Más?" she asks.

"Please," her mother says. So she returns to the kitchen and dips the cup in again.

CYRINDA LOVES TO SING. IT'S the best thing in the world, as far as she's concerned. She hears music, she feels music, and a power comes through her, an electroshock, and she opens her mouth and she sings. It's the best thing she's ever felt (with one or two exceptions).

Down the dusty paths she dances, head awhirl with words and music, barely aware of the others tripping along behind her. The last ten years seem to have melted into forever. When she first came here from Transway she thought she would go crazy from boredom. There was always something happening there – life and music and constant surprises. Her dad had the best wayvern on the strip.

Everyone came to Arlo's to eat and drink and to hear him sing and tell stories. He said she had a great voice, even as a tiny girl, and would let her get up and sing with him while Mair played the piano. People clapped and cheered and she loved every minute of it. When he passed it seemed all the joy of life went with him.

Her mother felt that way too, Cyrinda knew. Mair tried to pretend for a while, but she was sad all the time, and lonely. The worst was when she started acting funny and crying and saying she never should have left the ranchos. Did that mean she wished she'd never met Arlo? Thinking that made Cyrinda feel like her mother might wish she'd never had her and Nola either.

Things got even worse when Mair suddenly announced that they all were going to go live at Rancho Pescados. She and Nola had cried and begged to stay on Transway, but to no avail. Mair paid a visit to her cousin Jillyanne and they talked in hushed whispers until Jillyanne agreed to be their patron, as no expro was allowed to return permanently to the ranchos without one. Tia Jillyanne helped them, found a place for them and, as it turned out, for their new little sister.

Cyrinda didn't mind that part (she loved babies) but there was nothing else here except crumbling old houses and constant chores – endless hours spent transing dirt and water, pulling weeds, and sitting around with a bunch of kids learning how to breathe. It was stupid. She didn't blame Nola for leaving at all; she just wished she would have taken her too.

Nola stayed away for a good long time, but a trickle of gossip worked its way between Transway and the ranchos so Cyrinda had an idea of what her older sister was getting up to – at Maddy's now, dancing for the crowds, lots of techs coming out to watch. And when she finally did come to visit Cyrinda could hardly breathe from envy. Nola looked so gorgeous with that silver-white hair. And those clothes! Antique leather jacket, retooled and studded with beads of polished quartz and a clingy blue dress of the soft bamboo jersey the techs made. She had looked down at her own patched-up skirts and sighed.

Nola promised to bring her some nice things next time, and she had. Her sister brought lots of little trinkets after that – earrings, a bracelet, and a beautiful soft scarf in a shimmery blue-green color. 'I thought it would match your eyes,' Nola said. And it did.

A few years later there was a different kind of present: A small, silvery vial filled with freedom. 'How long will they make *you* wait?' Nola'd said, scowling. 'Just because you started 'scuela late? That was mom's fault. You're as good as any of those little shits and you should get to start at fifteen like everybody else. Don't tell anyone though or they'll take it away!' Cyrinda swore she wouldn't.

She'd felt proud and very grown up when she took transferon for the first time. Finally a real dose of it, like the other kids her age. They could snicker all they wanted; she was way ahead of them now. They all had to leave their transfers at 'scuela at the end of the day. She could take some whenever she pleased. And it was amazing. Transferon made the world so beautiful she wanted to throw her arms around it and never let go.

She spent a lot of time with Nola and Dex after that. Whenever they came to visit they'd hang out at the bonfires where everyone played music and danced. Maybe people had teased Nola when she was younger, but now they crowded around eagerly to hear tales of techs and Transway.

One night, Cyrinda saw a boy so beautiful that her heart stopped just looking at him. He rang joy from a beaten guitar; then he smiled at her and she couldn't look away. Taegh didn't treat her like an expro or make fun of her for being stuck in a class with younger kids. He listened to her talk about her childhood and how happy she'd been. She even told him about the transfer. He said he'd never tell. He understood secrets.

Today, she is high in the mountains with him and two friends from his 'scuela class, chores postponed or abandoned for the afternoon. Afterschool idylls are tolerated at their age due to the lingering effects of transferon when their lessons are over. The adults grin and look the other way, remembering when it was new, before they got used to it. Sun-struck, Cyrinda careens along the trail singing a feral, joyful song.

Seen the light of lunacy
Get away, away from me
They all thought that she had drowned
Didn't see her diving down

The sunlight splinters into a million facets; particles and waves drifting through the clear bright air and mixing with the sound of the song and the dense green shade of the trees. Taegh says songs are like spells being cast and so she casts her songs out into the living air and draws back meaning and form like little fish.

Sometimes our monsters protect us
Force the dangerous ones to reject us
Ain't got the dots to connect us
So they all fall down

She screams this last as the path opens out into a meadow, all waving grass and dotted wild flowers. Cyrinda bursts into the clearing, spinning around with yellow hair flying and eyes shining like old bottle glass in the sun. Finally, she tumbles to the ground and tips her head back, basking in the beauty around her. The others follow suit, stretching out and watching great white puffs of clouds roll by.

"Doesn't seem like it'll storm," says Saddler, squinting watery grey eyes.

"Nah," Lulin agrees, shaking out her silky black hair, intent on picking the choicest blooms to twist into a wreath.

"Used to be it stormed all the time," he continues. "Came out of nowhere, my abuelita says. Crazy wind, rain, lightning storms. Used to blast stuff to ashes." Reclining against an old tree stump, he swipes lazily at the brown frizz of hair crowding his vision.

"It's settling down now," says Taegh. "Can't stay like that forever. Too más energy to be loca all the time."

"Not for Rin," says Lulin. "I swear, you'd think she had as much trans as we did today."

Cyrinda laughs, snub nose crinkling under a smattering of freckles as she shoots Taegh a furtive glance. He grins, violet-blue eyes alight.

"Rin's loca all the time."

"We know," drawls Lulin, and they all laugh at that.

"You think the techs'll start coming out more now?" says Saddler. "Coming over here?"

"They've been coming to Transway for years," Cyrinda says. "They used to come all the time to watch us. To see the shows. They'd trade for all kinds of things we made. Probably take them home and show them off – 'Mira! Transer art, how quaint!'" Her tone is pure acid. "But they're too scared to come over here. Scared of the elders. They think they're brujas or something."

"Idiots," mutters Lulin.

Cyrinda shakes her head definitively. "They'd never."

"Maybe they're curious," says Saddler, crooking an arm behind his head with a smirk. "Maybe they think we're over here all aviados and chingada every day." He waggles his eyebrows lasciviously. "Maybe they want a piece."

"Yeah," says Lulin, "if all they ever see are people like…" She trails off, trying for tact and failing.

Cyrinda bolts upright, staring daggers. "You mean like *Nola*? She did what she had to do."

"Yeah, dance around and take off her clothes for the techs." Lulin's lip curls in disdain.

"So?"

"So she didn't *have* to do *anything* with them. She could have stayed here."

"And be treated like shit her whole life? You don't know what it was like! She was twelve when we came here and the elders said it'd be years and years before she would get a transfer. She was so far behind she would've been sitting there with four-year-olds until she was eighteen!"

Unconsciously she slips a hand into her pocket, fingertips brushing the illicit vial. "But she got one anyway. She got it and got out!"

"Well she sure didn't get it at 'scuela." Lulin sniffs. "Bet she stole it."

Cyrinda's hand jerks out of her pocket like there's a hot coal inside. It clenches into a fist.

"Expros have as much right to transfers as anyone."

She glowers fiercely until Lulin's plump form cowers and ultimately retracts.

"Rin, you know we love you," she says, twining stems together with studied nonchalance. "And it's totally unfair you don't have a transfer yet." She plucks a white columbine and adds it to her circle. "You're a brilliant singer. If you'd been here all your life you'd be first in our class, chanting away with the eldest elders."

Cyrinda's glare cracks and she sighs elaborately, flopping down in the grass and throwing her arms around Taegh. "It's not my fault where I was born," she says, voice muffled against his chest.

He slides a slow arm around her and she relaxes a fraction.

"None of it's any of our faults," he says. "It's the elders' fault. They didn't know what to do after Jane Lees died. Their council was a joke; they let that storm destroy acres of food. Then they said we could live on air if we tried hard enough. Pure prana from the Sun! I mean, maybe *they* could, sitting around meditating all day, but not the people who had to work out in the fields. They had to eat. Their kids had to eat."

Lulin grimaces. "Taegh, you really shouldn't say things like – "

"What? Like the truth?" He sits up, shaking fuschia

hair free from grass bits. "It was total bullshit. Everyone knows they were wrong, even if *they* won't admit it. All those Precepts hanging on the wall and they can't even follow them. People begged them to go, ask the techs for help, but they wouldn't. So the expros did. Even if it meant not coming back.

"You're total survivor stock, Rin. Don't ever think you're less than anyone because your grandparents wouldn't go hungry to satisfy some white-robed puritans." He looks pointedly at Lulin and Saddler, who actively avoid his gaze.

Offhand, he adds, "I'd like to go have a look at Transway myself someday. Play our songs at a wayvern. Bet they'd love us."

Cyrinda smiles and he gives her a wink.

"Yeah, that'd sure be a sight alright," Saddler says. He clears his throat. "My tio says we should shut Transway down. Move everyone back over here, no patrons required. There hasn't been another storm that bad in fifty years. There's no reason for people to still be living off the techs like that. Not learning proper transfiguration."

Cyrinda starts to protest. He holds up a hand to silence her.

"Nothing against you, Cyrinda, or your sister. But our people had been living outside for a century – dealing with all kinds of crazy weather and old world crap – before that big storm hit. The elders got caught off guard. It happens. But we'd already proved we could live life

14

our way. That we could live outside, that transferon worked. That's the reason we split from the techs in the first place; they wouldn't have anything to do with it. Rather stay inside and put bots in their heads. They're ridiculous. It's bad enough that some of us went begging to them when things got tough, and yeah, it showed a lack of faith. But enough already! Just bring everyone back over here and be done with it."

He thumps a fist on the ground like it's a final resolution. Lulin nods vigorously in agreement.

Cyrinda gets to her feet, bright hair rippling in the breeze like a banner, and pins them with a haughty stare. "Your concern is appreciated," she says, sardonic. "But a lot of people don't want to come back. They figure the elders are as bad as the techs. And Transway is their home." Then softer, barely audible. "It was *my* home."

"All the more reason to go," says Taegh, jumping up and looping a lanky arm around her shoulders. "I'm bored with this place. Let's do something interesting for a change."

"Really, Taegh?" Lulin says. "And how are you going to live there? Are they going to feed you every day just to hear your songs?"

"They *are* very good songs," Saddler points out.

"True," she says, "but music should be sacred. Not some dumb entertainment for people who don't really understand it."

Taegh waves this off. "Spoken like a true white robe."

"Yeah? Isn't one of those 'white robes' your abuelo? You're not an expro Taegh; no matter how much you try to dye your hair like Dex's."

Taegh looks stung.

Lulin continues briskly, "Besides, you have to wait until you're eighteen for your transfer to be released. And you could be chosen as an elegido. Bet you wouldn't want to leave then!"

"We can't go now anyway," Cyrinda cuts in. "Not with mom like how she is. I can't do the same thing Nola did."

"Not now," Taegh says, pulling her close. "But someday."

Cyrinda says nothing, but her face lights up like the sky on Liberation Day.

THE SUN IS SLANTING TOWARD the western horizon, smudging the sky with fiery fingers that suffuse the inside of the old brown house with shades of gold and rose. From the doorway, Celan breathes in the last of the warm, toasted air and anticipates the chill of evening as a sudden breeze snaps a green leaf off a cottonwood and sets it twirling. Inspired, she steps out into the yard and begins to spin around and around, throwing out her arms and whirling until all the world merges into a multi-hued centrifuge. Then dizziness and gravity descend and she drops, breathless, to the ground.

"Celan!" Jillyanne's raspy bark shouts from somewhere close by. "Qué haces, mijita? Get over here and help me with these things."

Celan jumps obediently to her feet, but a wave of vertigo hits as she steps forward and she staggers a bit to the left. The round figure of Jillyanne – leaning on a gnarled cane and lugging a straw basket – bounces into view as she tries to balance on the spinning earth. Oso, Jillyanne's great grey wolfhound, bounds over and she puts a hand on his back to steady herself.

"No aviados." Jillyanne scolds, but her crinkled smile indulges as she sets the basket down.

"I know. I was just happy. I saw a leaf spin and I wanted to, too."

"That's cute. But you were up there just for the sake of it."

"I was just having fun! I didn't hurt anything." Oso licks her face as Celan stoops to pick up the basket. Peeking under the cloth cover, she spies a big bowl of tomato and cucumber salad and a thick loaf of calabacitas bread. Yum.

"True," Jillyanne continues. "But you know what the elders say…"

"Healing is the highest joy, I know." Celan turns primly, all dizziness gone, and retreats into the house, where she stows the basket on the table.

In the doorway, the older woman frowns. "Too smart for your own good sometimes, mijita." Then, relenting, Jillyanne pulls her in for a hug. Celan relaxes into her tia's warm kitchen scent and sighs contentedly.

"Gotta get you to 'scuela mañana," Jillyanne murmurs, chin pressed against the top of her small head.

Pranascuela. Celan smiles at the thought of the name. It's a peaceful name – calm and clean and bright. She doesn't even mind the long walk. Tanny and Max always wait for her and she walks up with them. They're twins, the same age as she is, who've been living with their Tia Jillyanne and her woman Lena for as long as Celan can remember. They don't come up to her house much these days, but whenever she can she goes down to theirs.

Jillyanne releases her with a final squeeze and straightens, hands firm on Celan's shoulders. "Cómo está?" she asks, tilting her frizzy grey-brown head ever so slightly toward the back bedroom.

Celan shrugs. "Lo mismo. She woke up for a while. Drank some." Then she remembers the spilled water and the transfer and winces. Jillaynne would be mad if she knew she'd touched it. Hopefully, the crate is dry by now.

But Jillyanne doesn't bother to check, just bustles over to the table and starts setting out food – shoveling salad onto chipped plates and cutting thick hunks of bread – talking the whole time. "Your sister should be home anytime now. Saw her at the ponds earlier. Looking sour as usual, but she did her share. Took off with that boy after." She purses her lips disapprovingly.

"Taegh's nice," Celan says.

"Hmmph. Walks around like he's something special. She'll be staying home tomorrow though, so you get yourself to 'scuela. Where she should spend more time, if you ask me."

"Cyrinda doesn't like 'scuela," Celan says. She takes two cups out of the cupboard and dips them into the bucket, then carefully puts one in front of each of their places.

"Yeah, I know," mutters Jillyanne, handing her a full plate. "Too much like the other one. It'd do her good, though."

Celan sits and takes a bite of bread, chewing thoughtfully. Then she brightens. "Tell me a story about when you and Mom were little."

Jillyanne sighs. "I don't know if I can think of anything today."

"Por favor," she wheedles. "You can tell an old one. I don't mind." Big brown eyes blink winsomely from her moon-round face.

"Oh, I guess I can do that much – what do you want to hear?" Jillyanne plants her ample rear in a chair and scoops some salad onto her bread, covering it with another slice.

"Tell about the time you fell down the old well and Mom pulled you out."

"Oh yes." Jillyanne takes a bite of her sandwich as she gathers her thoughts. "We were being very naughty that day. Not listening to the elders." She stops and looks pointedly at Celan, who rolls her eyes. "Don't give me that look. Anyway, we were being bad and we got sent to the quiet room. But your mom, she wasn't gonna go quietly. She was mad. When they shut the door she yelled really loud for a minute. Then she grabbed my hand and said 'Jillyanne, let's get out of here.' I was scared but she wouldn't take no for an answer. Climbed right out the window and I followed. Maybe I thought I could keep her from going too far." She stops, misty-eyed, and takes a long drink of water.

"And so you went off into the woods," Celan prompts.

"Yeah, went right off, this way and that. Your mom, she was fast. I was running to catch up. Not looking out where I was going. Crashed through a bunch of leaves and twigs and then *boom* – straight to the bottom!"

"Were you scared?"

"I didn't have time to be scared I was so surprised. Then I hit the water. Ugh. It was dark and dirty and it stank. Whoo! Nasty. I was thrashing around and yelling like crazy.

"Then I looked up and saw your mom's face way up high at the top. She didn't look scared at all. She said 'Jillyanne be quiet, we got to breathe.' And so we did. It was harder for me, treading water like I was, but I quieted down and looked up at her. She had her eyes closed and her hands stretched out and she said 'Picture your hands touching mine,' in a pretty voice like an elder. And I closed my eyes and reached up and I could feel a pull – a prana – and just like that she had my hands and was pulling me out."

"Were you scared then?"

"Oh, I was shaking, but your mom said I'd be alright and she took my hand and we walked back to 'scuela together. Of course, they were all concerned and wanting to know what happened so I told them how she pulled me out. They were pretty impressed, but she still got in trouble. No class for a week; had to pull weeds and trans water."

Celan smiles. "She was really good at prana."

"But she didn't like to do what she was told."

"Is that why she went off to Transway when she got older?" Celan says, making hills and valleys of tomato and cucumber on her plate.

Jillyanne stuffs the last of the sandwich in her mouth and chews in determined avoidance. Celan watches her intently.

Finally, she swallows.

"She took up with Arlo," she says. "Then she left. Just been chosen as an elegida and off she goes with him. I warned her."

"He was an expro, right?"

"Where do you hear these things, mijita?"

"Cyrinda."

Jillyanne sighs. "Yes, he was a child of expros. Grew up over there. His parents had some wayvern. Got to be his once they got too old. Your mother grew up

21

here. Arlo's aunt and uncle were from de la Virgen and he visited them sometimes. That's how they met."

Celan takes a deep breath. "He wasn't my dad, though. He was Cyrinda and Nola's.

"Uh-huh."

"So who was mine?"

"She never said." Jillyanne pushes away from the table and begins gathering up the plates for scraping and rinsing. "She never said, and I never asked."

BY THE TIME FULL DARK has fallen Jillyanne is long gone – back down the dirt path to her house. Cyrinda hadn't turned up yet when she left, so Oso was charged with keeping Celan company. In the flickering candlelight, she curls up next to him on her old wooden bed, humming a song she heard her sister sing the other day. It's not a ranchos song, so either it's from Transway or it's one she and Taegh made up.

Celan used to think songs came out of the ether like some musical form of prana; all the ones the elders sing seem like they did. But Cyrinda says she makes hers up, and Celan believes it. Her sister's songs are different. Louder. Harder. More fun to sing.

Caught up in the tune, Celan doesn't hear any noise outside until Oso growls low in his throat. She isn't afraid though, only curious, so she lifts the curtain and peers out the cracked window. In the moonlight, she can see the shadowy shapes of her sister and Taegh in the yard.

They're huddled together, talking earnestly. She strains to listen, but can't make out the words.

"DO YOU THINK THEY KNOW?" Cyrinda says, eyes wide. "About the transfer?"

"Those payasos? They have no idea." Taegh gestures dismissively.

"But Lulin said she thought I had as much trans as you all did today."

"She was just kidding."

"You think? I mean, what if she went and told her sister that – "

"She won't. She doesn't know a thing. And," he adds, "thanks to Nola, we know things they can't even imagine. We know how to do it *right*."

"Taegh," she chides. "That was just that one time. With her and Dex. It was special. We can't be transfusing all the time." She twines her fingers through his and looks up into his eyes. There's an odd light there she doesn't recognize.

"Why not?" he says. "It's not like anyone's gonna know. They don't even know that fusing exists, and they never will if they don't make elegido. We already know what we're doing. We don't need permission."

Cyrinda puts her arms around him, nuzzling her head into his chest. "Taegh, please don't be that way. We'll do it again, I promise...sometime."

"You've been saying that for months." He gives a

huff of frustration and his warm breath puffs against the top of her head. A shiver of pleasure runs down her spine.

"I know what it is. You're worried because of your mom. But you're not her. And you're not Nola either. We have enough training between us to be safe. No aviados. Just more to learn without the elders breathing down our necks."

Gently, he takes her chin in his hand, tilting it so that she looks up at him again. All the sweetness of Taegh is back. It floods her mind like sunshine.

"Alright," she says, swimming in the desire to stay like this forever. "Next Sunday? We can go up to the peak – the old cabin up there."

"Now you're talking."

With easy grace he circles an arm around her waist and steers her toward the house. Overhead, the stars wheel like birds in the night sky and a sharp wind spins dust down the pitted track. In the window a small form is haloed; head on hand, waiting.

2

In the morning Celan is up at first light, stretching and yawning under her frayed quilt. Oso is gone; after Cyrinda came in last night he took off to Jillyanne's. Her sister murmurs on the other cot and Celan glances over – *so beautiful, even in sleep*. No wonder she has a man like Taegh. He's so cute and nice and funny. He doesn't even have to be gross about it like some of the boys she knows. They're always burping and farting and laughing like it's the funniest thing ever; then they sneak up on you and try to put bugs in your hair.

Taegh though, all he has to do is make a certain face or say something in a certain tone of voice and it's hilarious. And that hair! It's the exact same purple-pink as prickly pear mead. As soon as he did it she immediately wanted to dye hers the same color, but Jillyanne said no.

Celan swings her legs over the side of the bed and shrugs off her nightdress, wriggling into her worn hemp skirt and shirt. Slipping on sandals, she creeps softly into the back room where she notes the rise and fall of her mother's chest under the blanket. Then she heads for the kitchen. There's a fresh wash of morning over everything and on the shelves the old glass jars shine. She turns and grabs the bucket off the table, heading out the door for a quick pit stop at the latrine and a trip to the nearest spring.

At the pool she fills the pail slowly – watching the midges rise off the water in a cloud and dreaming of the possibilities of the day ahead now that it's Cyrinda's turn to stay with Mair.

A sudden squawk and flap of wings in the brush jerks her awareness to the present in time to see the sleek, smoke-grey form of a coyote padding towards her. It's rare for coyotes to attack humans, but this one is intimidatingly large. One leap and it could be on her. She bites her lip, resolving not to fear. Still crouching, she sets the bucket down and breathes deeply, pushing her awareness outward.

"Coyote, are you hungry?"

He sits, locking his gaze on hers. *Yes*, he says, the impression of the word echoing in her mind.

"I cleared the mouse traps yesterday. There's a pile of them. I can show you where."

I am tired of rats and mice.

"There are chickens at the casagrand."

The coyote seems to consider this. Then he shakes his hoary head. *They are too stringy and dry. I want something juicy.*

Celan takes a deeper breath. *Wall*, she thinks, *around me*, and in her mind's eye sees a blue glow rise from her skin and encircle her as the coyote leaps in a blur of sharp teeth and furry underbelly. But he hits the aura of protection like the side of a house and bounces harmlessly away, landing in the spring with a splash.

He gets to his feet and shakes out his fur, bristling with humiliation. He gives Celan another long look, as if trying to decide whether or not to take another run at her. Finally, he seems to shrug.

Where did you say those mice were again?

"Behind the house, down in the arroyo. We throw them back there."

The coyote stalks off and Celan, hugely relieved, lugs the bucket up to the house.

At the kitchen table, she transes the water and splashes her face and hands, drying them on a dingy towel. She dips in a cup and drinks the whole thing in one gulp, then thrusts it and a hunk of leftover bread into her pack and darts back outside, shutting the door firmly behind her and barreling down the track in a whoosh of exuberance for the morning, for being alive.

The sun creeps over the mountains, pulling itself up with golden fingers and peering into the canyons with joyful eyes. She raises her hand to blow it a kiss. This is her favorite time of year: No clouds; none of the rain that falls in waves during the cold season. She knows the water is needed to make the grains and vegetables grow; it's collected and hoarded in tanks and barrels for the times when none falls. Still, she likes the hot dry season better.

She pauses to chase a tiny green lizard but is stymied by a wall of brush. Undaunted, she kicks along the path until she sees Jillyanne and Lena's tidy house appear around the bend.

"Hey!" Tanny shouts, and Celan speeds up double time. Tanny is hopping around, alternately shoving Max and then dodging away when he lunges at her. She is as tall and fair as he is small and dark and it's always been a stretch of the imagination to believe they are really twins.

Breathless, Celan arrives in time to get in her own push at Max. He gives chase and she sprints away across the yard as Tanny eggs her on and Oso bounds after them, barking. They're rounding the corner of the house when Lena's frowsy head appears out of the bedroom window.

"You all better stop fooling around and get moving!" She shakes her ginger curls disapprovingly. "I don't wanna see you all back here in an hour 'cause you got sent home for lateness." The window slams shut with finality, putting an instant damper on the horseplay.

ATRAVESAR – TO GET ACROSS

They exchange guilty grins before giving Oso a couple of pats on the head and setting out past the shady fish ponds that give Rancho Pescados its name. Further on, they meet the dirt road that descends from the springs to Tijeras, where the bulk of Pescados residents live side by side with Rancho de la Virgen. Only a half dozen or so families live up at the springs; it's an extra hike, but Celan doesn't mind. It's a peaceful retreat from the bustle of the town.

Where the road bottoms out, they slip under the old highway that snakes through the pass between the Sandia and Manzano Mountains. Max inspects the beams reinforcing the ancient underpass and gives a hearty shout, enjoying the satisfying echo, and the girls follow suit. Then they break into a run, always nervous that their yelling might bring the whole thing down upon them. But they always do it anyway.

They turn left, entering Tijeras. Already the town is alive with movement – people cooking breakfast over open fires, pushing carts along the streets, and heading out to another day in the fields.

Max stares at a young woman hanging out some wash, her nightdress sheer in the morning light. He nearly trips on a chunk of broken pavement and the girls laugh. He kicks at it, annoyed at being caught out.

"I can't believe they used to cover everything in this stuff."

"I know," says Celan. "They were so stupid."

"They did a lot of dumb things in the old world," Tanny says authoritatively. "There were so many people then…millions and millions! Like ants. And they used to poison everything and try and make each other die all the time. That's why we had the transition. A big rock hit and then everything shook and the waves came up and drowned all their poison. Lots of people got sick and they didn't know how to heal it."

Max shudders. "I'm glad I wasn't there."

"Me too," says Celan.

"The elders say you could have been, though, in a past life."

"Well, I'm glad I don't remember it then!" he says and Celan laughs. "I'm glad I don't remember the old world, even if I was there. It sounds like it was scary, even before all that."

"It was," Tanny says. "Lena told me they used to have bombs. Big ones. Like fireworks but worse. They'd drop them on people and blow them all up."

"Ugh, Tanny. Stop!" Celan says, putting her hands over her ears.

Max gives his twin a shove.

"Ow! Stop being such babies," Tanny says, looking down her nose. She's easily a head taller than either of them. "I'm just saying what happened."

"It doesn't even matter," says Max. "That was ages ago, like our great-great-great-great-grandparents' time. I like things how they are now."

"Me too," says Celan, who's removed her hands, cautiously.

"Whatever. You started it anyway, Max, talking about the stupid road."

They shuffle along quietly for a few minutes, each lost in private contemplation, as the road begins to climb upwards. The sun inches higher in the sky and the air grows warmer. Another cluster of children appears up ahead at the juncture to Rancho Cangrejos, but they're too far away for shouting.

Celan breaks the silence by regaling them with the tale of her encounter with the coyote. Tanny rolls her eyes and Max shakes his head.

"Chale, he missed you on purpose."

"No, he bounced off. I swear!"

"Not because of anything *you* did, Celan," Tanny says. "That's like elder-level stuff and even they can't always – "

"He wasn't gonna eat you," Max cuts in. "He was just messing with you." A shrug. "That's what coyotes do."

She's still trying to convince them as they turn onto the dirt lane marked Rio Del Road. Through the pines, the graceful dome rises like a leviathan, light reflecting off intricately fitted panes of glass. Miraculous that it's never been shattered or struck by lightening in the violent storms of years gone by. That's what a lot of people say, but Celan doesn't doubt for a minute that it's perfectly natural – that a place so filled with elders and learning would be perfectly preserved, like the jars of food lining the kitchen cupboards.

They mount the broad stone steps reverently, hushing their voices, all childish things tucked away. Through the wide wooden door they enter a large hallway, joining a line of other children already formed against the wall. On the opposite wall, an enormous banner printed with words in curlicues of gold flutters in the breeze.

The Precepts.

Celan stares up at them, though she's been able to recite these words for as long as she can remember:

One – *Every living thing is imbued with the power of the Universe, which is love;*
Two – *The combined sum of that power is greater than the will of any individual person;*
Three – *When we face difficulties, we must always search for the answer in love, and in accordance with the Universal Will.*

On it goes, down the list of all nine – as they promise always to search their hearts and rid themselves of their false perceptions, make things right with those they injure either accidently or on purpose, and realign themselves with the Universal Will.

Such good and right things! Reading them makes her feel blessed. She leans against the wall and closes her eyes, enjoying the serenity of the moment until the sharp ring of a bell snaps her to attention.

A slender young elegida in a pale blue robe appears and ushers the children through a stone archway and down a steep flight of stairs. Celan feels moist heat rising up from below and shivers in anticipation.

Ushered into the partitioned bathing room – boys on one side, girls on the other – they strip off their dirty clothes and stow them, along with their packs, in cabinets carved with plain symbols. Celan's is marked with a crescent moon. Clutching slivers of soap, they approach the edge of a large underground pool. Steam rises from the surface, redolent with minerals. The light from the algalamps gives the water an eerie phosphorescent glow.

Stepping into the pool, the comfort of clear warm water creeps in increments from Celan's toes to her chest. Once immersed, she floats toward the wall. Then she ducks under to wet her hair, shaking off the dust of several days.

Surfacing, she searches for Tanny in the humid dark, but she is busy chatting with a short, skinny girl that Celan doesn't know, so she lathers up, taking care to scrub her neck and ears and the bottoms of her feet. Once rinsed, she closes her eyes, giving herself over to weightlessness until the chime sounds for the end of the bathing period.

Out and dry, she removes a folded cloth square from the top of her locker and shakes it out, pulling the garment over her head. The cool robe is tinted a faint sage color, and it brushes feather-light against her skin from neck to ankles. She lifts the sleeve to her nose and inhales a scent like a summer sky.

Another chime and the girls mount the staircase and ascend, merging with the boys. Jostlings and whispers begin to fade as they draw close to the arched doorway into the dome. At a raised hand from the elegida they fall silent and form a line against the wall.

The children emerge single file from the hush of the shadowy hall into the large radiant space of the central dome. The base is framed in burnished wood with multi-paned glass walls rising high above their heads in a sweeping curve. Slivers of sky kaleidoscope in blue and white interspersed with patches of green around the edges. Several doors around the base are open, allowing the soft breeze and smell of growing things to filter into the room. The central floor space is covered by a large white padded mat and empty save for clusters of cushions arranged at intervals.

A white-robed elder stands in the center of each cluster as the children proceed clockwise around the edge of the mat to the first available space and sit quietly in their places.

Celan settles onto a squashy blue cushion and looks up at their elder expectantly. Caron will be their guide today. She's glad. Almost all of the elders are nice, but Caron is one of her favorites. She's very old, with pale eyes and pearl-white hair that lend her an air of tenuousness, as if she were a last autumn leaf trembling on an empty bough. Her appearance is deceiving though, there is nothing fragile about her air of authority.

When all the children have been seated, Caron folds herself gracefully into a half-lotus and asks them to please lie back and close their eyes.

"Today," she begins, "we are going to astral to a coastal area to do some healing near a place that was called New Orleans in the old world."

Celan smiles. Astral travel is fun and the ocean trips are the best.

"Unlike the old west and east coasts, many places on the gulf coast were not scoured by massive tidal waves during the transition. The flooding was much more gradual. This place has been underwater for many years now, but there are many contaminants which were stored on the land and leaked out into the ocean. They have been poisoning the water ever since. Some of those poisons get pulled into the water cycle when storms come over the ocean and they fall on us as rain and get into our food and water and our bodies. That, as you know, is why we must transfigure everything we consume. Transing removes the poisons and leaves the food and water clean and safe for us to eat and drink."

Caron's voice is rhythmic and soothing, and although Celan has heard these lessons many times before she never tires of listening to the elders' words. In her mind's eye, she pictures the drowned city and the leaking poisons, evil-smelling things that foul the water around them.

"Over the years," Caron continues, "we realized that we were never going to get rid of all the poisons unless we traveled to their sources. It is too far and dangerous to go in our physical bodies, but our astral bodies can go anywhere. In our astral forms we can still trans whatever we touch. Never think that something is too big to be cleaned. There is no difference between a tank of oil under the ocean and a pail of water on your kitchen table."

Celan recalls the bucket from the creek this morning. *I'm ready*, she thinks, *give me the biggest tank you can find!*

Caron instructs them to fold their hands over their solar plexus and take long, slow, even breaths – in through the nose and out through the mouth. She intones a long vowel sound as she breathes out and the children follow suit, trying to match the rhythm of their breathing to hers. The room vibrates with the sound of many voices holding the same resonant note.

Celan's palms begin to feel prickly and warm and her whole body becomes lighter and lighter until she feels like she's floating slightly above herself. She basks in the weightless space like a warm bath, continuing to breathe and tone until she hears Caron say, "Eyes open."

Her lids fly up to reveal the astral forms of Caron

and most of the other children in her circle hovering together with hers near the top of the dome. A few have not made it out of their earthly bodies and are merely asleep, but that is to be expected. Looking down, Celan can see her body at rest on the cushion below.

'See me later,' is what Max always says at this point when she's in his group. He usually gets shushed by the elders, but it never fails to make her giggle.

"Everyone ready?" Caron says. The children nod in answer. "Alright, everyone join hands and don't let go."

Celan takes the astral hands of the children on either side of her and suddenly they're moving at incredible speed out through the dome and over the green and brown blur of land. Faster they go, here and there whizzing over the ruins of the odd city or town. Celan always looks for smoke, movement, anything to signal that another group like theirs still exists. The elders say there are a few that remain, but she has never seen one. They say they're far away, though, on the other side of the world. They never take the 'scuela groups near them.

A shock of blue interrupts her thoughts as the vast expanse of ocean opens beneath them. With the sun dappling the waves it looks so beautiful she can scarcely believe that there's anything actually wrong with it. Some things you can't tell by looking though. Down they plunge, through the tops of the waves and into the churning sea.

Underwater, they whirl through the swirling blue until the tops of buildings come into view below them, along with big tanks and other nameless old world machinery. *So much poison!* She'd have no idea where to start. Caron does however; she stops them short and makes a sound like a stuttering static whistle. She waits a moment, cocking her pearly head to one side as if straining to catch an answer.

Celan hears nothing and cranes her neck impatiently. Suddenly, flickering forms appear off to the left. Closer they come until she can see their sleek bodies and grinning faces. The dolphins circle the astral group in bodies that shimmer like glass, chittering excitedly as Caron questions them. After a brief back-and-forth they appear to reach consensus. With a satisfied nod she turns to the children.

"Alright everyone. Escúchame. We are very lucky today to be joined by some of our cetacean friends. Due to the poison, they no longer survive on the material plane of our Terra Madre, but they live on in others and so can meet us here on the astral. Grab hold, gently, of their dorsal fins and they will tow you to the spot we have identified for healing today. We are going to be traveling on from here and I want *everyone to stick together*."

A long snout nudges Celan's arm and she takes hold of the grinning creature's fin. Half on its back she feels a great surging tug and finds herself being pulled along at high speed through the shimmering deep. It feels like flying and she lets out a joyous cry, echoed by a series of cheerful squeaks from her companion.

When the velocity slows, they are far out in deep water. An ancient metal structure looms like a skeleton with the ocean floor around it scarred and stained. Solemnly, they circle the damaged area until Caron raises a hand, causing them to halt.

"The dolphins tell me this is a particularly bad spot," she says. "So this is where we will concentrate our efforts today. We are going to use a technique known as the healing vortex. Can anyone describe this method to me?"

Several hands shoot up.

"Celan?"

Proudly she recites, "The healing vortex is used to make our transing powers increase exponentially. There have to be at least three people present to make one. We join hands and circle – first counterclockwise to undo damage and then clockwise to add clean energy. It creates a circle of power that becomes a vortex allowing a deep healing over a large area."

Caron inclines her head approvingly. "Bueno. Can someone define 'exponentially' for us?"

"It means 'by a lot'," pipes up a dark-haired boy.

"Please wait to be called on," Caron admonishes. "But yes, it generally refers to an extremely rapid and steep acceleration. We will form an inner ring while the dolphins will assist with an outer ring. Now, is everyone ready?"

All heads bob in agreement.

"Alright, let's join hands and begin."

THE BLONDE GIRL SLOUCHES ON a kitchen chair, knees jammed up against the rim of the heavy table, eyes closed. Her hands are folded loosely in her lap and her bare feet dangle listlessly. A bead of sweat moves infinitesimally down her right temple but she doesn't seem to notice or lift a hand to brush it away. The silence is total except for the hum of insects; Cyrinda listens to them, humming along quietly, ribcage rattling with the vibration.

Days like this used to stretch out so dull. Even before she got this bad, mom wasn't always all there and Cyrinda often got stuck watching Celan. Marooned in the house she would pace restlessly, irritation snapping across synapses until it could no longer be contained and would explode outward at the nearest available target, most likely her sister or Jillyanne.

She often chided herself for yelling at Celan. She'd invoke the Precepts – admit she was wrong and apologize, try to make it up to her. It almost became a joke between them. 'Five, six, seven, whatever,' Celan would say, rolling her eyes, but Cyrinda really was sorry.

It wasn't her sister's fault, she was only a kid. Jillyanne, though, deserved it for filling Celan's head up with all kinds of crap about how wonderful their sainted mother was, even as she kept an evil eye on both of them just waiting for them to step out of line.

Cyrinda smiles slyly.

I've already stepped out good and she doesn't even know.

She slips a hand into her pocket and it closes reassuringly around the small, cool vial. Days like this are easy now. A few drops of transferon under the tongue and she can tune in to the sounds of the world and be content. Which reminds her – the transfer was looking pretty low this morning. She should probably refill it while she has the place to herself. Her eyes blink open at the thought.

Slowly unfolding long legs, she stretches feeling into them before placing them firmly on the floor and bending her willowy frame over the table. She tugs the half-full bucket towards her and pulls out the transfer, unscrewing the cap and tipping the last few drops into her mouth. She really should go and get fresh water from the spring, but she knows Celan transed this one earlier and it's clean.

Plunging the empty vial below the surface, she watches a few bubbles rise as it fills. When they cease her other hand screws the dropper on, still under the surface to avoid trapping air pockets. Cap secure, she pulls it out and neatly wipes it on a dish towel before settling into the chair again, closing her eyes and clasping the transfer firmly in her damp hands.

Now for the tricky part.

Cyrinda readies every nerve and muscle and takes a deep breath, drawing in the calm, still air of the warm noon and feeling a tickle of energy in her palms. Concentrating all her attention on the vial she thinks of a star and in her mind's eye sees it begin to glow – first faintly, then brighter and brighter until, with a sudden pulse, it releases and fades.

Success. She leans back, exultant.

Who knew it was so easy to make transferon? As a kid she never knew where it came from; it was always there like the sun and rain. But the adults were all so careful with it that she thought it must be something precious and rare.

She'd laughed when Nola showed her – 'It's just water!' But no, her sister explained, once transfigured it becomes something infinitely better. Cyrinda never had much interest in transing water as a kid but she has to admit the knowledge is useful now. Amazing what the right motivation can do.

She holds the vial up to a beam of sunlight and admires as the crystalline surface throws out rainbow prisms that jig giddily along the walls and table top. Funny how transferon makes everything like that, how it imbues jubilance into every atom of existence. It's so stupid that the elders won't let her have any. She wouldn't even bother to show up at 'scuela at all anymore if it weren't for the singing. Plus, she doesn't want to make anyone suspicious.

She sighs.

All the years of training are so unnecessary; she's only seventeen but she's totally fine doing it on her own. And it makes things so much easier, so much better. If it hadn't been for Nola, she doesn't know what she would have done.

But a little voice inside says, 'There's one lying right there on the bedside table.'

Cyrinda frowns, shaking her head. That would be really bad, not that her mother would even notice. It's much better that she has her own; it's tuned just right to her system – well, hers and Taegh's. She's always willing to share with him. She knows he'll keep it secret.

The thought of his arms around her makes the color rise in her cheeks. He's the only boy she's ever kissed, the only one she'd ever let touch her. Nola had all kinds of men and didn't care. 'Techs don't count,' she'd say, shrugging, but Cyrinda knows she could never do that kind of thing.

When we go to Transway, they'll pay to hear our music like they did for mom and dad.

That's what people around here didn't get: The wayverns weren't bad or evil. They were havens for music and dancing, plays and shows, art – all the beautiful things that people like best.

With a final flourish she pockets the transfer and gets to her feet, throwing her arms up and letting them wave gracefully down as a sinuous tune rings through her head. She spins, pirouetting, delighting in the moment. In her mind, the scratchy hemp skirt twirls out like flowing jersey.

Someday, she vows, *I'll have pretty things like Nola's.*

Then, like a top winding down, she reluctantly comes to a halt facing the back bedroom.

Time to go check on *her* again.

Ugh.

THE WOMAN LIES IN THE bed, seemingly half-dead. *Am I old or am I young?*

She's not sure what she is anymore. Sometimes she feels so small and delicate she thinks she's a child. Other times she feels like a mountain – massive, sleeping for thousands of years as the clock of geologic time ticks out the eons. Sometimes she's wandering through a world of wispy white.

It's not snow, she thinks, *it's fog. That's what they don't tell you.*

She raises a hand and it swirls away, elusive. She keeps walking.

Then the veil parts and Mair is blinking in the sunlight. Slowly, she takes in her surroundings: The kitchen at Arlo's, mid-morning. Not pregnant with Nola yet, she must have just turned twenty.

It's a strange feeling, being inside her body in another time and place; not able to influence or change anything but simply to experience scenes like she's living them all over again. This happens from time to time when she's walking. Sometimes she can live whole days, other times it's only a few minutes. She never knows how long it will last, but mostly it's pleasant. It breaks up the fog.

Mair finds herself chopping onions, inhaling their stinging scent and humming soft and sweet. From the other room she can hear Arlo pounding away at the piano and singing in his deep, ringing voice, and she taps her foot along with the music. He's been teaching her to play and she's taken to it easily.

Thunk, thunk, thunk. Her whole body falls into the rhythm as she chops. She's enjoying herself so much that she isn't aware that the music has stopped until the sound of Arlo's voice at the door makes her start.

"Mair, love?"

"Arlo!" she gasps, nearly taking off a finger. "Don't sneak up like that! You scared me half to death."

He laughs and swoops in, catching her around the waist in a big warm bear hug. He presses his face into her hair, breathing her in contentedly.

"I doubt that," he says. "The kind of girl who'd climb over Sandia Peak in the dead of night with a man she just met is not the kind of girl who scares easily."

She chuckles. "What a scandal we made."

"Terrible. Stolen from the elders right under their noses." He takes a step back and gestures dramatically,

45

sandy forelock falling across his broad brow as he quotes a line of old world poetry.

"Come away, o human child!"

Yeats.

Mair rolls her eyes. "Please, you didn't steal me. I just decided to try something different."

"Decided after you'd already been picked. You were one of the elegidas." As much as he pretends to disdain the traditions, she can tell he's still the tiniest bit in awe.

She lifts her chin, defiant. "A girl has a right to change her mind."

"Learning the secret ceremonias..." He crosses his eyes and begins to babble gibberish, waving his hands in a crude approximation of an elder.

"Don't be too pleased with yourself. What, do you expros get a prize for every innocent ranchita you lure over here?"

He stops clowning and regards her seriously, eyes brimming with pride. "You're the only prize in the world I'll ever need."

He embraces her with arms so strong and solid it feels like nothing bad could ever happen in the world again. That's why she wasn't scared to climb the peak, why she wasn't scared to leave even though she was one of the ones chosen to be consecrated to the elders and continue to the highest levels of sacred learning. She remembers being so nervous at the initiation, shivering in the long blue robe, not knowing what to expect.

Truth be told, it was pretty incredible.

But not as incredible as she felt when she was with Arlo.

3

The small wooden bridge spanning Tijeras Creek clatters under Celan's feet as she inhales rich wafts of baking bread from the hornos around the casagrand. Her stomach rumbles – the sandwiches provided at 'scuela have long since burned off. She, Tanny, and Max spent several sweltering hours weeding and transing crops after lunch. It is required that they eat and get their hands in the earth to ground them after the separation of their astral flights.

The twins had to head straight home after that, so Celan promised to record their work hours for them when she stopped in to report her own. She doesn't mind at all, it gives her an excuse to dawdle. As soon as she gets home Cyrinda will try to wheedle her into taking over with Mair so she can go be with Taegh, even though it's still supposed to be her day.

The hulking adobe building with its funky, red-peaked roof appears welcomingly around the creek bend. The water feeds the corn, hemp, potatoes, squash, and chiles grown extensively, and almost exclusively, by ranchos Pescados and de la Virgen.

It wasn't always this way. Back when the three hundred original transers were expelled from Albakirk, they settled in the East Mountains and everyone shared everything, including the manual work. Up in Cedar Crest, they organized the first ranchos along an acequia with the portion of seeds and starts the techs had allotted them when they left. However, as their numbers grew, division of labor eventually became a necessity. The elders still garden, tending their small plots meditatively, but these days the majority of staples come from the fields near Tijeras.

Celan digs around in her pack, feeling for her cup, and helps herself to a drink from a pump by the wide patio. Leaning against a tree, she transes the water and studies the giant, circular mural painted on the front wall of the building. She never tires of looking at the colorful figures, which tell the story of Jane Lees and how she came to discover transferon, the substance that helped them live with the changes to Terra Madre without having to hide indoors.

In the first panel, Lees is a serious young scientist working alone in her lab, surrounded by machinery but also plants and minerals, showing how she blended technical knowledge with that of the natural world. Next she is shown with a man, her lover and fellow scientist Javier Timanti, who initially helped her in her endeavors. Then the transition comes in a swirl of chaos and they are both shown working to help save the survivors of Albakirk. At the bottom of the wheel Lees is again in the lab, holding aloft the first transfer, her ultimate gift to a new humanity.

Climbing up the left side is a surreal picture of Lees and her followers, at first radiant but then turning darker as they bring down the wrath of Timanti and those who feared the effects of transferon, thinking it a cheat or a hoax. The final panel shows them leaving the city, heading out into the wild to face whatever Terra Madre had in store for them.

Their faith was not in vain – the vibrant center panel reveals a new community, alive and well and prospering in the edenic East Mountains. As always, Celan breaks into a smile at the happy ending. She's glad her ancestors were so brave. It makes her proud.

Downing the last drops of water she jams her cup into her pack and sidles over to the hornos, looking longingly at the loaves until a woman laughs and gives her one. She tosses it from hand to hand as it cools, crossing the wide patio and ducking around a pack of smiling de la Virgen women carrying baskets of apples from the orchards at Rancho Arqueros.

Inside, the building hums with activity – people bartering and laughing; trading clothing, candles, cider, furniture. Delicious smells float from the kitchens, where large vats of stew simmer on the big stoves powered by a solar generator. The generator also pumps hot and cold water throughout the building and helps fuel an ancient electrical system.

They'll light up this whole place for Liberation Day, Celan thinks happily, *and there'll be fireworks too.*

Ducking down a hallway, she finds a place in line outside the room where the casagrand's record keepers maintain the lists of the ranchos families and the amounts of time they devote to different tasks. Celan's mother's illness has been duly accounted for and only she and Cyrinda are expected to work.

Gingerly, she transes the bread and takes a careful nibble. Finding it sufficiently cool, she rips off a big chunk and sits with a bump on the floor.

"Tired, mijita?" An old man in front of her chortles. "Wait until you get to be my age. You'll be sitting down after every ten steps you take."

His ancient brown eyes twinkle merrily and his shoulders shake as he laughs at his own humor.

"What were you working on today?" he asks.

"Weeding," she says through a mouthful of bread. "The squash."

"And do you know what grew in that spot last year?"

"Leaf to root to flower to fruit," she recites, sing-song.

"So...beans maybe?"

The younger woman next to him says, "Oh, papa, let the girl be!" and with a wink he turns around, leaving Celan to chew contentedly.

The line is long and slow-moving, and she entertains herself by watching the legs of people tramping along the corridor. She invents a game – trying to predict what a person's face looks like just by seeing their feet. A pair of ragged sandals and wrinkled toes: Old man, white hair, wizened eyes. *Got it!* A graceful ankle with a swirl of blue skirts: Elegida. *That one's easy.* Tan, furry legs and sturdy hemp half-pants: *Could be anyone.* She looks up to find a young woman with a round brown face, laughing at something her friend said.

The game lulls her into a semi-hypnotic state, broken only by the occasional movement of the line and subsequent scoot of her butt closer to the door. Finally, she finishes the last of her bread and stands, brushing crumbs off her lap. Almost there.

At the next shuffle she enters the cluttered little room to find two harried women busily jotting notations. When the one behind the placard marked M-Z is free, she steps up and announces herself.

"Celan Mairs. Pescados."

The skinny, sunburned woman rifles through a stack of papers.

"Cuántos?"

"Two for me. And two each for Tanny and Max Elenas."

The woman marks her hours down, but doesn't look up. "A-L is in the other line."

"I know. But I can't be in two places at once."

The woman rolls her eyes but resigns herself to tapping the stout A-L woman on the shoulder.

"Misty?"

The stout woman turns her attention away from the old man and his daughter from out in the hall. They don't seem at all put out, though. They flash Celan conspiratorial grins.

"Yeah?" the woman named Misty says to M-Z.

"Tanny and Max Elenas. Two hours each."

Misty grimaces, flipping through papers. "I don't see an Elenas…"

"It might be under Jillyannes," Celan pipes up, trying to be helpful.

The stout woman flips a few more pages, scanning. "Yeah, I see 'em now. Name needs to be the household they live in, no matter who their mother is."

"Lo siento."

"And you know everyone is supposed to report hours themselves," she chides, giving Celan a reproachful look.

"They had to get home early."

Misty relents, sighing, and marks them down. Turning on her heel, Celan exits the office, marching through the corridor and out of the building.

She snags an apple from an unattended basket on the porch then ambles along the creek, tossing in leaves and and turning over rocks, searching for mayfly nymphs. By the time she crosses under the old highway the heat of the day has started to lift. A light breeze caresses her face as she emerges onto the gravel road, squinting in the late afternoon sun. No one else is around and she kicks at a rock, chasing it forward repetitively until it bounces off into the weeds. At the next to last bend she hears shouting and slows up to a walk.

Cetus, Joella, and Joella's little brother Mick are up on the rise, throwing a ball around and yelling at each other. Though it's really more like Cetus and Joella are taking turns throwing the ball *at* Mick, trying to hit him while he dodges, screaming. Still, obeying their command, he keeps picking it up and throwing it back.

"Hey," Celan says, "que pas'?"

They all turn.

"Oh, it's Celaaan," says Joella, drawing the name out mockingly and tossing her dark hair, nose in the air. "I thought I smelled something."

Cetus chuckles, lumpy head and shoulders bobbing, as Mick takes this momentary distraction as a chance to escape and sprints off, bawling.

"You better not tell!" Joella hollers after him. Then she whips around, hurling the ball with sudden force at Celan, who jumps sideways to avoid it. It rolls harmlessly off down the road.

"Better go get that, Joella," Celan says, and attempts to pass them as they strike up a chant.

"Tu hermana! La putana!"

They dance around tauntingly. Celan tries to ignore them, picking up her pace until Joella steps out in front of her.

"How many techs was your sister with?" she hisses. "Hundreds, I bet."

At that Celan reacts instinctively, burying a fist in Joella's gut and dropping her in the dust.

"Chingada!" she shouts, the worst word she knows, and feels a moment of triumph until she's grabbed from behind and spun around by Cetus, who throws a mean right hook that connects soundly with her eye.

Whirling in a circle, she manages to land a kick where it hurts before taking off at a run, not daring to look back until she's passed Jillyanne's house and is safely at the door of her own. Cyrinda is waiting there, foot tapping impatiently.

"Where have you – hey what happened?"

"I got in a fight. With Cetus and Joella." Celan rubs sullenly at her eye.

"Ven aquí. Let me trans it for you," Cyrinda says soothingly, leading her inside. Her sister plops into a kitchen chair and motions Celan to kneel, pressing a cool palm to her throbbing eye.

"Now what were you fighting about?" she says.

"They called Nola a whore."

Cyrinda shrugs. "Well she was one."

"That's mean," says Celan, pulling away. "I thought you loved her."

"Of course I did," her sister says, tugging her back into healing range. "But the truth is the truth."

Celan starts to protest again but Cyrinda cuts her off.

"Mira, Celan. Nola was what she was and there's nothing we can do about it. Believe me, I've beat a few of those bitches myself. It doesn't change a thing.

"But," she continues, "the one thing Nola *wasn't* was stupid. She was one of the smartest people I've ever known. I mean, on Transway they made us go to this tech school thing they had for the expro kids. I never paid too much attention, but Nola was so good at it! And she read more than anyone; any old world book she could find. She knew all about the old world. And she knew a lot about the techs, too. She used to tell us when she came over here. She'd tell me and Taegh all about – "

"About what?" says a voice from the doorway. Taegh is slouched jauntily against the frame, guitar slung over one shoulder, prickly-pear hair falling in his eyes.

Cyrinda breaks out a brilliant smile. "Hey, I was just talking about Nola."

He leans over and gives her a quick kiss.

"What happened to her?" he asks, cutting his eyes to Celan.

"I got in a fight," Celan says. "Cetus and Joella

called Nola a putana and I got mad – "

"And I was explaining that it's not really worth fighting over the truth," finishes Cyrinda.

Taegh cough-laughs and she shoots him a shut-up look.

"Nola was a really smart person though, someone Celan can be proud of," Cyrinda says pointedly. "No matter what a bunch of stupid kids say."

She removes her hand and Celan pokes tentatively at her eye. The pain has faded and the swelling is going down too.

"Nice work," Taegh says.

Celan scrambles up. "Are you guys going out tonight?"

Cyrinda looks to Taegh.

"Nah," he says, "let's stay here. Give us a minute though, OK?"

"Sure," Celan says.

He leans the guitar against the wall and walks out into the yard with Cyrinda.

Fight forgotten at the prospect of a night with Cyrinda and Taegh, Celan takes in the contents of the kitchen table – a small heap of potatoes and chiles and a couple of fish. Good dinner. And music too!

She jigs gleefully in place.

TENDRILS OF MIST TRAIL FROM Mair's fingertips, clearing the scene in front of her like a hand rubbing condensation from a window pane. She's seated at the old piano by the stage at Arlo's, playing a rollicking tune and smiling indulgently as the big man and little girl run through their routine one more time. Cyrinda, blonde curls bouncing adorably, grins a gap-toothed grin that lights up the whole room. Knobby knees bending, she jumps and twirls, spinning out the skirt of the frothy pink dress that's been weeks in the making.

She takes so much after her father – same hair, same eyes, same larger-than-life personality. Mair's own demeanor is more subdued, but she's filled with pride, not envy, as she watches her youngest child wrap her father's heart around her finger. She'll do the same to a packed house before the night is out.

Mair's nostrils twitch with the lingering scents of the food, drink, and smoke consumed in quantity here nightly. The room yawns behind her like a cavern with the bar along the left wall and booths on the right. The middle space is filled with round tables and chairs. All are deserted on this rainy Saturday morning, but they won't be for long.

The stage runs about three quarters of the way across the back of the room, leaving a clear space for the wait staff to get in and out of the kitchens. Performers use a stage door on the other side.

This side door creaks open as a pudgy, brown-haired girl slips into the room. Mair tries to catch her eye, feeling a pang when she responds with a diffident wave. Nola, her first born – dark moon to her sister's radiant sun. Mair knows she shouldn't play favorites, but she can't help feeling a special kinship with the girl.

So smart, the thought arises unbidden, *she should be at 'scuela.* She misses a note and shakes her head, cursing under her breath, as Nola sits quietly in a chair and buries her nose in a book.

THE FISH SIZZLE DELICIOUSLY ON the grill over the fire pit in the yard. It's too warm to light the clunky old woodstove in the kitchen this time of year. Cyrinda leans over a pan of potatoes spiced with chile and adds a couple more drops of sunflower oil to keep them from sticking, turning them with a fork. The rich smoky smell makes Celan's mouth water.

They had dragged the kitchen chairs out into the yard earlier and Taegh is perched on one now, playing an old campfire tune between swigs from a bottle of dandelion wine.

As I walked out on the streets of Laredo
As I walked out on Laredo one day
I saw a young cowboy
Wrapped in white linen
Wrapped in white linen as cold as the clay

I can see by your outfit that you are a cowboy
These words he did say as I boldly walked by
Come and sit down beside me and hear my sad story
I'm shot in the breast and I know I must die

It was once in the saddle I used to go laughing
Once in the saddle I used to go gay
First to the cardhouse and then down to Arlo's
But I'm shot in the breast and I'm dying today

He sings the mournful words with exaggerated pathos, expression downcast but eyes drolly alight, until Cyrinda says, "Stop being silly and go flip those fish."

Dutifully, Taegh parks the guitar on the side of his chair and saunters over to the grill, turning the fish with practiced skill.

"Almost done, how're the taters?"

"Just about. Celan, go get some plates."

Celan bounds up the rise into the kitchen; it's almost too dark to see and she gropes around on the counter until she finds the plates and forks. She's about to head back outside when she hears a noise from the bedroom.

A tiny knot forms in her stomach and she calls softly, "Mom?"

That noise again, like a helpless kitten.

Eyes adjusted to the dark, Celan hastily stows the plates on the table and sloshes a cup full of water.

"I'm coming, mom."

Light from the fire flickers in the window as she enters the room. Mair is half-sitting up in bed, snowy hair falling around her shadowed face.

"Did you want some water?"

Mair nods, clearing her throat and coughing, and

Celan hands it to her.

"What's that light?" her mother rasps.

"We're making dinner."

"Cyrinda?"

"Yeah. Me, Cyrinda, and Taegh."

"Taegh?" Mair says vaguely.

"Cyrinda's man. You know, you've met him," Celan says, impatient. "Do you need anything else?"

Mair shakes her head and Celan hurries back into the kitchen, snatching up the plates and utensils as she hears Cyrinda call her name from out in the yard. She darts over to where her sister stands holding the frying pan, looking exasperated.

"What took you so long? Do you want all this stuff to burn?"

"Mom wanted water," Celan says, placing her burdens on the tree stump that's serving as a table.

Cyrinda says nothing, just scrapes potatoes onto each plate, lips set in a grim line. She hands one to Celan, who then passes it to Taegh for a portion of fish. She does the same with the next two until, plates full, they sit in silence. Cyrinda stares mutely into space, picking at her food. The knot in Celan's stomach gets tighter with each passing minute until Taegh nudges her and passes her the bottle of wine.

"Give this to your sister," he says conspiratorially. "You're welcome to a sip too, if you want."

Celan takes a tentative taste, and then a long swallow

of the tart liquid. It's warm and funky-tasting, but it makes the knot loosen a little. She hands it to Cyrinda, who gives her a sour smile and downs the rest wordlessly.

4

Shadows stretch long across the trail on the ridge between the South Peak and Sandia Crest, but Cyrinda and Taegh are unconcerned. They're getting close to their destination and can afford to take their time and still reach it before dark. At ten thousand feet the panoramic view is stunning enough to make them want to linger. To the left, the land drops off abruptly down sheer cliffs that reach to the foothills of Albakirk. On the right, the gentler slopes of the East Mountains shimmer verdantly in the late afternoon sun.

Cyrinda had been nervous to ask Jillyanne to stay with Celan and Mair overnight, knowing their patron's dislike of Taegh. So she had put on her most innocent face and acted like she was going to sleep over with a couple of girls from 'scuela. She knew Jillyanne would like that and, much to her relief, it worked. Jillyanne said she would sit with them and leave Tanny and Max with Lena.

The hike up was long and hot, but Cyrinda isn't tired at all. The exertion has burned off the lion's share of her former anxiety and replaced it with a growing sense of freedom as expansive as the arching blue sky. Even her apprehension about what they plan to do at the cabin is starting to evaporate. It's like heaven up here and they can do anything. Anything at all.

She mounts a rocky outcrop and looks out over the vast ruins of the old city and the shining new one rising from of its southern end. It feels like she could take off and fly like a hawk on the wind, down and down, and land at her old house on Transway. She closes her eyes and sighs like a little girl making a wish.

"Rin?" Taegh's voice carries on the breeze over to where she stands. He was ahead of her on the trail and must have just realized that she stopped.

Slowly she turns and takes him in – intensely hued hair and eyes like a mural come to life, with the neck of his guitar poking up above his head where it's slung across his back with the rest of his pack. His brow is knit in pique, but the stoop of his shoulders is sweetly endearing and in that moment she does wish, fiercely, for him to stay just this way and love her forever.

"Yeah?" she finally says, shifting the weight of her own pack. They didn't bring much – a few blanket rolls and some food and water. Anything else they need they can easily forage.

"Qué haces?"

"Just thinking."

"About Transway?" He always seems to know what she's thinking.

She nods.

"We're going. I promise. We'll get a place of our own and then we can do whatever we want. We're gonna be the best thing they ever saw." His eyes glint with conviction.

"I'm glad you're so sure."

"I am."

Her mouth draws into a pout. "They won't even let us play at Liberation Day."

Taegh sighs patiently. "Not the big serious concert. That's for the elders. They like boring music, you know that. We can still play at the bonfires, or at the fiesta. There's music at every other booth that day. I bet we get the biggest crowd!"

Appeased, she hops off the rock and starts toward him, limbs swaying like tall grass in a breeze. He reaches out a hand, she takes it, and they continue down the trail together.

THE STONE CABIN PERCHES LIKE an aerie on a bare rise right before the land falls away into nothingness. It is ancient, almost three hundred years old, and made of rough white blocks stacked as clumsily as a child's snow fort. The effect is far from comic though, and the small hut glows like a temple to some forgotten god in the last rays of day.

Reverent, Cyrinda and Taegh mount the two large steps in front of the entrance, shrugging off their packs and placing them on the broad ledges that frame the steps on either side. Taegh pops the cap off his water bag and takes a long pull, then passes it to Cyrinda. Their eyes meet and they share a quick smile.

Ducking their heads through the stone archway they note empty-paned windows crossed by old metal bars and a small fire pit under a chimney in the right front corner. Unseen hands have left a few withered logs stacked against the wall. Other than that the room is completely bare. A slight chill pricks Cyrinda's skin and she rubs at her arms.

They sling their packs inside. Taegh props his guitar carefully in a corner while Cyrinda peers through each window in turn, examining the vista from all angles. They meet at the middle window in the back, which looks out over the edge of the cliff and the vast expanse to the west. He pulls her close into the warmth of his body as the setting sun bathes them in a pink-orange glow.

She sighs. "It's beautiful."

"Gonna be even better in an hour or two. But first we need to get more firewood and some dinner in us. Don't want to fuse on an empty stomach."

He chuckles, and Cyrinda's stomach does a quick flip. She tries to ignore it. They are completely alone here, and perfectly safe. No prying eyes for miles.

Outside in the dying light they scurry down a rocky slope and into the trees to gather kindling, scooping up deadfall and snapping off small, low-lying branches. It quickly becomes a competition as they each try to gather as much as they can hold without dropping any, racing flushed and laughing up the hill and into the cabin where they dump their piles next to the fire pit.

"Winner!" crows Taegh.

"Chale!" Cyrinda says, panting. But his pile is almost twice as big as hers and he shuts down her argument with a kiss. The touch of his mouth makes the heat rise in her and she pulls him close, legs suddenly loose. His tongue slides between her lips and she purrs softly with pleasure. Then, suddenly, he releases her.

"Let's get everything set up first."

He crouches to arrange the kindling, thin shirt stretched across his lean-muscled back.

Cyrinda huffs over to their packs and drags them to the center of the hut where she rummages noisily, removing blanket rolls and shaking them out with a snap. The one in his pack is strangely heavy though, so she unrolls it carefully to reveal a jug of cider.

"Taegh!" she says happily. "Where'd you get this?"

"Strung a few guitars for some guys from Arqueros.

Knew you'd like it."

"And you hauled it all the way up here?"

He shrugs. "D'nada," and returns to his kindling.

Pleased, she arranges their bedding then digs into her pack for a small pan and a stoppered bottle of sunflower oil. Tucking her legs under her, she settles gracefully on the stone floor and removes a couple of potatoes and calabacitas, along with a large onion and a few withered carrots. Utensils have their own pouch and she pulls those out too, selecting a knife and unfurling a strip of bark. She sets to work chopping and dicing.

After cutting a few potatoes, she pauses to pop the cork off the cider and takes a swig. It's warm, but sweet and delicious like a ripe orchard, and it fizzes in her nose and curls into her stomach, sending a joyful feeling right down to her toes. She sips again, watching as Taegh strikes his flint and the dry wood sparks and catches, coloring the inside of the hut a cozy rose. Blinking in the brightness, she tucks her hair behind her ears and picks up the knife again, carefully slicing long strips of carrot.

"Hey Taegh?" she says, after a minute.

"Yeah?" He's sitting and fanning the flames as smoke whisks up through the chimney.

"I'm glad we came up here."

He doesn't turn around. "You were worried before."

"A little. I mean, everything with Nola. And mom."

"Nola didn't die from fusing, Rin. Whatever Dex did

70

to that roller, they weren't meant to go that fast."

"I know, but she got so…different."

"She was working at Maddy's. That'll change anyone."

"But she didn't need to fuse like she did. I mean, all the time like that."

"So?" he says. "It was fun. You weren't scared when she first showed us."

"But I didn't know what we were really doing – acting like elegidos, like elders. And they only transfuse in an emergency, to raise their prana up real fast, not just for fun. What if it's dangerous?"

He shakes his head and turns to face her, livid shadows writhing in his hair.

"That's ridiculous. It's fine. What Nola said made perfect sense; how the elders like to keep us ignorant, keep us in the dark. It all goes back to Jane Lees – and she lived a hundred and forty years, transfusing the whole time. She thought everyone should know how, but the council didn't agree. They wanted to pick and choose. Decide who was most evolved. So now no one here even knows that fusing exists, except for the chosen ones and they'll never tell."

He leans forward, eyes avid.

"So even once our transfers were released, if we weren't elegidos we'd go our whole lives and never know what they could really do. And the elders watch us, judge us, you know? You think they're ever going to make you an elegida? Even with all your talent? Not an expro, they won't. And even if they did, do you think they'd actually let you enjoy it?"

He wags a finger in mock disapproval. "No aviados young lady."

She laughs.

"But now things are changing. All it took was one old expro who knew the secret. 'Cause secrets get told. And now any expro that wants to can be just like an elegido. We don't have to wait around for them to choose us. We can choose ourselves." A smirk. "And enjoy it."

"But mom…" she says, poking at a calabacita.

"That's not the fusing. It's her choice to be that way."

"And I guess it's her choice that I'm the only one who's ever seen her do it either?" she says bitterly. "How long until Celan or Jillyanne sees something? The elders gave Jillyanne all this 'walking in the snow' crap and she believes it. Thinks mom has some kind of holy sickness!"

"At least it's not contagious."

"That's not funny," she says, but a grin tugs at her lips anyway.

He regards her in silence for a moment then asks simply, "Didn't you like it?"

"Yeah," she says, "I did." And raises her eyes to meet his.

TAEGH SIZZLES THE VEGETABLES OVER the fire, hand wrapped protectively in a cloth, and they share the meal out of the hot pan on the floor between them, chasing it with cider, the serious mood that had fallen lightening with every draught. When they're finished they carry the pan outside and scour it with sand, placing it on the ledge as they stand for a moment in the doorway, gazing at the stars and the rising moon.

"Ready?" Taegh says.

"Uh-huh."

"Do I still need to twist your arm?"

"Twist away," she says, proferring the transfer.

They sit side by side on the broad stone steps. Cyrinda lays her arm across Taegh's lap and turns her head away. There's a soft click and a momentary twinge like a cinder on her skin and then the stars are all there is, larger than she has ever seen them, spinning like fiery pinwheels as she throws her head back, bathing in the radiance.

It's like the entire force of the Universe enters her at once, lifting her up, and she wants to fly out across the mesa singing the most brilliant song she can imagine. Like the whole world is one big stage and she's about to give the greatest performance of her life.

Then Taegh's hand is in hers and she tears her eyes from the stars and turns to see her bliss mirrored in his face. Slowly, he lifts his other hand and strokes her cheek, letting his fingertips trail sparks down her neck and lower, to the buttons of her dress. He pulls the top one open, his mouth on hers.

"*Now*," he says, and he is on her, a pure rush of sensation under the pulsing sky.

LATER, THEY'RE CURLED UP BY the fire, all tangled limbs and blankets. Cyrinda's not sure how they got inside. They were on the porch and then…a tremor runs through her, an aftershock. She murmurs deep in her throat and snuggles closer to Taegh. Outside, the wind has picked up and she can hear it moan. The floor rolls gently, like a boat bobbing on the tide. She's not sleepy, just supremely content.

Taegh nudges her, mussing her hair. "See?" he says. "That's why I wanted to wait. Last time we didn't get to do it after we did it."

This strikes her as absurdly funny and she giggles, first a little spasm and then harder until she's helplessly convulsed. The sight of her makes him start in too and then neither one can stop, egging each other on with silly faces. Finally, eyes watering, they sit up grinning like goons.

"Let's play," he says, reaching over to stoke the fire, blankets slipping, leaving his backside bare. She gives him a playful smack and he pounces, mock growling, and wrestles her to the floor. Pinned, she glares up at him prettily. He gives her a swift kiss.

"I love you."

"I love you too."

He rises, pulling her up with him as the room rocks beneath their feet.

"Do you feel that?" she says as they sway together.

"Mmm-hmm."

"Your eyes look so pretty right now. All shimmery."

"Yours too."

"Does that always happen?"

"That's what Nola said."

"And no one else can see?"

"No one but us fusers."

With that he ducks down and grabs a blanket, tucking it around his waist and reeling away to grab his guitar. He flips the strap across his back and strums an undulating rhythm that bounces off the stone walls and reverberates deep in Cyrinda's solar plexus.

She shuts her eyes and swings her hips from side to side, utterly unselfconscious, humming along for a minute before launching into song.

You don't look the type but what is the type?
Giddy light we cotton to
The little things look good on you

We're gonna get each other in trouble
Riding a wavelength much too subtle
For the naked eye to clearly see
But we hear it whistle jubilee

Taegh laughs and she twirls around, yellow hair flying.

I don't look the type but what is the type?
Ecstatic and refined
The world can make you lose your mind

We're gonna get each other in trouble
Riding a wavelength much too subtle
For the naked eye to clearly see
But we hear it whistle jubilee

The music throbs as she spins, throwing out her arms like they could take in the whole of the world and hold it all here in this room.

We don't look the type but what is the type?
Rara avis taking flight
Strike the match 'til you ignite

We're gonna get each other in trouble
Riding a wavelength much too subtle
For the naked eye to clearly see
But we hear it whistle jubilee

A brief coda and the rhythm grinds to a halt. Taegh is staring at her with such fervency that she shivers. Cyrinda picks a blanket up off the floor and huddles it around her shoulders.

"Let's go back outside," she says, "and watch the stars."

5

"You all better slow down!" Lena orders sternly, as she and a huffing Jillyanne stump after the three youngsters beelining toward the casagrand. Celan, Tanny, and Max just caught the first whiff of the fairgrounds and are bouncing with excitement despite the large packs they carry stuffed with items to trade: Dried salted fish – a huge treat for those visiting from the upper ranchos – and the buttons, beads, and trinkets the two women carve from stone and wood. Basic food and drink can be had for the asking, but specialties require some barter.

"I want frybread!" Max says.

"You just had breakfast," chides Lena.

He shrugs. "Still hungry."

"You'll all get plenty," says Jillyanne, "but you gotta wait for us."

They slow their pace and Celan falls in next to her tia.

"Can we each have a cider this year?" she pleads.

"Yeah," Tanny chimes in. "Please? You let us split one last year!"

"We'll see. That stuff's a little strong sometimes."

"Can we go up to some of the other ranchos later?" says Max.

"There's enough to see here."

"I heard Gemelos and Arqueros've got – "

"Whatever they got is no better than what we've got."

"Some people try to visit all the celebrations in one day," he points out.

"Well, we're not those people."

Max sighs, defeated. "At least there's frybread."

Celan dances a few steps impatiently. Next to Navidad, Liberation Day is her favorite holiday – the food, the booths, the crowds, and best of all, the fireworks. But they're going to have to watch them from the roof of her house this year instead of from the fairgrounds. They have to get home before dark to relieve Cyrinda of her Mair-watching duties and let her have a turn at the celebration.

She frowns, thinking of last year when her mother was still well and they were all together. Mair had made sure to hold Celan's hand during the explosions even though she wasn't scared a bit. *Mom loved the fireworks best, too*. Celan swallows hard against the lump in her throat, resolving to put it out of her mind. This is going to be a fun day no matter what.

She squints at the long row of pushcarts and old bicycles parked along the edge of the road – down at the end there are a couple of rollers, their shiny white bodies looking completely incongruous next to the tumbledown carts. Rarely does she see one of these sturdy, tech-made vehicles. Their silver solar canopies glint enticingly.

There must be expros here!

She tears off toward the rollers.

A similar thought must have occurred to Lena, who makes a face. "Don't see why they gotta come around here," she mutters.

Jillyanne gives her a hard look. "They have as much right as anyone. They've got families, too."

"They got trouble is what they got. You just help it along."

Jillyanne sighs. "We've been through this a hundred times, querida, and it's never gonna change. She saved my life, Mair did, and I'm not giving up on her and her girls no matter what."

"It was her own fault you were in danger in the first place. She only saved you from her own mistakes. It's not your job to save her from hers."

"And it's not your job to judge what I do for family." Jillyanne takes Lena's hand and squeezes it – sweet, but firm. "You know I love you, but you know my mind on this and it's been made up."

81

Lena grimaces. "I love you, too," she says and squeezes back. "I just hate to see you give yourself away on trash."

"It's my own business, what I give."

This is all lost on the three children, who are happily inspecting the rollers until a guy with a shock of green hair pops up from the back seat of the far one, apparently interrupted in a nap. He growls an epithet and they scream and take off running, laughing wildly. Right before the entrance to the fiesta they remember to stop and wait, again, for the adults to catch up.

A merry-go-round of color and sound unfurls as they pass through the gate. People rush to and fro, bent on business and pleasure in almost equal measure. Booths sprout like wildflowers, dotting the wide, grassy field that constitutes the fairgrounds proper. Some are elaborately decorated constructions with banners snapping smartly in the breeze trumpeting their purpose or wares, while others hunker more modestly, consisting of little more than the makeshift table and chairs issued to all participants.

"Ours'll be nicer than that." Tanny sniffs as they stroll past a particularly scruffy one where a pinch-faced woman is arranging equally pinch-faced wooden carvings. "Terra Madre! Those things are ugly – ow!"

A swift whack on the head from Jillyanne silences her, but Max pulls a face mimicking the carvings, and the children dissolve in giggles as Lena peels off from the group, marching over to a table in front of the casagrand to get their lot assignment. Jillyanne gives them a jaundiced eye as they wait, muffling the last of their laughter.

"You all think you're so cute," she says. "Not everybody's booth is nice as ours, but some are a whole lot nicer. You don't know what people's situations are so don't go making fun."

They look down, abashed. But secretly, Celan grins. Those carvings are awful, no matter what Jillyanne says. And so is that booth. What's the point of having one if you don't even try to make it nice?

They all worked hard enough on theirs, especially without Mair's contribution, and they ought to be able to take pride in it. Hours spent, backs bent, embroidering graceful ripples and delicate fish on the bolts of antique blue cloth Lena found in some old cabin. Her fingers ache just thinking about it. And it's not like the adults are so nice. They'll gossip for the rest of the summer about whose booth was especially pretty or shabby this year.

At that, she risks a defiant glance up, but Jillyanne is done with her admonishments and is busy inspecting a display of freshly-tooled sandals.

Tanny nudges Celan's arm. "Hey, you want to play the ring toss later? They have some good prizes."

"Bo-ring. Besides, those games are rigged. No one ever wins."

"Yes, they do. Max won a new pack last year at the

dunking booth, didn't you Max?"

"Yeah! I dunked the mayordomo," Max says, puffing out his chest.

"That one's different," Celan says. "They have to let people get dunked or no one would play."

"Well then they have to let people win all the games or no one would play them either," Tanny concludes, obviously pleased with her logic.

Further argument is cut short by the return of Lena, holding up their card triumphantly. Lots are assigned by the luck of the draw and a high number means being stuck at the back edge of the field where hardly anyone will see your booth, no matter how nice it is.

"Row 3, Lot 4," she says.

They all breathe a sigh of relief and lug the packs to an empty spot sandwiched between a cider stall and a jewelry maker. Jillyanne gives Lena a look. The jewelry is fine, might be good for the bead trade. But if the cider proves popular it could attract a rowdier crowd. Most of the serious drinkers head for the free beer up by the casagrand, but sometimes they're willing to barter for something especially tasty.

Lena shrugs like, 'what can you do?'

While the two women wordlessly converse, the children unpack with a practiced air, shaking out banners and setting wares aside for arrangement in attractive groupings – dried fish on one end of the table, trinkets on the other. There are other fiestas and smaller trading days around the ranchos throughout the year so they're used to the routine. Liberation Day is less a serious trade day, though, than a chance to show off what you do so people know to look for you the rest of the year.

Jillyanne settles herself in a chair as Lena and the kids hoist up the four poles of the canopy and secure them in place. Then Celan and Tanny clamber up on the table to string the main banner between them, draping colorful flags around the two front poles while Max tacks bunting along the edge at their feet.

He helps the girls down when they're finished and briskly sweeps their foot prints off the table with his shirtsleeve, mock polishing it as he grins winsomely at Lena.

"Adorable," she mutters, seating herself next to Jillyanne as the children swiftly arrange the goods on the table. As soon as they're done, they turn on the adults in a pack.

"Can we go now?!"

The two women burst out laughing.

"Go on, then," says Jillyanne, "and take a few things for trade. You all did good. Think that's a record."

Feverishly, they stuff buttons, beads and, in Max's case, dried fish into their bags and set out with a collective whoop onto the fairgrounds.

"THAT'S THE BEST DEAL OF the day so far," Celan says, running a hand over the soft folds of Tanny's new skirt.

Tanny grins, stuffing it in her pack as the latest booth recedes behind them.

"I know! I can't believe she wanted all those beads so bad!"

"Well, she's all the way back here. Probably hasn't had that many people come by."

"Quizás. You could've gotten one too, you know."

"Eh."

"You can borrow mine sometime, after I wear it," Tanny offers.

"Gracias."

The girls spot an empty bench and hurry over to claim it.

"I wonder where Max took off to?" Celan says as they sit.

"Who cares? Boys are annoying."

Celan nods, but privately disagrees. Max's gang is always up to something interesting. Maybe they all snuck off to check out another rancho. She sighs. She would've liked to go too, but Tanny would definitely tell Jillyanne if she suggested it. She closes her eyes, midday sun pressing hotly against her eyelids.

"We should go back to the booth soon," Tanny says. "They'll want us to watch it while they go eat. It's almost lunch time. They're probably wondering where we are."

"Órale," she says lazily. If they're good, maybe they'll get that cider.

A loud *tsk* from Tanny opens Celan's eyes in time to

see a couple of young guys lurch by, obviously having taken advantage of the free beer.

"Honestly," Tanny says, "it's barely even noon."

Celan grins. "They're not hurting anybody."

"Not *yet*," Tanny says, shaking her head. "Give them another couple hours and they'll be fighting for sure. Probably end up locked in the basement all night."

The basement of the casagrand is famous for serving as a makeshift drunk tank for rowdies during major fiestas. The mayordomo and his cronies will keep the peace by removing them from the crowd and leaving them to sober up until morning, when they'll all have to publicly apologize. Some of the basement stories are the stuff of Liberation Day legend.

Celan rolls her eyes. "You sound like Jillyanne."

"So?"

"Never mind," she says, getting to her feet. "Vámanos."

They skirt the edge of the fairground, hurrying until Tanny suddenly halts, gazing at a small crowd gathered under a copse of cottonwoods.

"Mira! What's going on over there?"

Celan shrugs.

"Que pas'?" Tanny calls to a woman heading in that direction.

"It's Trijon," the woman says, pointing out a dark-haired, white-robed man who sits like a statue under one of the trees. "He's channeling the entities!"

"Come on, Celan." Tanny says, tugging at her sleeve. "Let's go see. He might say something important."

Celan digs her heels in, forcing Tanny to pull harder.

"Since when?" she mutters, eyeing the breathless bunch skeptically. It's not that she doesn't believe in entities, not with all she's seen and done at 'scuela. She's just not sure she believes in Trijon. There's something about him, a kind of condescension that sets her teeth on edge.

"Isn't he kind of young for an elder?" she whispers.

Tanny looks scandalized. "It's not for us to judge them," she says, hustling Celan close enough to where any further conversation is impossible.

Celan looks furtively around the semicircle of faces, all rapt with attention, eyes fixed on the man's smooth face as he stares out past them at a spot somewhere far above their heads in the vast blue sky. A bird chirps, the wind stirs the leaves, a lizard skitters across his feet, but the man takes no notice.

Then, without warning, a voice from his chest thunders, "Buenas tardes, good people of the ranchos! I speak to you now from the dimension of all-that-is. I am one-who-is-eternal. I can see through the past and beyond the future and I can tell you, good people, Terra Madre shall be delivered! The time is at hand when helpers from the sky will come at last."

A chitter of excitement goes through the crowd and he raises an arm dramatically, pointing at a vision only he can see.

"Even now they are coming. They will help you restore your precious Terra Madre to health and wholeness. No more shall you scavenge upon the leavings of the old world. No more shall you and She suffer. You have proven that you love Her and now, you are to be the first of a whole new race, the true Madren race, who will finally join in fellowship with your fellow beings from across the stars!"

People scan the horizon eagerly. Despite herself, Celan takes a quick glance up, too; there is nothing there save sun and cloud. Very quietly, she snorts, ignoring Tanny's side-eye.

"You will know them when you see them. You shall not fear. And they in turn, will know you. And they shall welcome you at last like the brothers and sisters you are."

The man falls silent, chin dipping to his chest and then abruptly jerking upward as he stares at the crowd as if amazed to find them there. Everyone starts talking at once, firing questions, but the man smiles with exaggerated modestly, waving them off.

"I don't know," he says softly. "Only They know the answers."

"Let's go," Celan says, tugging Tanny toward the fairgrounds. "I think the channel's closed."

Tanny rounds on her, yanking out of her grasp. "You think you're so smart. Always know better than everybody else."

Celan takes an involuntary step backward, holding up a placating palm. "C'mon, Tanny. You know I didn't mean anything."

"Sure you didn't. That's the point. What the elders say, what the entities say, it means something. *You* don't mean anything!"

Celan reddens. "You really think helpers from the sky are coming?"

"And what makes you think they're not?"

"It's just…" She shuffles her feet uncomfortably. "If they really exist why didn't they come help us before? When all the bad stuff happened? Why would they wait until now?"

"Weren't you even *listening*?!" Tanny yells. "We had to prove that we loved Terra Madre first! Now that we have, they'll come help us."

"Claro," Celan says drily.

Tanny says nothing more, just stares daggers at her before turning and stomping off toward the booths.

"Fine!" Celan shouts at her receding back. "Go ahead and be that way!"

Tanny doesn't turn around.

Cursing, Celan weighs her options. There's no way she's going to the booth now. Tanny's going to get there first and tell on her and then she'll end up with a lecture from Jillyanne. Lena never lectures, just gives you a look like you're so stupid she can't even be bothered.

That's the last thing she wants right now – Tanny sitting there all smug while she gets fussed at. No way. If she's such a model ranchita let her prove it. Let her watch the booth by herself. This day is supposed to be fun and she's not going to let Tanny ruin it.

She surveys the field, looking for anyone or anything that might offer a diversion. She's so absorbed that she yelps and jumps half a foot when someone taps her on the shoulder, only to be met by a mischievously grinning Max. He's flanked by two boys she recognizes from de la Virgen – one tall and rawboned, the other short and squat.

"Max! Ugh! Why'd you sneak up on me?"

"I didn't sneak, you were standing right there."

"Yeah, well," she says, embarrassed at having been caught off guard. "Que pas'?"

"Gonna go check by the booth, see if they need anything," he says, all innocence.

"I think Tanny's got it under control."

Something in her tone makes him smirk.

"You two have a fight or something?"

"Something. I don't wanna talk about it."

"Well if you're trying to avoid her…want to go check out Arqueros?"

"Really?" she says, anger on hold at the prospect of an illicit adventure. "You think we'll get back in time?"

"We've got, like, hours," Max says. "Plenty of time if we run."

"Yeah," challenges the rawboned boy, "you scream like a girl, but do you run like one?"

"Chale! I'll see you there," she says, and tears off across the fairgrounds, the boys hot on her heels.

CELAN'S SANDALS SLAP THE CRACKED pavement as sweat streams down her face and neck and her breath comes short and fast. Ignoring the discomfort, she concentrates on Max's skinny legs. He passed her right before the juncture to Rancho Toros. The other two are still behind her, close enough that she can hear their pounding feet. Their initial burst of exuberance has turned into a real race.

Just a little bit farther...

One more bend in the road and she'll reach the juncture to Arqueros; she only has to hold them off a little longer. She concentrates with all her might, picking out destinations.

Just have to make it to that tree. Past that fence.

Relief blooms in her chest as the road curves to the left and Max hurtles onto the Arqueros turnoff. She careens around the corner in his wake and the contest becomes more challenging as the rutted dirt track fills with throngs of fiesta-goers. Now they have obstacles on their course. Almost on cue, she hears a cry and a curse as one of her pursuers collides with a body behind her.

She almost turns to look but is brought up short by a little kid darting out in front of her. She almost trips, then dodges deftly and continues her flight. The main gate is just up ahead. She puts on a final burst of speed. Maybe Max got tripped up too and she can still catch him.

But he's inside already, hunched over, hands on knees, panting and grinning. She skids to a stop in front of him only to be sent sprawling as someone charges full on into her back. She faceplants straight into the dirt, hearing Max's strangled laugh as he regains his breath. Furious, she scrambles to her feet, brushing off her clothes.

"What the *fuck*?" she yells, channeling Cyrinda when she's mad.

This makes Max laugh even harder, joined by the rawboned boy, the one who must have knocked her over.

She points an accusing finger. "Sore loser!"

"You stopped short!"

"I did not!"

"Did too. I was right behind you."

"Were not. I was way ahead of you. You're just mad I beat you."

"Celan," Max says, "I saw it. Gabe *was* right behind you. You stopped and he ran right into you. It was an accident."

"Well…" she says, examining herself for injury. There are some scratches on her hands but she's otherwise intact. "Alright. Just don't let it happen again."

Max exchanges a 'Girls, what can you do?' look

93

with Gabe as the fourth member of their party arrives, red-faced and chastened, obviously having been bawled out by whomever he bowled over.

"Damian, you loser," says Gabe.

All three unite in laughter at Damian's expense until, satisfied with the establishment of their small hierarchy, they turn toward the fairground.

It's much cooler here than at the Pescados/de la Virgen fiesta. Ancient, sprawling apple trees form a canopy over the fairgrounds, filtering light through their leaves as the acequia burbles around the perimeter like a little canal. Planks straddle it at intervals, letting people cross to the other side. Some jump straight into the ditch, splashing in the cool water. Celan wonders how many ciders they've had.

Max must be thinking the same thing. "Man, I'm thirsty. Maybe we can get ciders up here – the good kind."

"Yeah," Gabe says, "theirs is the best. And it's free – all those apples they got. I could drink a barrel."

Celan sneers. "Riiight."

"Watch me."

"Well, first we have to get some. They don't give the hard stuff out to kids. Not unless an adult's with you."

Gabe gives her a look like she's so stupid, but Damian nods his head in agreement. "Yeah, they're never gonna give us any."

"How do *you* know?" Celan snaps. The last thing she wants is to be lumped in with Damian, the loser.

Gabe grins. "I got an idea."

"What?" the rest chorus, and stop to huddle under the edge of an awning. The booth it's attached to displays glassware and grown-ups cluster thickly around the table; no one pays their group any mind.

"OK, well," Gabe starts. "They got the hard cider and the soft, sabes?"

"Yeah, yeah," Max says, impatient.

"And they look pretty similar, don't they? The soft's a little less fizzy but once people get to drinking it they don't really notice as much, right?"

"True." Max makes a go-on gesture.

"So we go get ourselves some nice soft kiddie ciders and then go sit down over there." He points to a phalanx of long tables where people sit engrossed in eating, drinking, and conversation. "Not all together. One by one. We find someone drinking a hard cider and we sit down next to 'em all casual-like. Put our drink down next to theirs. Then, suddenly we see someone we know, we wave, and we get up, taking their drink instead of ours."

"Órale!" Max says, and he and Gabe fist-bump.

"What if we get caught?" Damian worries and is treated to the you're-so-stupid look.

"Duh," Celan says. "That's the whole point. Most cups don't look that different. So we picked up the wrong drink. Oops. Lo siento. Made a little mix-take."

Max and Gabe laugh. Not at her, though, more in

appreciation. She smiles, reveling in it.

"Alright," Max says, snatching back his leader's mantle. "Are we ready to go then?"

"Yes!"

"So, vamanos!" he says, and they scatter, intent on their mission.

THIS IS EASY, CELAN THINKS, snatching cider number two off the table behind her unsuspecting victim's back. She doesn't feel the least bit bad about it either. The guy is with a bunch of his friends and they're all saying really rude things about some girl they know. Just because she slept with two of them. With Nola for a sister, she's heard enough putana jokes to last a lifetime.

Kiss your drink goodbye, cabron, she thinks as she saunters away.

She takes a sip, savoring the fizzy sweet-tartness. She drank the first one fast, being seriously thirsty from the long run, and found her head feeling swimmy in response. It was a nice kind of swimmy though, like the whole world was swaying underwater. She liked it. But she figures she better slow down on this one.

She peers out over the fairgrounds, searching for the others. They've been studiously avoiding each other for the duration of their heist, but she thinks she sees Max over by the food stalls, munching on something. Maybe he'll share a bite if she gets to him in time.

With another swallow of cider, she skirts the outside

of the table area and maneuvers through the crowd until she's right alongside him – without spilling a single drop. A fast elbow jab gets his attention.

"How many'd you get?" she asks.

"This is my second," Max says proudly, taking a big bite of a burrito and hoisting the purloined cup in his other hand.

"Me too."

"You got two, too?" Max echoes and they both chuckle.

"Hey can I have some of that?"

"Sure." He passes the food over.

Celan tastes savory potato and beans, but seconds later a wave of heat engulfs her tongue and her eyes start to water.

"Wow, this is spicy." She gulps at her cider.

Max laughs. "Extra chile."

"Ouch," she says, but takes another bite.

"Hey, there's Gabe and Damian." Max points over to where the two seem to be arguing. Gabe gives Damian a shove.

"Uh-oh," Max says, and speeds off in their direction. Celan trails him, still chewing.

"Hey, que pas'?" Max says, as they reach the two boys – Gabe sweaty and red-faced, Damian stoic. "How many'd you get?"

Damian shrugs. "One."

Gabe hiccups, staggers a little. "Well I beat you all.

I got four."

Celan and Max exchange a nervous glance.

"And now," Gabe announces, "I'm going to go win that game!"

He points waveringly to the left, where a line of round targets is set up in a clearing, each marked with concentric circles orbiting a red center. People are shooting at them with bows and arrows. It looks like a pretty serious contest.

Max smothers a laugh. "Maybe that's not the best – "

Gabe cuts him off angrily. "What? Afraid I'll beat your ass?"

"Not exactly."

"Think you're so fucking great, Max, don't you? Always the winner." Gabe's right up in his face now, practically spitting.

"I – uh." Max looks to Celan for help.

So she does the only thing she can think of.

"Yeah, Gabe. He totally does," she says, taking him by the arm and steering him toward the targets. "But you'll show him, right?"

"Thas' right," slurs Gabe, leaning heavily on her shoulder. His bulk is not a welcome sensation and it almost unbalances her, but she grits her teeth and hauls him along.

"Now you just sit right here," she says, depositing him under a big tree a short distance from the game field. "And we'll get you some nice bows and arrows."

Gabe's head dips to his chest. After a few seconds, he looks up again vaguely, then turns to the side and vomits in a gush.

"Ugh," she says. "What a loser!"

Max and Damian materialize on either side of her.

"What are we gonna do now?" Max frets. "We can't carry him all the way back to Pescados like this."

"Don't worry," Damian says sagely. "My tios do this sometimes. He'll sleep for an hour or two then wake up grouchy and thirsty, but he'll be able to walk. I'll watch him, make sure he's OK."

Celan sighs, relieved. Maybe Damian isn't so bad after all.

"Well," Max says, "now that we've got that settled, you want to go try it?"

He gestures toward the archery range, and she shrugs, nods.

Might as well do something interesting.

"You sure you don't mind?" she says to Damian.

He waves her off, plunking down under the tree next to Gabe. "Yeah, he's my cousin. You guys go ahead."

She and Max chug the rest of their ciders, shove cups in their packs, and stride in the direction of the booth. There's only one person ahead of them – a salt-and-pepper haired man hoisting a basket of arrows, who takes an enormous bow from the man behind the counter and struts purposefully off toward the targets.

The counterman trains his gaze on them. "Can I

help you?" he says, smirking.

Max hesitates, so Celan speaks up.

"Yes," she says, swallowing her nerves. "We'd like to take a turn, please."

"Ever shot before?"

"Not really, but we'd sure like to learn."

"Fair enough," the man says, then turns and hollers. "Lang! Raf! Ven acá! Got some newbies for you." Then, addressing Celan and Max, "They'll help you get set up, shoot a few, have a good story to tell at your rancho, OK?"

They both nod as two figures swagger out from the back – boys, a couple years older than they are, punching each other in the arm and laughing.

"Great," Max mutters.

The boys circle around to the front of the booth and stop in front of Max and Celan, appraising them. One is long and lanky with a prominent nose while the other is shorter but well-proportioned, with a face so beautiful he could almost be a girl.

"I'll take the boy," the beautiful one says. "He looks like he's tough."

Celan sighs, disappointed. The lanky one snorts. His eyes are a pretty green color, but he looks obnoxious.

"Whatever," he says. "This girl's gonna kick his ass." He punches her arm. "Right?"

"Right," she says, with the most superior air she can muster.

Both boys laugh. Then the skinny one says, "Cuántos?"

The beautiful one turns serious. "Orchard hours. Una semana."

"No way."

"Thought you said she was gonna kick his ass."

"Whatever. Three days."

The beautiful one's lip curls derisively. "Three days then. But only half an hour practice. Then we're gonna have them shoot it out."

"Órale."

The beautiful boy hustles Max off behind the booth as the green-eyed boy turns Celan in the opposite direction.

"OK," he says, slapping a friendly arm across her back. "What's your name?"

She shrugs him off. "Celan."

"From?"

"Pescados." She stares straight ahead, hoping her short answers broadcast her displeasure.

"I'm Lang," he says importantly, but then notes her mood. "What's the matter?"

"I wanted to shoot an arrow! Not be part of some stupid bet!"

"Well, we gotta keep it interesting somehow."

She pouts. "Why can't we just practice by ourselves?"

"Well, I'm very sorry, miss," he says, mock solicitous, "but that's the way we do things. Safety first. Can't let first timers loose with sharp objects. Especially," and here he crinkles his nose and sniffs, "when they've been drinking cider."

Celan flushes, taken aback at being caught out. "I only had a little!"

"Don't worry," he says, soft in her ear. "Me and Raf had a couple few too."

She glances up and they share a sly smile.

They're just like us, she thinks, and her anger evaporates in a flash.

THE NEXT HALF HOUR IS a frustrating blur; shooting an arrow is much harder than it looks. Even with a child-size bow, it takes all her arm strength to draw it properly. The first few arrows she tries to notch drop straight into the dirt. Celan is close to the edge of her patience when finally one shot succeeds, lodging in the extreme edge of the target. Nowhere near the center, but at least it hit somewhere. Maybe she won't totally embarrass herself.

"Nice one!" Lang says encouragingly.

She gives him a rueful look. "I'm awful."

A shrug. "It's not easy. It takes years to get good."

She wipes her brow on her sleeve.

"I guess Max isn't doing much better then?" she adds hopefully.

Lang grins. "I doubt it."

"Alright," she says, "let's get this over with."

Leaving the training target they emerge onto the main field, veering off from the adult section and into a more child-sized area. Still, the competition looks way beyond her limited skill. But the expression on Max's face as they approach him and his trainer tells her he feels the exact same way.

"Three for three, Raf?" Lang says by way of greeting.

Raf nods. "Let's do this. Ladies first?"

Lang smirks. "Guess that means you."

Raf starts to protest but Max rolls his eyes. "Whatever," he says, and steps up to the line.

He draws and notches fluidly then lets the arrow fly, lodging the point at the edge of the target, right about where Celan's best shot went. She frowns.

"Your turn," Raf says smugly.

She steps up to the line, drawing the bow back more easily than it seemed in practice. Her hands are shaky though. She takes a deep breath, notches the arrow, and squints at the target.

Thwang! It misses wildly and Raf barks out a laugh.

What a jerk.

She can't believe she thought he was cute. Even for a minute.

Celan steps aside for Max and again he hits smoothly, getting two rings closer to the center than on his first shot. Raf pats him on the head. She looks over at Lang and he gives her an encouraging thumbs up. But she's already feeling defeated, and though she manages to aim and shoot, she barely grazes the edge of the target.

Max's last shot must be infected with her frustration

because his arrow misses the mark entirely, flying off into the trees. He grunts, aggravated.

My feelings exactly, she thinks, coming up to the line for a final time. She eyes the boys; they aren't even paying attention. As far as they're concerned, the contest is over.

Oh well.

She draws back the bow and notches the arrow. Relief floods her veins. One more shot and it's done. Drained of all nerves, she stares calmly down the line of sight, straight at the center of the target. She lets it fly.

Thunk. Right in the red center. She lowers the bow in disbelief. Behind her, Lang lets out a triumphant whoop.

"Nice shot!"

He bounds over and gives her an enthusiastic clap on the back. "We won!"

"But I only got one."

"And one bulls-eye's worth three shots on the outside! He only got two." He jostles her again. "You got good aim! I knew it."

She beams. "Gracias."

She and Max hand over their bows, leaving the boys to argue about whether Celan got lucky or not. Returning to Damian and Gabe, Max is quiet and Celan doesn't gloat.

"That was stupid," she finally says.

"Yeah."

"Imagine Gabe, though? He would've been terrible."

Max laughs, pantomiming a drunken Gabe taking aim at the target. When they reach the real Gabe he's sitting up, drinking water, and holding his head like it hurts. Damian's crouched next to him, sanguine.

"Ready?" Max says, noting the tilting angle of the afternoon sun. "We better get going."

Gabe gives him an evil look as Damian gets to his feet and extends a hand.

"Let's go, borracho," he says.

Gabe glares again, but takes the offered boost and Damian hauls him up. Celan and Max lead the way across the fairgrounds in the direction of the main road.

No one says much on the way home.

6

The woman's white robe is stained crimson by the light of the setting sun as she stands solemnly on a platform before the crowd. She raises her hands and silence falls. It's time for the address, one elder at each rancho speaking the litany of liberation, the words they drink in eagerly on this day each year.

"On June 3, 2059, twelve years after the massive changes wrought upon on our Terra Madre forced all to huddle in the remnants of Albakirk, living like rats on the scrapings of the old world, one heroic woman led three hundred brave souls out of the dark and back into the light of the sun and glory of our beautiful land of enchantment. It was this woman's goal, in fact, her life's work, to re-enchant a world lost in destruction, fear, and mourning."

She pauses, letting the cultural resonance sink in, though none alive is old enough to have lived through the actual events.

"To that end, she spent long hours during the years inside, devoting what little free time she had to the creation of what would become her greatest gift – the hope of humanity – transferon."

Scattered cheers.

"This gift she shared freely, with all who dared to learn how to open the channel to the free use of their natural gifts and abilities, abilities hated and feared as supernatural occurrences by those of limited vision.

"And so this gift was rejected by many of those it could have helped, those who preferred to remain in the dark, cogs in an ever-growing machine, instead of opening their minds and hearts to the benefits this miraculous substance could bring them: True union with Terra Madre!"

She closes her eyes then, smiling, seemingly lost in the wonder of it all, but when she opens them again her tone is all business.

"So they forced this woman, this visionary leader, to make a terrible choice: Either to lie, to renounce the creation for which she had shed her very lifeblood, or to leave the safety of the enclosing walls and walk away into a world with a dangerously unstable climate and a poisonous environment to face whatever fate awaited her there. And not only her, but all those who followed her as well."

A pause for effect.

"And so on that fateful day, this third of June, the woman I speak of, the great Jane Lees, made that choice. And three hundred brave souls followed her. So on the anniversary of that momentous occasion, we gather together to celebrate her, and our, successes – our society, our achievements, and yes, our liberation, while across the mountains, those inside still grind hopelessly away – "

"This is boring," Taegh whispers. "Let's go get drunk."

Cyrinda grins and takes his hand and they push through the crowd, earning annoyed looks from those trying to listen until they emerge out of the crush into the mostly deserted booth area.

"Perfect timing," Cyrinda notes with satisfaction. "No lines."

They amble over to the beer booth and hand the woman behind the counter their cups, which she fills to the brim. After slurping off the top few inches to avoid spillage, they carry their drinks over to an unoccupied bench and sprawl out contentedly.

"Now this is more like it," Taegh says. "Beats listening to all that tired old shit."

Cyrinda laughs and clinks her glass to his as a voice behind them pipes up, "Bet you wouldn't say that in front of your abuelo."

They turn to see Lulin and her sister Susila, every

inch the pious elegida in her pale blue robe. Though a year older than Lulin, she's a head shorter with thin, waifish limbs. Her stern demeanor, however, is anything but delicate.

Taegh curls his lip. "I sure would."

"I'm sure you wouldn't," Suslia says archly.

Lulin shifts her weight. "C'mon, Su, he's only joking. Let's go up closer." She tugs at her sister's sleeve.

"Yeah," Taegh says. "Why aren't you down front with all the other little azulies?"

"I had *work* to do," Susila says. "Which is more than I can say for you. Lounging around with this one." She indicates Cyrinda dismissively.

"What the fuck is that supposed to mean?" Cyrinda half-rises, fixing the elegida with her deadliest stare.

Susila is undaunted. "It means," she says, "that he knows better. He has ancestros, and he'd better start acting like it if he wants a chance at this." She indicates her robed attire.

"Who says I do?" Taegh challenges, with an insouciant slug of his drink. "I don't even care."

Susila breezes past them, hurried along by Lulin. "Sure you don't," she says, then taunts over her shoulder. "You're always such a good boy at 'scuela."

THERE'S NO WARNING NOW, ONLY a stirring of the air, a quickening. The veil parts and Mair finds herself in the kitchen. But not the one at Arlo's. Her kitchen in the ranchos, where a white-haired girl eyes her angrily.

"I think you're being selfish, Nola," Mair says. "What about your sisters? What kind of example do you think this sets for them?"

"Example?" Nola snorts. "And you say *I'm* selfish? What kind of example were *you*? An elegida, running off to Transway? Marrying an expro?"

Mair winces. "I made mistakes, I know that. I just wanted to give my girls a chance – "

"Your girls. Claro. Cyrinda and Celan, you mean. It's always been about them. You never gave a shit about me! First it was all about little miss adorable. Then it was all about the baby. You dragged me to this fucking dirty chicken coop of a house and left me to rot so they could be 'raised right'. You didn't care how you raised me."

Mair looks at her imploringly. "Nola, I never meant to – "

"What? Hurt me?! Is that what you were going to say?!" She's shouting now, gesticulating wildly. "I'm sure you didn't, for the five minutes you ever thought about it! What the fuck did you think I was going to do in this place? Bake bread and pull weeds for the rest of my life?"

"You could have gone to 'scuela. You could have learned. You were always so smart. But you never even tried – "

"Tried? Tried what? 'Try to be nice, Nola. Try to

make friends, Nola,'" she mocks acidly. "Like any of these fucking little shits ever gave me the time of day. They treated me like a disease."

"Now you're exaggerating."

"You think so, huh?"

"Yes," Mair says, crossing her arms firmly over her chest. "You never even gave them a chance."

Nola dips into the pouch at her waste and begins to roll a smoke. She cocks her head insolently.

"You really have no idea, do you?"

"About what?" Mair challenges. "You think we're so backward here, so stupid? I once thought so too. But I was wrong. And I've been trying to make it right for my girls."

"Make it right?" Nola strikes her flint and drags deep, blowing out a cloud in her mother's direction. "Don't you get it? You can't wave your hands and 'make it right' just like that, just 'cause it's easier for you."

"If you think this is easy – "

"Yeah." Nola tosses her head. "It's so hard telling your daughter you hate her."

"I don't hate you."

"Yes you do. You think I'm bad, that I'm a bad influence. Well, chingate. My sisters see my way, and they see your way, and they can choose for themselves."

"You better not – "

"Oh, don't worry. I'm not going to corrupt your little darlings. Especially that tech baby." She pops her eyes, mimicking her mother's shocked expression. "Oh, you thought no one knew? Your bad. But I'll keep your little secret. You really think I want anyone to know I'm related to one of *them*?"

And with that, in a puff of smoke, she is gone.

A GOOD-SIZED CROWD HAS GATHERED by the time Cyrinda and Taegh swing into the finale of their impromptu set with a rousing rendition of 'The Three Hundred,' a Liberation Day standard. Fueled by beer and adrenaline, Cyrinda swaggers and swears, passionately recounting the tale of Jane Lees, voice rising above the ringing tones of Taegh's guitar as the crowd claps out the rhythm. She holds the final note as long as she can, drinking in the applause and the shouts for more as her eyes sweep over the blur of faces, spying three multihued heads clustered off to the side. Expros. She sidles over to Taegh.

"Hey," she says, "let's do that Aetherworld song."

Taegh grins wickedly. It's a song by an old expro band that Dex taught them, about as far from 'The Three Hundred' as you can get. He strums a few bars of off-kilter syncopation before Cyrinda swings into the verse.

I feel so frail like a ghost faded pale
I feel so light like a thief in the night
You look at me can't believe what you see

Big open chords ring out the chorus.

I don't think you really wanna know just what I am
I don't think you really wanna know just where I stand
Wanna go to heaven but you just don't wanna die
Throw your wishes in the well and then you'll never have to try

Look 'cross the line but that line's in the sand
When the wind blows, I got no place to stand
I am defined by the ties that I bind

She throws herself full throttle back into the scathing chorus as the watching eyes register unease. No one walks away, but the applause is considerably muted at the end. Cyrinda stands panting and defiant as Taegh marks the show's end by flipping his guitar around, adjusting the strap across his chest so it rests against his back. The crowd disperses, muttering.

"Hey," says a voice, "check out these ranchitos – think they're at Arlo's or something."

"Awww, so cute."

"Where'd you learn that song little ranchita?"

It's the expros – a tall, muscular guy with bluish-black hair and two others, heads dyed red and green, respectively; less physically imposing, but still with the same slightly menacing air. Unfazed, Cyrinda marches right up to them.

"I am *not* a ranchita," she says, right in the big guy's

face, "and I've gotten nothing but shit for it since I was seven years old. So I'm sure as fuck not going to take it from any of *you*.

"Arlo, as in *Arlo's*, was my father," she says proudly, "and Nola Mairs was my sister."

The guy does a double take, impressed.

"Cyrinda Mairs? No shit! So what are you doing back here with this payaso?" He jerks a thumb at Taegh.

"He's not a real rancho either."

"Cyrinda," Taegh warns.

She whirls, hands on hips. "Well it's true, Taegh. Maybe you were raised in a fine old family but you sure weren't born in one. You told me how they found you. Right here by the casagrand. I'll bet you anything your real mother was an expro."

Taegh grimaces.

The big guy rolls his eyes. "So? Your puta madre doesn't give you the right to walk around looking like this." He tugs at a lock of his own hair. "We don't do this to look pretty. We do it for a reason."

Taegh's stare could put the sun on ice. "Mine's as white as yours under this," he says quietly. "I fuse all the time."

All three faces register shock. The leader recovers first, stepping past Cyrinda and looking hard at Taegh.

"You ain't fucking fused right now, ese. I can't see nothing in your eyes."

"We were waiting for the fireworks."

115

"Yeah? Let's see your transfer."

Taegh draws Cyrinda's vial from his pocket and displays it open-palmed; the guy grunts, satisfied, and he stuffs it back in before anyone else can see.

Then the leader's tough mask drops and he laughs, slapping his palm against his side. "Tomás, güey," he says, sticking out a hand.

Taegh pauses for a moment before taking it and offering his own name.

"Jenner and Brophy." Tomás indicates red and green. They all shake.

"And you already seem to know Cyrinda," Taegh says, placing a proprietary hand on the small of her back.

All three nod respectfully.

"Well shit, what're we waiting for?" says Tomás. "Vamos aviados!"

As they trail the gang away from the fairgrounds, Cyrinda drops behind, plucking at Taegh's sleeve.

"My hair's as white as yours?" she hisses furiously. "Just because I let you have the transfer sometimes you better not be – "

"Of course not," Taegh says. "I just said that to shut them up."

"I don't want to fuse with them," she pouts.

"You don't have to if you don't want to." He gives a small, put-upon sigh. "But I don't have a choice now. You're the one who had to get in their face and tell them all our business. They probably would have gotten bored and left us alone."

"They *probably* would have kicked your ass if I hadn't told them about your mother."

"We have no idea who my real mother was," he says flatly.

"But she probably was an expro – couldn't get a patron so she left you here for a better life and all. It happens. Why is it such a big secret? Kids get raised by different relatives all the time."

"Not like this. They still have ancestros. I thought I did too, until I found out the truth."

"Yeah, because your sister is a pinche little bitch," she says, shaking her head. "She only told you because she's mad she didn't make elegida, even with all that pure ranchos blood in her veins. She can't stand the thought of you still having a chance."

"If she knows, then my grandfather knows, then all the elders probably know," Taegh says glumly.

"So? Why do you act like it's something to be ashamed of? I'm an expro! Are you ashamed of me?"

"Of course not," he says, eyes softening as he touches her arm. "It's just – "

"It's the only reason Dex and Nola trusted you. They thought you were just some snotty ranchito until I told them."

"Maybe it helped with them," Taegh allows. "But these guys don't care. They only backed off when I showed them the transfer. And now I gotta show 'em I know how to use it."

Cyrinda mutters disgustedly; it's clear that machismo is going to trump reason. Taegh merely shrugs and grabs her hand as Tomás turns to look at them and they hurry to catch up.

THE ELEGANT MAN SMILES AS Mair stretches out on the messy bed – his warm brown eyes are flecked with gold and a stray forelock of dark hair falls earnestly across his furrowed brow. After Arlo died, she didn't think she would ever touch another man again. It hurt too much to even think about. This one was so kind though, so understanding. And so different.

But she never meant for things to go this far, to get this serious. It was a novelty at first, a little fling that wouldn't cause a lot of talk since he had just as much reason to hide it as she did. Or so she thought.

He sits on the edge of the bed, stroking her hair.

"I know it sounds radical, Mair. But imagine the possibilities."

"It'd be too hard. Too hard on my girls."

"You won't be stigmatized, if that's what you're afraid of. Your daughters either. They'll have so many opportunities to learn that they'd never have in Transway. The oldest is what, twelve? Making good progress in our expro school, apparently. Think of what she could accomplish with a real education."

Mair says nothing, staring past him at the ceiling and

trying to avoid his relentless gaze.

"I don't think I could live inside like that."

"Don't be silly. There's no lock on the door. Look at me. I'm out now, aren't I?"

He spreads his arms wide, pleased with this display of self-evident truth.

"But they track you," she counters, sitting up. "With those bots in your head. You told me yourself. They probably know you're here right now."

"So?" he says. "I told you. No one's sitting at a screen and watching our every move. It's not like that. The bots transmit to the Bank, where information is saved in case something goes wrong. Just think, even in an emergency you'd never have to worry. You could find out where your girls are like that."

He snaps his fingers.

Mair sighs. "It's just not natural to have those things in your brain."

He springs to his feet, raking a hand through his hair in frustration.

"Natural?" he says, pacing up and down beside the bed. "What's 'natural' about Transway? You eat our food. You drink the water we pump in here. The rollers you ride. The lights in your wayvern. You've been here, what, fifteen years now and you're pulling this right-off-the-rancho stuff? Increíble!"

His face is full of thunder.

"Theodore," she says, placating. She's not scared,

not exactly, but she doesn't want to rile him further.

He softens, sitting and taking her hand in his.

"I love you, Mair. You know that. And I just want what's best for you. You'll see. It's high time the expros starting reintegrating back into Albakirk. Just think -- you could be the first fully reconstructed transer. An example for the others."

He smiles encouragingly but she cringes inside, barely managing a faint grin in return.

"Why would you even want me though?" she says, trying for a light, teasing tone. "If what you tell me is true, you're going to be one of the biggest bosses in the whole city. What are you going to do with a transer wife?"

"Adore her," he says, squeezing her hand, "and have everyone else adore her, too."

She rolls her eyes. "And if they don't?"

"They will."

He grins again, but there's something behind his eyes that makes her shudder.

"Don't be scared," he says. "It'll all be fine."

"I – I'll think about it, but I can't promise anything," she hedges. "I need some time."

"How about three months?" he says, getting to his feet like it's all been decided. "That's how long I'll be in Winnipeg."

"Quizás."

He places a soft peck on the top of her head, like she's a sweet but stubborn little girl, then tips her chin up with long fingers and places another, considerably less chaste kiss on her lips.

"When I get back," he says, "you can let me know your answer."

One last smile – with the confidence of one who knows exactly what that answer is going to be.

"MIRA." TOMÁS LAUGHS, LOUNGING AGAINST a tree. "Look at this guy – aviados, tres, and cuatros." Idly, he strums Taegh's guitar. "Gets a pretty good sound out of this thing, though."

Taegh is sprawled on the grass with his head in Cyrinda's lap; face a mask of rapture, gaze fixed heavenward. The fireworks are in full bloom, colors bursting on an inky canvas as the crowds in the big field ooh and aah at the display. Their small group is hunkered in a sheltered knoll by the creek bend. It's been quiet with the guys all lost in their fuses, but they seem to be coming around now. All except Taegh.

"Híjole!" says Jenner. "His eyes look like that sky up there right now."

Brophy draws lazily on a smoke, exhaling a fragrant blue cloud as he scratches at the wispy beard on his chin. "That was a big bang for a little ranchito."

Taegh doesn't even blink, absorbed as he is in the firmament. Cyrinda sighs, pulling him closer.

"So how'd you guys learn to fuse?" Jenner wants to know.

"Mi hermana."

"The lovely and talented," Tomás gibes.

"Spare me," Cyrinda snaps. "I've heard it all."

"No offense," he adds. "Nola was great."

"Hmmph." She grunts, only slightly pacified.

"Serio," says Brophy. "She used to come around my cousin's place all the time. Talking about the techs. She said the only reason they have their whole food-growing operation is because of Jane Lees. She was the one with the whole seed bank before the transition, saved all our asses, and they act like we should be kissing theirs for giving us something back. She was fucking brilliant."

"Right on," says Jenner.

"She told us all that, too," Cyrinda says.

"She knew all about the elders, too," Brophy continues. "How they all fuse, how they hide it. They don't want anyone knowing all their secret shit. It's how they keep control over here."

He takes a deep drag and passes the smoke to Jenner. "They think they know the Will of the Universe, right? The way I see it, no one's known that since Lees died. She was the real thing. And a fuser to the bone. But you don't get another Lees when you only pick the ones you think you can control. The ranchos are fucked. The expros are the future." He leans back on his elbows, nodding with conviction at his own words.

"Órale," says Jenner. "That's how it is."

From under the tree, Tomás chuckles softly. "You're a

fused-up fucking philosopher, güey."

They all laugh and then fall silent, staring up at the sky.

"You two aren't bad, you know, with the music," Tomás finally says.

"You think?" Cyrinda says eagerly.

"We got a band, too," adds Jenner, tapping out a rhythm against his thigh.

"Really?"

"Claro que sí. We're at Alamora right now, but we've played Arlo's."

She looks wistful. "I miss it."

"You should come and play," says Tomás. "You're wasting your time around here."

"Oh, we're gonna. There's some family stuff going on though, you know?"

"Yeah."

"But we're gonna," she says firmly as the explosions wind down, "for sure."

Darkness descends once more, settling velvety soft, the hush broken only by the gurgling of the creek. The smell of sulfur hangs in the air. Tomás rises slowly, brushing dirt off the seat of his pants as he flips Taegh's guitar across his back. The other two stand as well and they all look down at Cyrinda.

Jenner flicks the smoke to the ground and stamps it out. "Want some help with this guy?" he says.

"Thanks," she says, relieved. Jenner and Brophy pull

Taegh upright between them as Cyrinda scrambles to her feet.

Tomás pats a hand against Taegh's cheek. "Hey, ranchito, you still in there?"

"Hnnmm…"

"We're gonna walk now. Think you can handle it?"

"Yeah, m'fine." Taegh's eyes open and focus momentarily before consciousness greys out again.

"Bueno. We can put him in the roller."

"Where're we going?" asks Jenner.

"Back to my house," Cyrinda says. "He'd be, like, disowned if his folks saw him right now."

"Huh," says Brophy, digging in the pockets of his jacket. He pulls out a flimsy knit cap, pulling it firmly over Taegh's bright hair.

Cyrinda gives him a quick smile. "Nice."

They keep to the path along the creek, well away from the bulk of the crowd and any curious faces. A passed-out ranchito at the fiesta is hardly an anomaly, but one being carried by expros would definitely warrant a second look. Cyrinda finds herself holding in a breath that she doesn't fully exhale until they are safely on the road.

It's cramped in the back of the roller with Taegh stretched across her and Jenner's laps as they twist up the road toward the springs. Despite the sturdy wheels, the ride is still bumpy and the only solid things to grab onto are the bars that hold up the solar canopy. Cyrinda keeps one hand on a bar and the other on Taegh but every steep turn strains her shoulders. Once, their headlights reveal several walkers up from the fiesta. They wave hesitantly. She's glad it's not a full moon.

They're coming around the last bend when Taegh jerks awake. "Hey," he says, scrambling to sit up. "What the – ?"

Jenner grabs his collar, pulling him flat so as not to upset the weight distribution. "Don't worry güey, está bien."

"We're going back to my house," Cyrinda says. "It's fine."

At the end of the road Brophy brakes and Taegh lurches forward across Cyrinda's lap.

"Ow!" she yelps, whacking him in the head. The cap flies off but he doesn't seem to notice.

"Sorry," he mumbles, running his hand vaguely through his hair as he staggers out of the roller.

She jumps out after him, snatching the cap up off the ground while Jenner stretches his legs out with an elaborate sigh of relief. Tomás and Brophy share an amused look. Cyrinda smiles and tosses the cap to Tomás. In return, he hands her Taegh's guitar.

"Thanks for all your help," she says.

"D'nada. Glad we met. When you two get out to Transway ask for Fused Up! at any wayvern. They all know us. We'll put you up."

"Gracias."

She positions the guitar across her back and grips

Taegh's arm, gently steering him toward the ponds as the roller whirs away behind them, tires spitting gravel. As soon as the expros are out of earshot though, she gives him a shove. He stumbles, almost falling into the brush.

"Why the fuck did you do that?" she demands.

A pained look. "What?"

"What do you mean *what*? You know exactly what."

"Aw, c'mon Rin," Taegh says, rapidly recovering his faculties in the interest of self-defense. "Don't be like that. It was an accident. I didn't know that was gonna happen. I've never done that much before." He smiles to himself. "It was pretty great, though."

"I'm so glad you had a good time," Cyrinda says, caustic. "But you were completely out. Those guys could have done anything."

"Do you think I would have done it if I thought they were dangerous? We were perfectly safe. And look, now we even have a place to stay on Transway. That's what you wanted, isn't it?"

"Yeah," she concedes, "but I don't want you like that all the time."

"I won't be, Rin," he says solemnly. "I swear."

Arms crossed, she continues to glare as he edges toward her, eyes all apologies. He slides an arm around her shoulders and gives her a squeeze, a kiss on the cheek. She sighs. He's right – everything did turn out for the best.

And everyone makes mistakes.

She turns her face up, kisses him back.

ATRAVESAR - TO GET ACROSS

IT'S DARK IN THE ROOM where she's been for – *how long?* Mair doesn't know. It all swirls around her like a kaleidoscope – everything that's been in a series of flickering images. One turn and she's a child, running down a dusty road with the sun on her face bright and hot, trying to make it to 'scuela on time. Another and she and Jillyanne are fourteen, lazing under a tree after a long day's work in the fields, confessing their first crushes in giggling whispers. Jillyanne's was on their friend Belinda, Mair's was a boy named Ramón. He was an artist. He drew her a picture of a scarecrow in a field and she tacked it up on her wall.

The face of her abuelita, alight with pride when she made elegida. Her mother, crying at the public ceremony. Then Arlo – the night they ran away over the mountain under the full moon, hand clutched in hand, confident they couldn't take a false step.

Her mother never spoke to her again.

But there was so much joy on Transway. So many nights of song. And then her girls, kissing their sweet faces as she put them to bed. The smell of their hair. Their soft baby skin. Her cheek against Arlo's chest as they lay in the night and counted their blessings. Before it all got dark. Before it all went wrong. Before he died and left her alone.

And then that man, Theodore. What had she been thinking? Going with a tech like some Maddy's whore. But she needed someone to hold, to soothe the empty ache in her chest. 'Techs don't count,' the Maddy's girls all said and maybe part of her believed that – so much so that she didn't bother to trans herself properly afterwards.

Careless. Stupid. Pregnant.

She knew that if he found out he'd never let her go – and she couldn't stand to live inside those cold, unnatural walls. She would go crazy.

She laughs then, a wheezy sound deep in her throat. *Crazy* – looks like she went anyway. The laugh stops as abruptly as it started.

So many mistakes.

Nola gone; Cyrinda pulling away the same, still angry that she had to leave Transway, not knowing that it could have been so much worse. Maybe she should have told them straight out what happened. But she couldn't. And everything she did that she thought would make things better only ended up making them worse. Every twist and turn, like a rat in a trap. Never able to claw her way out.

It's all her fault. She must be wrong, rotten.

Cursed.

She ran away from the elders, from her duties, and this is her punishment. The Will of the Universe. It must be. Maybe her last girl will be safe if she leaves now; doesn't pass the curse on.

A shadowy form touches her hand, a daughter.

"Mom! Did you see them? The fireworks? Weren't they beautiful?"

She can't see anything anymore, except for an odd illumination in the window and a man stepping through it; a tall blond man, smiling.

"Mair, love, it's time to go."

She lets go of her daughter's hand and reaches for his.

"Arlo, I'm coming."

She rises and steps through the window.

The breath in her body ceases.

"Mom?" Celan shakes her shoulders. "Mom?!"

JILLYANNE'S SOFT ARMS ENFOLD HER, hold her close and safe as they walk outside, both sobbing. Tanny and Max look up, their eyes big and solemn in the firelight. They're huddled next to Lena around the small blaze she started to ward off the evening chill.

Neither of the adults had said a word when Celan and Max arrived, breathless, just as they were starting to pack up the booth. And Tanny was oddly conciliatory on the walk home. She said she was sorry for their fight and so did Celan and that was the end of it.

Mair had been as she normally was when they returned from the fiesta; they all went up on the roof to see the lights. When they came down, her breath was ragged. And now she's gone.

Wordlessly, the three stand and surround the grieving ones, drawing them into the circle of warmth and light. Jillyanne lowers her bulk to the ground, her back against a solid log. Celan clings to her as Oso curls up at their feet and Tanny hugs her from the other side. Lena puts her arm around Max's shoulders. They all stare into the fire. No one speaks for a long, long time, until the murmur of voices somewhere on the path below the house incites a flurry of barks from Oso. Two heads pop into view, blonde and pink in the firelight.

Celan scrambles up and runs headlong toward them crying, "Rin! Mom's gone. She's passed. Rin!"

7

Mair's body lies on the pyre ringed by a small semi-circle of family and friends. Arms folded peacefully across her chest and wearing a long white robe, as is custom in death, she is flanked by three equally white-robed elders, whose duty it is to escort people out of this world. In dying she is restored to life, to purpose; and liberating the dead is a purpose they all understand.

The middle elder looks kindly around the circle. "Speak, please," he says. "Say what you need to say."

"She was good," Jillyanne affirms, hugging Celan close. "A good woman, she just couldn't take it anymore. She made her mistakes, sure, but she was loving."

"I remember," says a grizzly-haired man, "she helped me when I was hurt. I'd had a little tussle with a cougar." He lifts up his pant leg to show the proof. "Terrible thing. I was laying in the trail like to die. And then she came and she transed me, and it healed up just like this." He indicates the scar with tears in his eyes. "A good woman, like you said, and powerful prana."

A middle-aged woman attests, "She healed my daughter, too. She'd been off somewhere. Touched something bad. Some old world poison. Thought she'd die that day she got so sick so fast. But Mair was there and she healed her. My daughter's got daughters now." She sniffles.

Lena hesitates before saying, "I didn't always think so well about her, but I know she was good in Jillyanne's eyes and that's enough for me."

She bows her head solemnly and Jillyanne starts to cry. Celan pulls away from her and stares fiercely around the circle.

"She was my mother, so I guess I get to say something too. She loved me and my sisters and she taught us about a lot of things. She was good. And she loved fireworks."

Cyrinda stifles a laugh. "Yeah," she says, a jagged edge to her voice. "She sure did."

This earns her a few raised eyebrows, but she doesn't elaborate, only frowns down at her feet until Taegh embraces her and they retreat up the path from the burial grounds.

Celan looks to Jillyanne, confused, but her tia just shakes her head and sighs. The elders share a meaningful glance. Finally, the one on the right clears his throat.

"If there are no more speakers…" When no one replies, he strikes a flint, lighting the torch in the middle elder's hand.

As the other two chant the final prayer, the torch-bearer lights the pyre. Later, they will scatter Mair's ashes in sacred places around the ranchos. Even if she didn't spend her whole life here, she was born here and she died here and it is her due.

"A LOT MORE HERE THAN there were down there," Jillyanne says sourly, mopping her brow with a towel as she collapses, legs akimbo, in a kitchen chair.

Her house is filled with people partaking in the funeral feast. The smell of savories wafts temptingly as she and Lena are nearly run to ground with the cooking and serving.

Celan and Tanny and Max help, running back and forth with platters and pans, the adults mildly solicitous of Celan but not treating her with pity, as is custom. People pass on and their souls are at peace. There is no need to mourn, only to celebrate what life they had when they were here.

A few of the guests strike up a tune out in the yard, and the old song drifts in through the window as the beer and wine begin to flow.

Lena stoops over the kitchen stove, stirring a big pot of posole and brushing humid locks out of her eyes.

"So what's it gonna be with the girls?"

Jillyanne grimaces. "Gonna watch 'em, same as always."

"That Cyrinda, she's not gonna listen."

"Doesn't matter, I'll do my best."

"They gonna live here with us?"

"I don't know."

"I think Celan should," Lena says, suddenly earnest amidst the steam. "Let the other one choose, whatever she wants to do."

Jillyanne stares, wondering and grateful, then gets up and embraces her.

"I always knew I picked you for a reason," she says, chin nuzzled into Lena's damp neck.

"Yeah," Lena grunts. "Bueno."

IT'S EERILY QUIET UP AT her house but Cyrinda's glad of that; here she and Taegh have their space. They ate their fill of the feast at Jillyanne's and drank some wine, but now it's time for some private recreation. She's sick of people watching her, whispering. It's been like that all day; *all* the days, really, since her mother got sick. It never stops. But now it will.

Taegh has some cider stashed in his pack, which he uncorks with a pop and they sit, propped against the outside wall, legs hugged up tight against their chests. He takes a long swig and passes it to her. She does the same.

"So what now?" he says. The question hangs in the air.

"We'll go," she says, staring fixedly into the distance,

"to Transway."

"When?" He traces a long finger around the mouth of the bottle until she yanks it out of his hand and takes another pull.

"In the morning. I'm done with this. All of it."

"Tomorrow?"

"Yeah," she challenges. "What are you, scared?"

"Of course not. It's just…what about your sister?"

"She'll be fine. She's gonna live with Jillyanne and Lena. They love her; they don't love me," she says flatly, lips a tight line.

Taegh eyes her thoughtfully. "I love you," he says.

Her face softens and she slips an arm through his, snuggling closer. "I love you too."

A sudden breeze stirs, brushing fingers of cool night air velvet-soft against Cyrinda's cheek. A memory: She's six and sick with a bad fever, her mother's cool hand on her forehead. For the first time that day she feels like she might cry.

But she bites her lip. She won't. She won't give in to it. All these tears all day from people who pretended they knew her, who pretended they cared. All worthless.

She chose to die and didn't give a fuck about anyone she left behind.

That's the reality. And all the tears in the world won't change it.

She buries her face in Taegh's neck, breathing in his salty sweet scent like a tonic. He presses his lips to the top of her head and begins a run of small pecks across her forehead and down the side of her cheek until finally his mouth is on hers, kissing her so soft and deep that she shivers. She pulls him closer, wanting total immersion in this good feeling so that the bad ones can't get in. Finally they break apart and his face, big as the moon, smiles down at her.

"We should wait," he says softly, brushing a strand of hair out of her eyes, "until my transfer's released. It's only a few more months. It might be good to have an extra."

"Why? We only need the one." She digs deep in her pocket, takes out the vial, grins up at him.

"Let's fuse," she says. "They can't do anything to us now."

One Year Later

8

The afternoon blazes white-hot, but it's pleasant in the shade; Celan sits at the edge of a tree-lined pond, drowsily feeding the fish and half-listening to their silly chatter.

Too bad Tanny and Max had to go weed the chiles today, we could have had a good time up here.

Idly, she trails a hand along the water's surface, rippling her reflection then letting the water go still so she can see her face.

Older, she definitely looks older. More mature. Definitely. A week ago today she turned eleven.

Secretly, she loves the number, the way it looks – two straight lines, so strong and clean. She dips in an index finger, tracing them in the water, then laughs at her own folly as they immediately disappear.

Insects drone around her in a dull hum and she

swipes at them lazily until all at once she becomes aware of another sound – a strange whirring and crunching from out on the road. Wiping her hands on her skirt she stands, craning her neck around the gaps in the bushes to spy a roller moving slowly up the dusty track with a blonde head and a purple-pink one bobbing inside.

"Rin!" she cries happily, careening around the brush and dashing headlong toward the sturdy, four-wheeled tech vehicle.

"Hey!" says Taegh. "You wanna get run over?"

"By that thing? I can run faster than you drive."

He leans on the horn in reply and Celan screams and takes off for the safety of the trees, giggling wildly.

The roller jerks to a halt, kicking up a cloud of dust, and her sister and Taegh disembark, Cyrinda hastily smoothing her wind-blown hair. She's wearing a tight jersey top and a fluttery pink skirt that swirls prettily above her knees. A long scarf trails from her neck and her shoes look new. Celan eyes them admiringly as she steps in for a hug.

"Hey ranchita," Cyrinda says, "how're all things Pescados?"

Celan sighs. "Same old."

"That good, huh?" says Taegh, swinging his guitar of the roller's back seat. His face is slightly drawn but still reassuringly handsome, eyes crackling with humor. He's traded in his sandals for a pair of motley patched grey boots.

"It'd be better if *some* people came to visit a little more often."

"Well, we're pretty popular these days. Hard to get away from the adoring crowds."

Cyrinda rolls her eyes. "It's a long walk, you know? But now that we've got the roller…"

"Is it yours?"

"It's the Arlo's roller, but we can use it whenever we want. And so we had an idea." She pauses, beaming. "How'd you like to come visit *us* for a change?"

Celan's eyes widen. "Really?"

"Just for a couple of days," she adds hastily. "We've got a big show coming up and stuff and we have to practice. We have a drummer and bass now and everything. And we have our own little place at the wayvern – it's so perfect! We can get our hair done and get you some pretty clothes."

"To feed fish in?"

"You're a girl," Cyrinda says. "You should get to look cute." She twirls, using her own outfit as an example.

"Will there be techs there?"

"Claro," says Taegh. "But they're really not all that interesting."

"Do they really have things sticking out of their brains?"

Taegh smothers a laugh.

"Honestly, Celan, where do you hear this stuff?" Cyrinda says, shaking her head. "They look just like us."

Celan regards her dubiously.

"You met Dex, right? He had bots. Did he look any different?"

"No, I guess not." A shrug. "I forgot about that."

"So do you want to come or not?"

"Órale!" She throws her arms around her sister's waist. "I can't wait."

"Bueno." Cyrinda laughs, disentangling herself. "Let's go tell Jillyanne."

"ABSOLUTELY NOT." JILLYANNE'S FISTS ARE planted firmly on her ample hips and she fixes each of them in turn with a ferocious stare, commanding center stage in her cluttered kitchen. A pot boils on the stove, ready for canning tomatoes.

"But it's only for two days!" Celan wails, near tears. "I'll be back in time for 'scuela!"

Jillyanne ignores this, addressing Cyrinda and Taegh.

"You're not taking this child over there with all those crazy people and techs running around and that's that. You and your sister, that's what you wanted, fine. You're too old for me to tell you what to do."

"I'm not Nola!" Cyrinda says hotly, stung. "I'm not doing anything but singing and there's nothing wrong with that."

"I don't know what you're doing over there and I don't need to. But it's no place for Celan."

"Oh, but it was fine for me and Nola, fine for Mom."

142

Jillyanne grimaces. "You all were old enough to make your own decisions. Maybe I didn't agree with them, but there wasn't anything I could do to stop you. Even your mother in her day – I warned her. But Celan's still a child and she doesn't need to see all that." Under her breath she mutters, "Got enough ideas of her own already."

"I don't know what you think goes on 'over there,'" Taegh cuts in with steely politeness, "but there isn't a whole lot to see that she couldn't just as easily see here."

Jillyanne regards him with frank distaste. "There's plenty and you know it."

"It's not like we're going to take her to Maddy's or anything," Cyrinda argues. "There's not going to be anything dangerous. Just a little music. Just for the weekend. She'll only be gone a couple of nights."

"Please," begs Celan, truly sobbing now.

Jillyanne looks at her and sighs. "No." Then she turns to Cyrinda and Taegh, dismissing them. "You can say goodbye later. You two go on now and let me talk to this child alone."

CELAN FINDS THEM BY THE ponds – Taegh hunched on a log bench with Cyrinda stretched out languidly, her head in his lap. They look so lovely and peaceful that she has to swallow hard against the disappointed lump in her throat. Her downcast expression broadcasts her failure before they even ask.

"No luck, huh?" says Cyrinda.

"I begged and begged, but she still said no." Celan scuffs at the dirt with the toe of her sandal. "I really want to come but she won't let me."

"And you always do everything you're told," Taegh notes drily.

"Jillyanne loves me," Celan says, a little defensive. "If she says it's not safe then I believe her. She doesn't lie."

Cyrinda and Taegh exchange a glance.

"What?" Celan says.

Their eyes meet again but they say nothing.

"What was that look for?"

"Forget it," Cyrinda says lightly. "It didn't mean anything."

"Did too." Celan shifts her stance uneasily. "Dígame."

"Celan, seriously, it's nothing." Cyrinda disentangles herself from Taegh and gets up off the bench, sidling over and slipping an appeasing arm around her shoulders. Celan jerks away, arms crossed.

"Tell me."

"Celan…"

"Tell me what that look was for."

Cyrinda bites her lip and looks down at the toes of her shiny new shoes, sun-kissed silk brushing against freckled cheeks. Finally she half-raises her head and peeks out through a fringe of bangs.

"Did Jillyanne ever tell you about Mom? About how she got the way she was?"

"She said she got sick," Celan says, matter-of-fact. "She got sick and she died."

"Do you know what 'walking' means?" Taegh cuts in from his place under the tree.

She regards him with mild interest.

"Those who walk out into the snow…" he starts.

"Yeah, I know. I heard people say that so I asked Jillyanne. She said it meant Mom was gone, walking on the astral. It was a holy sickness. They tried, but they couldn't cure it. Sometimes you can't."

"Celan," Cyrinda says, shaking her head. "It means that she transed and kept transing and didn't stop. Even when it made her get like she was."

Celan gazes up into her sister's sea-change eyes and feels like she's being sucked underwater. "That's not true," she says, struggling for some kind of footing. "Transferon can't kill anybody. All the grown-ups take it. The elders take it!"

"Transferon does whatever you want it to do." Taegh's voice again, impassive.

Celan looks back and forth between Cyrinda and Taegh with growing horror. "You can't – she didn't *want* to die."

"No, not that she wanted to," Cyrinda says soothingly. "Not on purpose. She just lost control."

Celan feels the pull of a current so swift and deep that she knows it, inexorably, as the truth. But still she struggles, yelling, "No she didn't! She was *sick*," and

145

on that last word she chokes and the hot tears rise. She turns and runs blindly, ignoring Cyrinda's shouts.

She dives into the trees, branches slapping her wet face and twigs snapping underfoot as her chest heaves, mind swirling with sudden fragments of realization like a familiar puzzle whose pieces have been tossed into the air and are now falling together in jagged new shapes.

Jillyanne said mom's sickness wasn't catching but she wouldn't let Tanny and Max come over anymore. She let her have the transfer, she could have taken it away. Why did she let her keep it?

And worst of all —

That's why she's always watching me. Why she's always saying 'no aviados.' She thinks I'm like that, that I don't have control.

Faster she runs, as if she could burn the knowledge out of her head with the force of sheer speed; but it won't be denied. Finally, gasping and spent she leans against a tree, legs shaking. She stands like that for a long time before wiping her nose on her sleeve, stiffening her spine, and marching out of the woods and up the path toward Jillyanne's. By the time the house comes into view her eyes are as dry as the sky.

Celan slams inside and stomps into the kitchen, where she stands glowering in the doorway, staring daggers into Jillyanne's back. Jillyanne stiffens, but doesn't turn around; she continues chopping tomatoes and onions on the wide counter.

"You better turn around right now and come in this house softly, mijita," she says.

"No."

"I'm going to count to ten..."

"You can count to whatever you like. How about you start counting all the lies you told me?"

Jillyanne freezes. Then, slowly, she turns, and whatever she sees in Celan's face stops her dead.

"Qué pas'?" she says carefully. "What's the matter with you?"

"You told me my mother got sick. That's why she died. Not because of her transing!"

"What did Cyrinda – ?"

"Don't blame her. I made her tell me. You're always blaming her and Taegh but they didn't do anything wrong. At least," she adds, "they always tell the truth."

Jillyanne gives her a pitying look. "Celan, escúchame. Your mother *was* sick – a sickness of the heart, the spirit. She never got over Nola dying. Never. She blamed herself. She'd been through a lot, your mother."

"You could have stopped her. You could've taken it away!" The tears are rising again. Stubbornly, she blinks them back.

"No," Jillyanne says. "I couldn't. I wanted to. When she first started getting like that I went to the elders, asked them what I should do. They said there was nothing – once they get like that there's nothing for it but to wait. If they're gonna come back, they do. If you take it away they're just gone."

Celan says nothing for a minute. Then, voice low and angry, she cuts to the heart of it.

"You think I'm like her. You think I'm like Cyrinda and Nola, too."

"Celan, no, that's not true," Jillyanne stammers. "You're a good girl, a smart girl, you're different." But Celan can sense she's really hit home.

She regards her tia coldly. "I'm going," she says. "I'm going to Transway with Cyrinda and Taegh and there's nothing you can do to stop me."

And with that she turns and is gone.

HURRYING BACK TO THE SPRINGS, Celan hopes against hope that they're still there, that they haven't left yet. She bursts into the clearing by the fish ponds calling their names. It's totally deserted. But out past the bushes she thinks she sees the roller still sitting up by the road and picks up her pace, pounding around the wall of brush until she emerges, scattering pebbles in her wake.

Taegh is perched on the hood of the squat vehicle playing guitar, eyes closed. At the sound of her footsteps he opens them and smiles.

"Coming with us after all?"

Celan's mouth turns down and begins to tremble.

"Hey," he says. "Don't be upset, ven aquí."

He slides over to make room and she scoots up next

to him, dejected.

"I called her a liar. I was so mad. I said I was going with you no matter what she said." She sniffles. "Now she probably won't ever want me to come back."

Taegh gives her a comforting nudge. "Don't sweat it. She did lie, right? She's earned a little scare. Hang out with us for the week. We've got a big show next Saturday. It'll be fun and by the time you show up again she'll be so happy to see you she won't care what you said."

Celan draws a shaky breath and reclines against the roller's warm hood, staring up at the sky and watching puffs of clouds race each other past the sun. Taegh plays a slow, dreamy tune, singing softly along with the music in his ragged tenor.

Into the west and my heart's begun
To roll out toward the setting sun
On a boat that smells of salt and sea
And a big warm wave to carry me

I can hear you
But I'm not coming back
I can hear you
But I'm not coming back

She watches his pale, skinny elbow bob with the rhythm as it pokes through a hole in his frayed shirt.

"Taegh?"

"Yeah?" He doesn't miss a beat.

"That's pretty."

"Thanks."

"Taegh?"

"Yeah?"

"Can transferon really make you die?"

He stops playing and regards her seriously. "No, of course not. I trans all the time. So does your sister. So does everyone."

"But Mom…"

"Your mom had a lot of bad things happen to her. She couldn't handle all of it so she lost control."

"You mean like Nola dying?"

"That, and other things. Before you were born."

She ponders this for a minute, torn between asking him to explain and not being sure she really wants to know. Finally, she changes tack.

"Do a lot of people lose control?"

"It happens," he says, "but it's rare. Look, you do really well up at 'scuela, right?"

She nods.

"Well, then you've got nothing to worry about. When it's your turn, you'll be fine."

Celan sighs, lacing her fingers beneath her head and turning questions over in her mind like rocks. She picks up the most intriguing one.

"What's it like?"

Taegh considers this. "It depends," he says, "on how much you do and how you do it and why. It's different for everyone."

"But for you?"

The question hangs in the air as he absently plucks a few strings, violet eyes gazing into the middle distance.

"For me, it's…" He pauses and grins, color rising in his cheeks like he's heard someone say the name of his secret crush. "Just like bliss really, happiness. Everything feels so easy, but realer somehow, too. Better."

"I want to do it."

He chuckles. "Jillyanne would have fits."

"Just a little bit. Just to see."

"Haven't you had enough rebellion for one day?"

Now it's her turn to look sheepish.

He shakes his head, frowning with mock disapproval while his eyes shine with amusement. "First she runs away from home, then she goes straight for the transferon."

"Well you're not supposed to be aviados either, you know."

Taegh turns toward her, suddenly earnest. "That is *not* what we're doing. We're not aviados, we're learning, just not at 'scuela. They wouldn't let Rin have a transfer, even though she was old enough, so we did our own thing instead.

"Besides, what we do is different than what anyone here does. Some people blow glass, some people make clothes – this is what I do." He flourishes a riff. "And sometimes that takes a little more trans than sewing buttons."

Celan's next argument is cut short by a shout from Cyrinda, flushed and aggravated, struggling toward them with a big jug of water.

"Need any help with that?" Taegh says, but he makes no move to put down the guitar. Celan laughs and jumps off the roller, helping to heft the jug into the back seat.

Cyrinda cocks her head to one side. "So what's the story, hermanita?"

AFTER A BRIEF DETOUR TO de la Virgen for some food and barter they head west into the long shadows, Celan tucked in with the now half-empty jug and Taegh's guitar. At first she takes in the scenery excitedly, but the scrubby trees on the side of the road are no different than they are in Tijeras. Eventually, the combined effects of a full stomach and the novel feeling of being in a moving machine lull her into drowsiness. But as she starts to drift off she hears Cyrinda's voice, low and insistent from the front seat, and perks up her ears.

"I can't believe you, Taegh! It was only supposed to be for the weekend. What is she going to do for a whole week?"

"Shhh, she'll hear you," says Taegh, jerking the wheel to the right to avoid a buckled section of pavement.

"She's sound asleep." To prove her point Cyrinda

turns and softly calls Celan's name. Celan responds with a delicate fake snore. "See?" she says.

"You worry too much."

"Well somebody has to. What about Saturday? The show? It's Arlo's thirtieth anniversary. It's gonna be crazy. How are we gonna keep an eye on her?"

"Give her a tambourine and let her dance around. She'll have fun."

"And the rest of the time?"

Taegh sighs, exasperated. "We do what we normally do. Why does it have to be such a big deal? We eat breakfast, play music, show her around. She's not going to be the only kid on Transway."

"What we *normally* do?" Cyrinda mocks. "I hope you're not planning on doing what you normally do."

"What's that s'posed to mean?"

"It means no más fusing."

Taegh throws her a wounded glare. "You know I wouldn't do anything in front of her."

"I know. But just to be sure I'm holding the transfer this week."

"I can't believe you don't trust me."

Cyrinda says nothing, foot tapping impatiently against the dashboard.

"Bueno," he says, shoving a hand into his pocket. He pulls out the vial and drops it in her lap. "All you."

"I didn't say you couldn't have *any*."

"No, you're just going to make me feel like shit if

I ask."

"That depends on how many times you ask," she snaps. Then, softer, "I don't care if you *trans*, Taegh, I just don't want you fusing. Not in the house. Not while she's here." She tips her chin toward the back seat.

"I said I wouldn't."

"Then we're good."

The roller rattles on towards Transway, but its passengers are silent for the rest of the ride.

CELAN JOLTS AWAKE TO A tremendous lurch as they bounce down a crude sort of ramp leading off the crumbling highway. She rubs her eyes, wondering that she really did fall asleep after all. She had intended to stay awake for the whole ride in case Cyrinda or Taegh said anything else interesting. She's dying to ask what they meant by 'fusing' but it's obviously something they don't want her to know – so it's probably smarter to be quiet and listen.

Off to the left, the lights of Albakirk blaze white-hot against a soft black sky. She'd thought the casagrand looked impressive when it was all lit up on Liberation Day, but that was nothing compared to this. This is that times a hundred, a million even – sleek pyramids towering up into the sky like so many spaceships preparing for landing. There must be thousands of people in there.

What do they all do?

Celan sits up, uncramping stiff arms and legs. Her left arm seems to have fallen asleep and she shakes it, tingling, to life as Taegh steers them onto a broad street lined with old storefronts and houses – some decaying and in ruins and others rebuilt and reclaimed. Many buildings are lit up and welcoming, with people coming and going in a brisk trade.

Celan tears her eyes from Albakirk and peers around at these more prosaic surroundings.

"Are those the wayverns?" She leans over the front seat to ask and Cyrinda turns, startled.

"Oh, you're awake. Yeah, that's what they are." She sweeps an arm out grandly. "Home sweet home."

"Which one's Arlo's?"

Cyrinda points out a large tan adobe structure painted with a swirl of murals. These aren't the familiar bucolic images of the exodus of Jane Lees, but garish scenes of wild celebration. Celan's heart leaps with nervous excitement.

"Nice, huh?" says Taegh, aiming them toward it. He beeps the horn at a couple who are standing and kissing in the middle of the street. The two part, first annoyed then waving in recognition. Taegh gives them a nod as he pulls the roller into Arlo's side alley and parks. They all climb out.

"Is this where you live?" Celan asks, spinning around to take it all in.

"Allá," says Cyrinda, gesturing to the end of the

alley. "Everyone who works at Arlo's lives there too. We have some gardens and stuff, so we don't need to get everything from the techs."

"Kind of like home then?" Celan says tentatively.

"It really is. It's like a family. It's not like what people think."

A side door slams open, releasing a burst of music and laughter and a haggard-looking man who staggers past them blindly.

"Well, mostly." There's a wry tilt to Taegh's brow as he lifts his guitar out of the back seat. He gives Cyrinda a quick kiss. "Gotta go talk to Brophy for a minute. You two go ahead." Then he vanishes through the same door that the staggering man came out of.

Cyrinda stares after him for a long moment before reaching into the roller and removing her pack and the water jug. Then, with forced brightness, she takes Celan's hand and gives it an affectionate squeeze, saying, "Let's go and see the house."

They dive deeper into the gloom of the alley, punctuated by a small square of light from a grimy window and a larger one from a screened kitchen door. Mingled smells of food and refuse and shouts and bangs of pots and pans drift out into the night. A young man in a grubby apron leans against the door jamb, smoking listlessly, lank, bluish hair falling around his gaunt cheeks. He nods briefly as they pass.

"He has hair like Taegh's," Celan whispers.

"Yeah," says Cyrinda, "there's a lot of that going around." Celan looks up, questioning, but her sister is staring straight ahead, jaw set, and doesn't elaborate.

The alley ends at a large courtyard where a central garden can be made out in the dim glow from the windows of the surrounding buildings. They are all long and low and built of the same material as the main wayvern. Some doors are open and people lounge outside in the cool evening – laughing, drinking, and chatting. A few play various instruments.

Cyrinda circles the yard briskly on the hard-packed walkway, then stops before one of the darkened doors, plunking down the jug and dropping Celan's hand before rummaging in her pack for the key.

"Cyrinda!" calls a guy from a group huddled a few doors over. "Que pas'? Wanna drink?"

The two girls sitting with him beckon as well and Cyrinda abandons her search, grabbing Celan's hand again. Celan snatches it away, not wanting to seem like a baby in front of her sister's friends.

Cyrinda gives her a look and opens her mouth like she's going to say something, but then seems to change her mind. When they reach the group – three cheerful expros perched on a couple of beat-up chairs and a makeshift crate – she just says, "Hey, this is Celan, my sister."

The door behind them is open and a light from inside bathes them in a golden glow. The guy is slightly

157

pudgy with sunny blond hair and friendly hazel eyes. The girls could not look more different – one lush with copper curls and very skimpy clothing and the other slim in a modest jersey shift with inky hair tucked neatly behind her ears.

They are passing a bottle around and the guy offers some to Cyrinda, who takes a hearty swig.

"Can I have some?" Celan says.

They all laugh.

"I can see the resemblance already," the guy cracks good-naturedly, as Cyrinda hands the bottle to Celan and she takes a careful sip.

Dandelion wine.

Still nasty, but it tastes like home. Wiping her mouth on her sleeve, she passes it back.

"Nice to meet you," she says to all of them.

"Cap's our bass player," Cyrinda tells her. Then, for the group adds, "Celan's gonna be staying with us this week. A little trouble at home, you know how it goes."

The girls exchange sage glances.

"You a ranchita?" Cap says, and Celan nods. "Well, nice to meet you, too. This is Eris and Zita."

"*Aman*zita," the redhead corrects him.

"Whatever." He brushes her off. "Thinks she's a big deal now she's working at Maddy's."

The girl punches him in the arm, but not hard.

"Ow!" the guy says with obvious exaggeration.

Celan giggles and Zita gives her a congenial grin.

"What rancho you from, hon?"

"Pescados."

"My people were de la Virgen back in the day."

"*Way* back," says Cap, winking.

Another punch, harder this time.

Ignoring their antics, the girl named Eris addresses Cyrinda. "Hey, so how do you want your hair done for the show? It's like a week away now, right?"

"Yeah!" Cyrinda brightens, interest piqued.

Eris scoots over on the crate and Cyrinda settles in next to her. They put their heads together, conspiring over hair and makeup. Celan plops down cross-legged on the ground with a sigh.

"Cheer up," says Zita, passing her the bottle again. "You're gonna have a great time."

AN HOUR LATER (OR MAYBE more – time seems to move at a different speed on Transway) Celan is curled on a narrow cot in the main room of Cyrinda and Taegh's apartment; a little loopy from the wine, but not in a bad way. They only let her have a few sips.

She snuggles under the blankets, suspended weightless in a patch of moonlight, thinking about how luxurious it all is: Their own place – with a sink and an algalamp and a hot plate where they can cook things for themselves without building a fire. Tons of people to play music with whenever they want.

Even the latrines are nice. Cyrinda took her to

159

wash up before bed and it was so clean. There was even a shower, and a box on the wall that blew out air so you could dry your hair. No spiders lurking like in the creaky old shack at home.

And, best of all, they have a radio. It's like magic, a box that plays music! There's a building around here where they play the songs and the waves go through the air and then they come out of it. According to Cyrinda, there used to be millions of them in the old world.

"And if you like this, wait 'til we go in the wayvern," she'd added. "They have big screens in there where the techs come on and make speeches and lectures. It's like they're right in the room with you but they're not really; they can send pictures through the air too."

Celan can't even imagine. Wait until she tells Tanny and Max! But that makes her think about Jillyanne and a bad feeling creeps into her stomach and stays there until the creak of the front door jolts her out of her thoughts. She bolts upright, heart pounding. But it's only Taegh, looking shifty.

"Hey," she says.

His head turns. "Sorry." A wince. "Is Rin asleep?"

"Think so." Then, after a beat, "Where were you?"

"Oh, just out. Ran into some friends, you know? Band stuff." Shrugging off his guitar he shuts the door and drops a small bundle on the counter. "What'd you two do?"

"Met your neighbors. They gave me some wine."

Taegh smiles, face angel-bright in the moonlight.

"Good night," he says, heading for the bedroom, a slight sway to his step.

There's a lot of that going around...

"Taegh?"

He pauses, hand on the door knob.

"Are you and Rin OK?" Celan says uncertainly.

"Huh? Of course. Why wouldn't we be?"

"I don't know. Just – " She pauses, not wanting to give away any knowledge of having overheard their talk in the roller.

"Is she mad?" Taegh presses. "Did she say anything?"

"No," Celan says, shrugging. "She just gets grumpy sometimes."

Taegh chuckles. "That she does." It seems like he's waiting for her to continue, but when Celan says nothing more he turns the knob and pushes open the door. "Good night, hermanita."

"Good night," she says, as it shuts behind him.

9

In the morning Cyrinda is raring to go. "Wait'll you see the Saturday market," she says, digging into the sack Taegh brought back last night. She pulls out a roll and munches it with gusto. "They have so much great stuff there. That's where we got the algalamp."

Celan eyes the roll longingly. "Can I have some?"

Cyrinda digs in again and tosses her one. "Claro. You don't need to ask, take whatever you want." She scoots up on the counter, swinging her legs impatiently. "Anyway, like I said, it's great. I'm gonna bring a bunch of my old scarves and stuff and try to trade 'em in for something nicer. Plus, we have a few chits if we need to buy anything."

"Chits?"

"Yeah, it's what the techs give transers who work

for them. And what you use if you want to get something from them. Or from anyone selling anything, really, everyone uses them now. We get some from Arlo's if we pull a good crowd. They're little round – " She pokes around in her pocket. "See?"

She's holding up a flat, circular chip that looks like something from a children's game. She tosses it to Celan who examines it suspiciously.

"People give you stuff for this?"

"Yeah, it's weird. But everyone does it. Like, that one's blue so it's worth five. White ones are only one. Red ones are ten."

"Weird." She makes to toss the chit back but Cyrinda waves her off.

"You keep it, but put it someplace safe and don't lose it!"

Celan pockets the chit as Taegh emerges shirtless and sleepy-eyed from the bedroom and shuffles over to Cyrinda, putting his arms around her and burying his head in her neck. She laughs, hugging him back.

"I was telling Celan about the market. Are you coming with?"

"Nah." His voice is muffled. "Promised Brophy and Jenner I'd help them out today. They're still working on the generator."

Cyrinda raises an eyebrow. "Taegh Francisco Gwens! When have you ever volunteered to do any extra work for *anybody?*"

"It's for the show," he says, smiling up at her innocently. "I'll meet up with you guys after."

"Bueno," she relents. "But let's all get going then. It's getting late!"

FRESHLY WASHED AND DRESSED, CELAN and Cyrinda set out across the courtyard, Celan feeling slightly uncomfortable in one of Cyrinda's old dresses. It's too big and hangs, sack-like, past her knees. But her sister had summarily dismissed her ranchos clothes, saying 'They smell like fish' and wrinkling her delicate nose, and that had been the end of the discussion.

In the alley, Cyrinda pauses to rap on the wayvern's rickety kitchen door. A stout, scowling woman appears, but when she sees them she manages a thin smile.

"Hey, Alice," Cyrinda says, all girlish charm. "You got any more of those sandwiches?"

"Yeah," Alice grunts, shifting her bulk and scuffling over to a large cooler, where she rummages around unhurriedly.

Celan shoots her sister a questioning look and Cyrinda whispers, "She and Paulo run Arlo's now. She's the head cook. She gives us stuff when they have extra."

The woman reappears with two thick sandwiches wrapped in wax paper and cracks the door open, passing them out to Cyrinda, who stows them in her pack.

"Gracias," she says. "Hey, this is my sister Celan. She's staying with us this week."

Alice gives Celan a short nod before wheeling around and shuffling off without another word.

"She's really pretty nice," Cyrinda says as they head for the street. "Just grouchy in the morning. She likes us. I think she has a crush on Taegh."

Celan grins, reveling in the intimacy of this grown-up gossip.

At the end of the alley Cyrinda makes a quick turn onto Transway. It looks different in the daylight, Celan notes, considerably shabbier than the nighttime dazzle. They step lightly around broken glass and trash as faces rush by on the sidewalk, some grim, others oddly blissful. Rollers whir up and down the main drag and she gets her first glimpse of what must be techs – po-faced figures dressed in identical tan uniforms. She gapes after them until a swift smack on the head from Cyrinda brings her up short.

"Stop staring! They're just people."

"But –"

"Mira, Celan. It's not a big deal, OK? They do their thing, we do ours."

"But I wasn't –"

"Do you want to look like you're right off the rancho?"

Celan relents. "I guess not."

A few blocks further and the street opens up into a large grassy field filled with booths, like a fiesta. Celan bounces happily as Cyrinda browses among the stalls, studying a dress here, some shoes there. Occasionally, her sister strikes up a barter – trading a scarf for some pretty earrings, an old belt for a new skirt. Initially, the process is interesting, but as time drags on boredom sets in and Celan begins to look around – out past the stalls, over to the mountains, towards the ranchos.

Does she miss me or is she glad I'm gone?

Hurriedly she turns away, searching for something else to focus on. Then, finally, she sees it – the shining city rising above Transway like a leviathan. Last night she mainly saw the lights, but now it's revealed in all its glory, swoops and whorls of dun-colored architecture punctuated by towering pyramids shining like the dome the elders live in, but multiplied a hundred times. She draws in a breath. It looks like it holds wonders, treasures untold. She tugs at her sister's arm, pointing.

"Can we go in there next?"

"Why would we want to do that?" Cyrinda says, dismissing the idea. "There's nothing to see. It's boring."

"But I want to see it."

"Well, we can't anyway."

"Why not?"

"Because they have scanners. If you've taken any transferon within the past twelve hours they can tell and you're not allowed in."

"You took some?"

"Of course," she says briskly, snapping out a shirt and holding it up, scrutinizing the cut. "Everyone takes a few drops in the morning."

"But where'd you get a transfer?"

"Never you mind," Cyrinda snaps, obviously annoyed with herself for having given this bit of information away.

Celan is silent for a moment. "But why do the techs care if you took some?"

"They don't like it."

"Why not?"

A shrug. "I don't know. They just don't."

"But how can they tell? I mean, how do the scanners work?"

Cyrinda sighs impatiently. "Something to do with your eyes."

"They scanner your eyes?"

"Scan. But, yeah. They scan everyone's eyes. Even their own."

"They *trans*?" Celan says, incredulous.

"No. Some of them have *gotten* trans – put in their drinks at the wayverns. The people who did it got in bad trouble. So now they scan everyone."

Celan contemplates this. "But how does it work?"

"I told you. I have no idea. Find a tech and ask them."

"Maybe I will."

Cyrinda shakes her head and turns to the vendor, holding out a pretty metal pin in the shape of a flower. "I hate to let this go," she says. "It's been in the family for ages. But I really like that shirt."

Celan tunes her out and lets her eyes search the market, finally alighting on a couple of figures in slate-blue tech uniforms. They are cutting through the crowd, headed this way. As they pass the booth she jumps out in front of them.

"Hey!"

The two men regard her with mingled surprise and amusement.

"Yes?" the taller one says.

"How do you scan our eyes?"

The man smiles – first at his companion and then at Celan. His close-cropped dark hair and neatly trimmed beard and mustache lend him a distinguished air. "You look a little young to have to worry about it."

She waves that off. "Oh, I'm not worried. Kids don't take transferon. But Cyrinda said we couldn't come see your city because of the scanners, so I asked her how they work and she wouldn't tell me. She said to ask a tech. So I'm asking."

The shorter man laughs but the distinguished one addresses her question thoughtfully.

"Well, it's a complex process," he says, "having to do with the refraction of light in the eye. The ingestion of transferon causes a temporary excitation of the rods and cones, resulting in a characteristic halo effect that is visible on the ultraviolet spectrum. That is what our scanners are built to detect."

Celan regards him intently. "What," she starts, "is a refraction – " when she's grabbed by the collar from behind.

"Lo siento," Cyrinda cuts in, deferential. "My little sister has a big mouth." She gives the two techs a rueful smile and tugs at Celan's hand. "Come on, Celan. Stop bothering them."

As they walk away, the tall man watches, a musing expression playing across his elegant face as they meld seamlessly into the crowd.

Out on the main boulevard Cyrinda explodes. "You don't go walking up to techs and asking them questions!"

Celan is unrepentant. "You told me to ask a tech and I did. What's the big deal?"

"Really, Celan. We don't talk to them unless we have to. Especially the ones in blue."

"You never told me the difference."

"The blue ones are the bosses – the Ens. Engineers. But we don't talk to any of them. Not unless we have a good reason to."

"I thought you said they were just people, just like us."

Cyrinda shoots her a withering look. "I meant they're not some kind of freaks to stare at. But that doesn't make them our best friends either."

"Well don't tell me to do something unless you mean it."

Cyrinda exhales, exasperated, and struts ahead as Celan doubles her pace to catch up. But as soon as she does, her sister stops short in front of a cheerful shop; a riot of overflowing flowerpots festoon the sidewalk and several lovely dresses drape languidly in the window.

"Aren't we done getting stuff yet?" Celan says.

"Stop fussing." Cyrinda purses her lips. "I just remembered. I promised Trina I'd come by for my last fitting today. My dress for the show. It'll only take a minute."

"Claro," Celan mutters. Once her sister gets going on clothes it could be hours. "I have to go to the latrine," she announces.

Cyrinda's hand is already on the doorknob. "OK, but come right back."

"I know."

"And don't talk to any more techs."

"I *know*."

With a huff, Celan stomps off down the street as the shop bell chimes silver at her sister's entrance. There's probably a latrine in the courtyard right behind the store, but she presses on to a wayvern at the corner, passing a guy with a red bandana on his head hefting a big drum and two slouching, skinny girls who look like tired servers headed off to their shifts.

Eli's, the wayvern's sign says. It's smaller than Arlo's, a bit shabbier and considerably less well-trafficked.

A couple more techs scoot by in a roller and Celan eyes them clandestinely. A man and a woman in tan – interchangeable, drab and pale, but still human. It's disappointing that they don't have machine parts after all. Just the bots in their brains, but you can't see those.

171

She scuttles down Eli's kitchen alley and meanders through the courtyard to the garden. A patch of pretty red blooms bobs enticingly in the breeze and she's bending to admire it when she sees something that makes her freeze.

A hunched figure sits propped against the garden wall, legs crossed loosely in front of him. He looks like he's asleep with his chin dipped down to his chest but he could be dead or drunk or something, so she backs away nervously. She's almost around the edge of the wall when she realizes who he is. A knit cap covers his head but a fringe of fuschia rings the bottom edge and those are definitely his boots with their mismatched patches.

"Taegh?" she says, approaching hesitantly, not sure if she should try to wake him. Maybe she should go get Cyrinda. She's about to turn and run when his head jerks up and his eyes fly open. She hops back, surprised.

"Wuh?" he says, blinking, bleary-eyed. "Oh, hey Celan."

"What are you doing down there? Aren't you supposed to be helping Brophy?" she demands, secretly relieved, but poised with hands on hips, channeling Rin at her bossiest.

"Uh…finished early. Took a little siesta, you know?" A theatrical yawn. "Nice afternoon…sitting in the sun… got a little sleepy."

"Well," she says, "While you've been goofing off, *we* did a lot today. Rin's at her fitting now at Trina's. I had to use the latrine."

"And you came all the way down to Eli's?"

"I…"

"You were trying to escape the endless beautifyings for a few minutes, weren't you?" he teases. "I know how that goes."

He grins, and she smiles in spite of herself.

"I didn't really have to go."

"I didn't think so. Help me up here and we'll go tell Rin we're gonna get some snacks. Go watch the techs on the screen. Throw popcorn at 'em."

Celan laughs, wrapping her small fingers around his bony wrists and tugging as Taegh rises, groaning like an old man. She sniffs surreptitiously but doesn't smell any drink on him. Maybe he really was resting.

Once upright, he leans against the low wall for a minute, rubbing at his eyes.

"You must've been really tired," Celan says.

"Yeah," he says, "exhausted. That generator was a pain in the ass."

He shakes his head and the motion flings his cap to the ground. Slowly, he reaches for it, stretching like a cat in the sun. As he straightens up he perches the hat on Celan's head and appraises her shrewdly.

"Looks better on you," he says and she cocks her head sideways, posing.

Taegh tugs the bottom edge over her eyes and pushes away from the wall.

"Race you! I'm starving."

Hastily recovering her vision, Celan chases his loping strides through the alley and out onto the street. Outside Trina's shop he pauses, saying offhand, "Hey, you're not gonna tell Rin you caught me napping, right?"

She eyes him keenly. So he *was* doing something he wasn't supposed to. Maybe he was fusing – whatever that is. Index finger on her lips, she pretends to deliberate, then finally shakes her head no.

"Don't worry. I won't tell."

He proffers a humble bow of thanks and sweeps the door open with a gallant gesture.

"After you."

She glides past him, giggling.

10

Cyrinda stretches an arm across the bed and finds nothing but empty space. Fumbling for the clock, she mutters a curse. It's two in the morning. Where the fuck is he? They went to bed together, had a real good time in fact. But now he's gone.

She knows where he is, though – out fusing with the rest of them. Every day another explanation and another excuse. But it's her own fault.

Not in the house. Not while she's here.

Why did she even say that? Giving him an out. She should have said *not at all*. He could stop this shit if he really wanted to, if he really cared.

But maybe he can't, creeps a voice around the corner of her mind. There's been all of kinds of talk about fusers lately, about how some of them can't stop or they get really sick. Zita had told her the other day, when she took her aside at Trina's.

At first, Cyrinda didn't understand. 'Like walking?' she'd asked, eyes wide, too scared to even think of it; Taegh – like her mother. She'd started to cry.

'No', Zita said, petting her shoulder, 'not walking. It's like a cold or flu. It happens sometimes. To the ones the techs call Class E. As long as they get another fuse, they're fine. It's some kind of thing in their brain. They can't help it. Don't be mad at him.'

But then he came in laughing with Celan, not a care in the world, and she was still mad.

Zita said more though, later that night, about how the ones that don't have transfers or friends get desperate sometimes. Might steal things. Or start testing – let the techs do experiments on them. Cyrinda had shivered then, but knew it was impossible; Taegh had lots of friends and they all had transfers. He wasn't suffering any.

After the show, when Celan went home, they'd talk about this. She'd tell him what she knew, what she suspected. She'd make him cut it out; it couldn't be that hard. She transfused sometimes and it never made her sick.

He just has to learn not to do it all the time.

Until then, she'll let him sweat it. This is all his own fault – it was only supposed to be for the weekend; he was the one who told Celan she could stay a whole week. She should've stopped it, but she couldn't let her sister down, not after all that fuss with Jillyanne. The poor kid had suffered enough.

But if he hadn't done that, she wouldn't have had to make him give her the transfer and he'd be here in bed, not running around at all hours begging fuses off of people.

She flops over, face in the pillow. *Let him sweat it.* She has every right to be mad.

CELAN TROTS ALONG CHEERFULLY AT Cyrinda's side, lugging a sack full of corn kernels for popping, as they tramp up a twisting path behind a bunch of ramshackle houses. It's a fine, cool evening and the first stars wink shyly in the indigo sky. Celan inhales the piney scent of the trees and dances a few steps happily. Almost the whole week has flown by already and she never wants to leave. Every day she's spent on Transway has been a taste of some new flavor of fun.

Sunday afternoon they'd watched roller races out on the mesa – dust and wind whipping their faces as the sun went down in a blaze of red rays and the souped-up vehicles roared by faster than she'd ever thought rollers could go. They were all painted up with designs and pretty colors too, not like the techs' boring white ones. She'd cheered herself hoarse for the nicest one.

Then there was the poetry contest – five contestants painting pictures of life with the rhythm and vision of their words, as real as if they'd painted them on the wall.

Life in Transway, longing, love. It was dizzying. Everyone had listened raptly and clapped for their favorite and the winner got a small pot of chits for her trouble.

Yesterday, it was the radio station. Cyrinda and Taegh sang a couple of songs right out over the airwaves. She'd been fascinated by all the buttons and dials and peppered the operadors with endless questions until Cyrinda told her to go sit down and be quiet.

She shakes her wrist, reveling in the jangle of borrowed bracelets. With these and one of Cyrinda's old dresses, hemmed up and taken in and tied at the waist with a pretty blue sash, she feels almost entirely grown up.

"What kind of party is this one?" she asks.

Cyrinda grunts, hefting a bag full of bottles of wine and cider that clink together merrily.

"A casaviejo."

"Huh?"

"Sometimes the guys find a sweet old house up in the hills and clear it out. Have a big bonfire. Food, music. Don't have to clean up after."

"Are you gonna sing?" Celan asks.

"Quizás." She shrugs. "It's not a real show, just fooling around."

"Was that where Taegh was all day? Clearing out the house?"

Cyrinda rolls her eyes. "Allegedly."

"What does that mean?"

"Never mind," her sister says, and falls silent.

The house is a huge gated affair surrounded by a crumbling adobe wall, but they can smell the smoke and see the flames licking skyward from outside. Celan's pulse quickens. Through the gate the first notes of tuning instruments reach their ears and they emerge into a large courtyard buzzing with heat and noise, at the center of which roars an enormous bonfire.

A small constellation of hand drummers clusters off to one side, tapping out syncopations while dancers swirl around like dizzy satellites. Around the edges there are smaller cooking fires, where tortillas and vegetables sizzle on grates. Celan spots a boy and a girl she met at the roller races sitting by the nearest one.

"Hey!" she says, and they both look up, smiling in recognition.

"Can I go talk to them?" she asks Cyrinda.

"Sure, give me the corn. I'll be over there."

Cyrinda cocks her head toward a tumbledown gazebo on the other side of the fire – the source of the random bursts of music – where some familiar figures are setting up equipment. Celan goes to join the kids as Cyrinda trudges off in that direction.

OVER BY THE GAZEBO, CAP and a guy with a thick moustache sit with their basses slung low on their laps, running through some chord changes with Tomás on guitar. A skinny girl with orange-streaked hair hunches on an overturned bucket, beating out the rhythm with drumsticks on a ratty old snare.

"Que pas'?" Cyrinda says. "Where's Brophy?"

"Quit," Tomás says, not looking up.

"Quit what?"

"Fused Up! Fusing. Everything. Said he 'just can't do this anymore.'"

"Are you serious?" she says, stunned (but still putting her bags down carefully).

"Yep. That payaso thinks he's gonna go work for the techs. Learn a trade, he says." He rubs frustrated fingers against his temple.

"But the show's in two days!"

"Yeah," Tomás says drily. "I know."

Cyrinda turns to Cap as the full ramifications of the situation begin to dawn on her. "And what do you think you're doing?"

"Don't be mad," he says hastily. "Me and Stino are just trying to help out. Gonna play a few songs each with them tonight, see if one of us can fill Brophy's spot for the show."

"But you can't!" she wails. "What about us?"

"I'm not quitting you guys. Don't worry. I'd only be helping them out for the night. It's the anniversary show, you know? They can't blow it off."

"But then you'll be tired by the time we play."

Tomás smirks. "You're still the openers, chiqui, recuerdas? He'll be tired by the time we play."

She lifts her chin, defiant. "Nothing's definite until they post the boards."

"And come Saturday morning, we'll definitely be at the top of the list. Like always."

"Hey," says the drummer girl. "It's not that big a deal. Taegh said it was alright."

"Oh, he did, did he?" Cyrinda snipes, hands on hips. "And how aviados is he, Aleta?"

Tomás and Stino laugh, but Cap says soothingly, "He's fine, Rin. Really."

"He's what now?" says a voice behind her and Cyrinda turns to see Taegh grinning impishly, drawing on a smoke, Jenner beside him. She scans his face, but he looks calm and composed, not dazed and confused. She gives him a quick peck on the cheek along with a guilty glance for being caught out talking behind his back. Taegh drapes an arm around her shoulders.

"Relax, Rin, we're all trying to work together here."

She crosses her arms in front of her chest but doesn't shrug off his embrace.

"Yeah, well," she says. "What about the generator? That was Brophy's thing. How are any of us gonna get the sound we wanted without the extra juice?"

"No problemo," Jenner cuts in smoothly. "I know how to do everything. It's easy."

Cyrinda regards him skeptically.

"Don't worry," Taegh says. "It's all taken care of. We got it running great. Gonna test it out tonight."

"What? Here? How'd you even get it up here?"

Taegh waves his free hand mysteriously. "The wonders of prana…"

If her eyes rolled any harder they'd fly clear out of their sockets. "Please."

Taegh shakes his head. "Always underestimating me."

"Whatever."

Muttering under her breath, she plunges into a sack and yanks out a bottle of dandelion wine.

"Might as well get this started," she says, straightening up and cadging Taegh's smoke, taking a long drag.

Jenner grins broadly. "Órale."

THE TWO KIDS SLIDE OVER to make room for Celan on their makeshift bench. Between bites of tortilla-wrapped vegetables the nearest one says, "If you want some, go ask her," and gestures with his elbow toward the grill, where a frowsy woman with a flushed face pokes at the food with a long fork.

"Do I need a chit?"

"Nah, it's free," the boy says, wiping his greasy face on his sleeve.

At that she gets up and marches over to the woman, who wordlessly hands her a wrap.

"Gracias," she says and sits down with the others, tucking her skirt neatly beneath her.

"So," the girl says, "you're Celan, right?"

"Yeah," she says, biting into the wrap. It's piping hot

and delicious and she exhales a sigh of pleasure.

"Cyrinda's sister?"

Celan nods, leaning forward so the drippings won't spoil her clothes.

"She's so beautiful," the girl says longingly, "and such a good singer. I wish she was my sister."

"When I grow up," the boy says, "I'm gonna have a band too."

Celan chews and swallows. "What are your names again? Lo siento. I met a lot of new people this week."

"Emmeline."

"Josh."

"Well nice to meet you. Again."

They all eye each other.

"So," says Emmeline, flipping long black hair off her shoulders. "You're a ranchita, right? You go to 'scuela?"

"Yeah," Celan says, leaning in for another bite, "do you have 'scuela here too?"

"Not like yours."

"I go to tech school," Josh pipes up proudly.

"What's that?"

"The techs have a school for expros. We learn reading and typing and science. Someday, we can do real jobs if we apply ourselves."

Emmeline snorts, derisive. "My mother doesn't believe in that. She teaches us at home." She looks pointedly at Celan. "I know how to heal, just like you."

"So do I," Josh says quickly. "A little. But I know

other things too."

"Stupid things." Emmeline sneers. "Who needs all that stuff?"

"Science is important," Josh says defensively. "It's how the techs heal. With their MedLabs. I went to one when I was sick one time and I got better right after."

"That's not *real* healing," Emmeline says. "You don't need their help if you can trans."

Swallowing the last of her food, Celan looks back and forth between them, not sure what to make of this turn in the conversation.

Emmeline eyes her appraisingly. "Is it true you know how to astral travel?"

"Claro. But it's not really that hard. The elders take us out with them."

"The elders!" Josh says. "You actually listen to them?"

"Well, we kind of have to."

"My mom says that the elders are a bunch of elitist theocratic hypocrites," says Emmeline, pronouncing each big word carefully, like it's something she's memorized.

Celan gapes at her.

"It's true. They were going to let us starve and they didn't even care. Say it was the Will of the Universe. Do they teach you about that at your 'scuela?"

There's an awkward silence.

"Well," Celan says. "It's been nice talking to you, but my sister said to come right back after I ate."

With that she jumps up and tears off, circumnavigating the fire, heels kicking up dust. Breathless, she arrives at the gazebo, running smack into Taegh.

"Hey, where's the fire?" he quips, and she snickers as he hoists his guitar and heads over to join the group getting ready to play.

"What happened with the kids?" Cyrinda asks.

"They were weird."

"Huh. Well, forget 'em then. The music's about to start." She takes a swig from the bottle in her hand.

"Is that cider?"

"Dandelion wine."

Celan makes a face. "Ugh."

Cyrinda smiles warmly, resting a light hand on her shoulder and bending close to her ear. "There's some prickly pear mead over on the table. I hate that sweet shit, but I brought some 'cause I know you like it."

Celan brightens. "Gracias," she says, fumbling in her pack for her cup.

"Anytime, hermanita."

The band strikes up as she pours out the vivid liquid: Taegh and Tomás sharing guitar and vocals, Stino on bass, and Aleta at the drums. They beat out a jumpy rhythm as people press forward. Some grab hands and start to dance, others jig in place. Taegh's eyes glint mischievously.

"This is an old world song," he says into the mic. "Heard it on the radio." He and Tomás break into a tight harmony.

Well I twine and I mingle my waving black hair
With lilies so white, then red roses so fair
Or juniper bright with an emerald hue
Or pale amanita so violently blue

Celan snakes her way through the crowd to her sister, who's right down in front bobbing her head and rapping her heel in time with the music. She takes a sip of mead as Cyrinda shouts into her ear.

"Wanna learn to two-step?"

"Yeah!"

She shuffles from foot to foot as Cyrinda takes the cup out of her hand and crouches, stowing it behind an amp along with her own bottle. Then she jumps up and grabs Celan's hands, spinning her around as the song's spell takes hold.

She told me she loved me and promised to love
Forever and over all others above
But I woke from my dream and my idol was clay
Her promise to love me had vanished away

The bouncy beat belies the sad lyrics and Celan follows Cyrinda's steps as best she can, messing up a lot but laughing. No one can ever hurt her when she's with Cyrinda and Taegh.

They're perfect, she thinks, *and everyone loves them.*

HOURS LATER, CELAN RETURNS FROM a short trip to the latrine that was dug earlier behind the house, savoring the memories of the impromptu concert – Cyrinda and Aleta doing an a cappella number that brought people to tears, Taegh dancing like a dervish before sinking to his knees before the bonfire, Jenner pounding the drums like a man possessed.

Rounding the corner behind the gazebo she spies Cyrinda and Taegh locked in a clinch, so she draws back and waits for them to finish. After what seems like forever they finally pull apart.

Cyrinda's still clutching the bottle of dandelion wine; she takes a quick swig and steps backwards giggling and swaying unsteadily until Taegh gently takes it from her and puts it on the ground, saying, "Maybe you wanna slow down on this a little, huh Rin?"

She stares at him in astonishment before breaking into a harsh laugh. "You're fucking kidding me, right? You can't go half a day without a fuse and you're gonna tell me I can't have a little wine?"

"I wasn't telling you anything," Taegh says mildly. "I was only suggesting – "

"Well, I *suggest* you shut the fuck up. You think I don't know where you've been disappearing to all week? Why don't you go find one of your little friends and vamos aviados? Or are they sick of you asking them already?" Lowering her voice to a nasty whisper she hisses, "Gonna start testing next?"

Taegh winces. "That's a shitty thing to say."

Cyrinda's bites her lip like she realizes she's gone too far.

"How could you even *say* that?"

"I didn't mean – "

"Yeah, you did. Is that what you think of me? That I'm that pathetic?"

"No. I don't, really. I'm sorry, Taegh!" She reaches for his hand. "You know I'd never let that happen to you."

He jerks away like she's burned him. "*I'd* never let that happen to me," he says and turns on his heel, stalking off without another word.

Celan slips deeper into the shadows as the smash of a bottle is followed by a storm of tears. Now is definitely not a good time to make her presence known. Silently, she creeps back the way she came. She can go the long way around the front of the house.

She's hurrying along in the dark when a tall shape rears up in front of her. She lets out a small cry, flattening against the wall until a familiar voice says, "Celan? What are you doing out here?"

It's Taegh. Her knees buckle in relief.

"I was coming back from the latrine and, uh, you and Rin were fighting. So I came around the other way."

"Fuck. Sorry you had to see that." His shoulders slump. "Did you hear everything?"

"Some." She shrugs. "Rin's real upset."

"Yeah, she gets like that sometimes."

"I don't like when you guys fight."

"Neither do I," he says heavily.

Silence falls and Celan's not sure what to do. His shadowy profile blots out the stars. Finally, Taegh clears his throat and reaches out a hand.

"C'mon hermanita, it'll be alright. Let's go on back inside."

11

The sun's already high when Celan wakes on Saturday morning, belly rumbling. Dress rehearsal went late last night. She scoots off the cot and makes her way over to the bedroom, pressing her ear against the door.

Nada.

She can't hear Taegh's staggered snore at all. She turns the knob and peeks in – Taegh isn't there and Cyrinda's asleep. She doesn't want to wake her sister but her empty stomach insists.

"Rin?" she calls softly, then louder, "Rin?"

Cyrinda stirs, cracking an eyelid, grumbling. "What?"

"Can we get breakfast soon?"

"Celan, I'm exhausted, OK? And tonight's the show. Give me another hour."

"But I'm hungry *now*."

"Go ask Alice to give you breakfast. She knows you're with us."

"By myself?"

"Just come right back after. Read a book or something." With that, she flops over with a final grunt.

Celan scuffs across the silent courtyard and raps tentatively on Arlo's kitchen door, but Alice is in a good mood and quickly supplies her with a bowl of corn mash and chiles and a slice of bread. She wolfs down the food and is outside in minutes, surveying her options.

She could ask Alice if she has any books, but somehow she doubts there's anything to read in the kitchen (aside from maybe recipes). Maybe she'll find something more interesting on her own, tucked away in one of the uninhabited nooks and crannies of the old buildings. The thought brightens her...*exploring!* As long as she returns before Cyrinda wakes up.

Her first stop is the garden, her favorite place in the mornings. Lush rows of tomatoes gleam ripely in the sun and she reaches forward to pinch a few leaves between her fingers. They tickle her nose as she breathes in the tart, green scent for a long moment before releasing them to the compost pile.

Then she squeezes her eyes shut and spins slowly in a circle – *round and round and round she goes and where she stops, nobody knows*. At the rhyme's conclusion she opens them to find herself facing an alley that exits the rear of the courtyard to the left. She sets off in that direction.

The alley funnels her into a long, narrow stretch with walls rising blankly on both sides. It's chilly in the shadows and she hurries to the end where it opens out into another courtyard, this one showing fewer signs of habitation than their own.

She tries a few doors and finds them all dishearteningly locked. But just as she's about to give up, the last one on the left creaks open at a touch and she peeps cautiously inside. It's empty, save for an old table and chairs. Still, there's a closet that might be worth a look.

Shutting the door neatly behind her she circles the table and yanks open the closet door. Sure enough, there's a stack of disintegrating books. Old world stuff. She kneels down and starts to sort through them, trying to find one still intact enough to read.

She flips through a thick one with a lot of dense text. *Boring*. But the thin one underneath it has a picture on the cover that makes her stop and stare: A man standing on a board and skimming down a giant wave. His hands are held out in a balancing gesture and it looks like he has wings.

Celan has never seen an old world image quite like it. It looks like – like she felt holding onto the dolphin, flying through the water. But this is different. This isn't an astral body, it's real. And he's flying *on* the water, a wall of water that could crush him at any time. In spite of this, there is no trace of fear on the man's face; it is filled with fierce joy.

She pores over the image, trying to imagine what it would feel like – the spray on her skin, the water beneath her feet – until the sound of voices brings her reverie up short. She strains to listen and is rewarded by the sound of Taegh's familiar mild drawl and another raspier voice she can't quite place. Then the magic word 'fuse' floats clearly out of the blurry muddle of sound.

On instinct, she scoots into the closet and shuts the door in time to hear their footsteps cross the threshold and the scrape of chairs as they sit down at the table not three feet from where she's hidden. Stooping slightly, she peers out through a crack, seeing Taegh's lean back and the profile of another, heavier-muscled guy with blue-black hair and an aquiline nose. Tomás, from Fused Up!

"Yeah so,"Taegh says, his offhand tone undercut with a note of strain. "Been short all week. Rin's got it locked down. Doesn't want me fusing around her sister."

"She's holding your transfer?"

"Well, we've only got the one. But it's obnoxious how she's being so righteous. It's not like she's never done it."

Tomás shakes his head. "You should get your own, ese."

"If they were that easy to get believe me, I would."

"Shoulda stayed at 'scuela, then, right? Don't they give 'em away to you ranchitos when you're eighteen?"

Taegh shrugs, wiping his nose and sniffling. "I'm done with all that shit. I'll get another one though, someday."

"Yeah, maybe someday when you're not opening for us anymore."

"Where you been, Tomás? We got the top spot tonight."

"The fuck you do."

"Take a look at the board, *ese*." He drums long fingers on the table top. "Read it and weep."

Tomás leans forward and starts to rise. "Yeah, maybe I'll go take a look right now." He narrows his eyes and seems to read something on Taegh's face. Then he laughs and sits back down. "Just kidding."

"You're a funny man."

"Yeah well, might as well get to it then, sabes?" Tomás reaches into his left breast pocket and pulls out a transfer. Taegh turns sideways in his chair and rolls up his sleeve.

Celan is riveted, heart pounding, not daring to breathe, as he taps at the crook of his elbow with two deft fingers while Tomás unscrews the top of the transfer. Pinching the bulb, he draws up some fluid. When it's about half full, he hands it to Taegh, who gives him a plaintive look.

Tomás grunts. "Too early in the morning to be hauling your ass up off the floor."

Taegh frowns, but takes the dropper and digs his fingernail into a groove on the cap. There's an audible hiss, like air being pressurized, and the bulb expands by a fraction. He takes a deep breath and places the end of the dropper against his arm, flush with a blue vein.

"Getting better aim these days," Tomás says.

"Cállate!" Taegh snaps.

Inhaling again, he focuses on the dropper, as if gathering some kind of force or momentum. Then, without warning, he squeezes the blub and there's an odd, quick flash. He jerks like he's had a slight shock and his head rolls on his neck.

Celan blinks. The fluid is gone from the dropper, but it's not dripping down his arm either. It's gone inside, she's sure. Into his vein.

After an extended moment, Taegh straightens up and hands the dropper to Tomás, who screws it onto the transfer and returns it safely to his pocket.

"Better?" he gibes.

"Much." Taegh sighs. He presses a hand over the spot where the transfusion went in and rolls down his sleeve.

"Let's go check out that board then. I still don't believe it 'til I see it."

Tomás shoves away abruptly from the table and heads for the door. Taegh follows slowly, pushing himself up with both hands, a little unsteady on his feet.

"Gonna make it, aviador?" Tomás says, "or do I need to carry you?"

"Chingate," Taegh says, waving him off. "I'm good." Balance regained, he steps over the threshold and they both move off, still bantering.

Celan waits, reeling in the dark for another few

minutes until she's sure they're not going to return. Then she slips out of the closet and into the chair Taegh recently vacated. It's still warm from his body and she draws her knees up to her chest and wraps her arms around her legs, rocking meditatively.

Bliss – the thought rises and expands. *Everything easy.*

Dazed, she slides off the chair and wanders back through the alley to the house. The bedroom door is still shut and the silence weighs heavily. Hunkering on the floor, she grabs Cyrinda's bag of scarves and trinkets and starts to sift through it, examining each piece distractedly. She's picking at a spot on a red scarf when her sister finally emerges, yellow hair askew, shielding her eyes from the brightness streaming in through the window.

"Morning," she says, yawning. Then, noting the bag, "Anything interesting?"

"Not really," Celan says, bowing her head so Cyrinda can't see her triumphant smile.

"SOUNDS LIKE IT'S GONNA BE some show tonight," Eris says, wiry form hunched over a pot of pungent purple dye.

It is late afternoon and Cyrinda lounges languidly in the makeshift salon as Eris fixes her hair in a ring of colorful braids wound around the crown of her head with the rest hanging loose and blonde and lovely. It's intricate work and Eris has been at it for over an hour, working piece by piece so the dye doesn't bleed into the rest of her hair and ruin the effect.

"I know!" Cyrinda crows. "I just knew we'd get the top spot. The biggest show *ever*. And it's gonna be the best!"

"And Yale's opening?"

"Yeah – it's them, Fused Up!, and us."

"And they got everything set up at Arlo's?"

"Yeah. Jenner and Taegh rigged the generator up to the sound system last night." She waves an airy hand. "I have no idea how it works but it sounds amazing."

"Yeah it does," her little sister affirms. Celan is curled like a cat in a big, squashy chair, head close to the radio, blissed out on some old world jazz.

Cyrinda smiles at her approvingly. "And wait 'til you see my dress. Trina's been working for weeks. It's gorgeous!" She shuts her eyes and sighs happily.

"I heard Tomás has been talking shit all day," Eris says, carefully applying more dye with a tiny brush. "Says they only picked you guys over them cause you were the real Arlo's daughter. 'Cause it's the anniversary. Nostalgia and all."

Cyrinda shrugs. "He's just jealous. I mean, I love Fused Up! and he's a great singer and all, but our songs are better."

"The best since Aetherworld, that's what some people say." Eris dips into the dye pot again and blots the brush on the side.

"Lots of people," Cyrinda says as the door flies open

and a small, cheerful woman with short brown hair bustles in, toting an oblong sack on a hanger.

"Trina!" Cyrinda says, almost knocking Eris' brush out of her hand.

"Cuidado!" Eris swears colorfully. "Do you want me to mess this up?"

"Sorry," Cyrinda says, chastened.

Trina smiles. "Bet you can't wait to put it on," she teases. "But you gotta wait until your hair's dry."

"Just hold it up, please," Cyrinda pleads. "I just want to look at it."

"Bueno," Trina says, hanging the sack on a peg and undoing several buttons.

Waves of artfully cut purple jersey cascade from an antique black leather bodice patched together from several old world sources and stitched together seamlessly. Two long, gauzy strips are attached at the top to wrap around her long neck for a halter effect. The overall look is gracefully tough.

Perfect.

Cyrinda gives a squeal of joy and claps her hands like a little girl. Trina and Eris laugh. Celan murmurs appreciatively and the dressmaker winks, reaching back into the bag for something hanging behind the beautiful dress.

"And for you," she says, pulling out a patchwork skirt in varying shades of blue and lavender sewn onto a wide belt.

"Oh wow," Celan marvels. "It's great. Gracias!"

She hops out of her chair and takes the skirt from Trina, holding it up against her waist.

"Can I wear it now?" she begs.

Cyrinda grins. *Trina's so thoughtful.* Everyone is these days. But this is how it should be, how she always should be treated. With respect, deference even – not like the stupid freak they made her out to be in the ranchos.

If they could see me now...

They can't, of course. But her little sister can. And Celan will tell all those snotty ranchitas what she saw when she goes back there. There'll be no more putana jokes; now they'll all be jealous of her other, brilliant, sister.

"Claro," she tells Celan. "Go ahead. Just be sure not to get it dirty!"

THE BACK COURTYARD OF ARLO'S, so quiet when they left for Eris' salon, is now abuzz with life. Almost all doors are open and people mill about – clustering around a small fire pit, talking excitedly, and blasting music in tandem from several radios as the pre-show anticipation builds in the glow of the setting sun. Everyone here belongs to Arlo's in some capacity and even if they're not in one of the bands, this is their show too.

A few people whistle and shout when they catch sight of Cyrinda and she waves grandly, the ring of braided purple atop her head looking for all the world like a crown.

"Your hair looks really good Rin," Celan says.

Cyrinda's smile widens as she hugs the bag with the new dress in it to her chest.

"I'm not gonna change until right before the show," she says, as if it's something she's given a lot of thought to. "I want it to be a surprise when everyone sees it all together."

They reach the front door of the apartment as Taegh stumbles out, unlit smoke in hand, in a rumpled shirt and loose hemp pants with prickly-pear hair falling in his eyes. He appraises Cyrinda with amusement. "Well, will you look at that," he says, lounging against the door jamb. "She's finally gone and gotten her fuse on."

"Oh, hush," Cyrinda half-chides him, glancing at Celan, who looks away with apparent disinterest. But then she relents and gives him a hug, her mood too good to be spoiled by his folly.

"It's only around the top," she points out, "and it's not staying like that after the show."

"That's what they all say," Taegh says, striking his flint and taking a deep drag. "Better watch out or you'll be looking as crazy as me."

"Madre forbid. And I hope you're going to change those clothes before the show. It looks like you slept in them."

"So what if I did?"

"Honestly, Taegh – "

"Not everyone has to get all prettified to go on

stage," he says, with a winning look. "You're pretty enough for both of us."

She preens. "Just wait 'til you see me in my dress."

Cyrinda stows the bag in the house and leads Taegh and her sister across the courtyard and over to a clutch of faces ringed around the fire. Celan settles in next to Cap and stretches out her hands to the crackling warmth. He gives her a friendly nudge.

"New skirt?" he says.

"Trina made it for me."

"Well, it's very nice."

"Gracias," she says, cheeks aglow.

Cyrinda beams with pride.

"We should go do it now," Jenner is saying to Tomás. "Do it up and then come down a little before the show."

"Adónde?"

"We can go to my place," says Aleta, sleek in all black with orange hair livid like flames against her face.

Jenner eyes Cyrinda and Taegh. "Vamos aviados?"

Cyrinda shakes her head no. "Not tonight," she says, pointing her chin at Celan.

"The lady refuses," Taegh says, and everyone laughs.

"Not like you, güey," Tomás says.

Taegh grins. "I'm always re-fusing."

Cyrinda rolls her eyes, but says nothing. It's totally pointless to argue about this tonight, with all of them doing it. And anyway, Celan seems uncharacteristically incurious about the whole thing.

Thank Madre for small favors.

"Hey Cap," she says. "Pass me some of that wine."

He cheerfully obliges as the others amble off after Aleta, followed at the last minute by a jittery Stino.

"Great," Cyrinda says, glaring after him. "Another one down."

Cap laughs. "He's in Fused Up! now – gotta walk the talk."

She cracks a half-smile despite herself. It really would be fun to be fused for the show, but with Celan here she just can't.

A little wine though, she thinks, taking a long swig, *never hurt anybody.*

LAMPS IGNITE ONE BY ONE around the courtyard as the gang straggles back – first Jenner and Aleta, laughing and miming drumbeats; then Stino, stringing along behind them in a daze. Taegh and Tomás bring up the rear – arms slung over each other's shoulders like the best of friends, passing a smoke back and forth, all rivalry temporarily at bay.

"Hey, Rin," Taegh drawls, "almost show time."

She rises slow and majestic from her place by the fire and turns to Celan. "Come help me get dressed," she commands.

Celan jumps up eagerly as Taegh disentangles himself from Tomás and grabs Cyrinda's hand.

"Let *me* help," he says throwing an exaggerated leer

to the crowd around the fire.

But Cyrinda coolly draws her hand away, taking her sister's instead. She and Celan walk towards the apartment, sashaying a bit for good measure. Taegh follows. At the door, Cyrinda pauses like she might shake him off. Instead, she turns and smiles an invitation.

"So, this is gonna be – ?" starts Taegh.

"Amazing," Cyrinda says as they step inside.

Loosening the ties on her old skirt, she lets it fall to the floor. Taegh settles on the cot, watching appreciatively. Cyrinda pulls her shirt off over her head and motions for the bag she'd laid out earlier. He passes it over and she unbuttons it, pulling out her prize with a flourish. She steps into the dress and shimmies it up, positioning the bustier around her chest. The strings dangle down, tantalizing.

"Tie me up?" She giggles, lifting her hair off the nape of her neck as she turns around. Taegh tugs at the strings with relish.

FEELING A LITTLE AWKWARD WITH this display, Celan busies herself gathering up Cyrinda's discarded clothes. She'll put them in the bedroom and give those two a few minutes to themselves. As she picks up the skirt, however, her hand closes around a hard lump in the pocket. She knows the shape by touch.

A transfer!

She can hardly believe her luck.

Fusing is all she's thought about all day – *What would it be like? How does it feel?* – but had resigned herself to the fact that she probably wouldn't get a chance to find out. Here, at least. At home people didn't guard their transfers so carefully.

At home though, it wouldn't be as fun.

And someone might find out; she might get in trouble. If she's going to do it, it needs to be here and *now*.

Heart pounding, she glances at Cyrinda and Taegh. They're totally preoccupied.

Perfect.

She ducks into the bedroom, closes the door behind her, and lays the clothes on the bed. Then she sits, pulling out the vial and holding it up to the light. The fluid inside has a welcoming glow.

She weighs it in her palm, thinking of Taegh with his slow drawl and twisting smile. Ringing exultant sounds, prickly-pear hair falling in his eyes.

Brilliant.

In her mind's eye the whole past week flashes by like a magic carpet ride. She thinks of them all laughing, joking about it – they all do this. Even Rin. It's not dangerous. And if only she does a little, maybe they'll never even know.

Celan stares into the soft phosphorescence of the algalamp in the narrow room, breathing in the close smells of human as she unscrews the cap and draws up a tiny bit of fluid. She finds the groove and presses.

The bulb expands. She pauses, dropper poised above the inside of her wrist.

I just want to see what it's like.

Touching it to a blue line, she draws in a breath.

Inside, she thinks, *right there*. She feels a surge of electricity race from her mind to her hand. Then the bedroom door flies opens with a bang.

In the split second before Cyrinda or Taegh registers what's happening, she squeezes the bulb as hard as she can and a tiny jet of liquid light pierces her flesh. She feels a moment of triumph at their stunned expressions. Then the fuse hits her.

First, all the lights go bright. A glittering rush of exhilaration explodes in the stem of her brain and she feels like she could run a hundred miles barefoot. She grits her teeth. It's almost too much. But just as she thinks she's going to scream the intensity peaks and breaks into a churning wave and she's flying down it, like the man she saw in the picture, riding it effortlessly until it rolls and stretches out onto the warm safe sands of calm.

Her head lolls forward and she almost rolls off the bed until, leveling out, she catches herself and stares at the cracked floor – seeing patterns, fractured and swirling labyrinths of inexplicable complexity, color, and depth. After a minute (or an hour for all she knows) she lifts her head to see Cyrinda watching her with apprehension, and Taegh with a kind of anticipation.

These are the two most beautiful faces in the world.

Behind them the algalamp is pulsing, sprouting vines and leaves out of its blue bowl like a large, hydroponic plant. The vines amalgamate into a vaguely human shape – a woman with long ropes of glowing hair. Her face coalesces and two tiny white buds sprout in place of eyes. The buds pop open to reveal violet centers. They start to spin; first clockwise, then counterclockwise. Suddenly they stop and the right one winks at her. She grins.

"This is...."

"Amazing, right?" Taegh says hopefully.

Bubbles are rising out of the lamp and Cyrinda's hair floats like seaweed. *We're all underwater!* The room rolls and pitches like the deck of a ship and Celan grabs the edge of the bed again to steady herself.

"Are you OK?" her sister demands, leaning in anxiously.

"Don't scare her, Rin." Taegh says.

Celan nods, not quite ready to speak.

"I can't believe you, Taegh!" Cyrinda turns on him, eyes stabbing daggers.

He raises his hands in a gesture of innocent protest. "What the fuck? You think I showed her? I didn't do anything. *You* had the transfer."

Cyrinda continues to glare.

"You said not in the house and I didn't, I swear." He seems genuinely baffled and her fury relents a fraction.

"But you talk about it constantly – "

"I do not. And anyway, talking's not showing. Besides, she's a genius, right? A prana genius. It won't hurt her."

Cyrinda puts her hands on Celan's shoulders, shaking her lightly. "Celan, dígame. Are you OK?"

"Claro," she says, recovering the power of speech. "And no one showed me either. I learned it *myself*."

"You see?" Taegh says. "It's not my fault."

Cyrinda snorts. "It never is."

He ignores this and scoops cap and vial off the bed where Celan dropped them in those first stunned moments. Screwing the transfer together, he pockets it.

Celan looks up at him wonderingly. "Your eyes…" she says, marveling at a novel radiance that makes the violet-blue glitter like sunlight on the surface of a stream.

"Oh yeah," he says, grinning. "Everyone's eyes look like this when they're fused up. But you can only see it if you're fusing too."

"Are my eyes like that?"

Taegh nods.

"Can I see in the mirror?"

"Later. First," he kneels down next to her, "you've got a little healing to do."

Cyrinda makes a derisive noise but says nothing, moving out of the way.

Gently, Taegh takes Celan's hand in his and exposes her wrist – where a strange, burn-like bruise has formed at the place the transfusion went in. He takes her other hand and places it over the wound.

"Think of your skin. Think of exactly how it looked before the transfusion."

Celan thinks, *This is healing. This I know.*

Automatically she breathes in, she breathes out. She sees the shimmering stars and hears the ripple of sound. She removes her hand and the wound is gone. She looks at Taegh.

"Always cover your tracks," he says, and laughs.

▭▶ 12 ◀▭

In the hall behind the stage at Arlo's, every facet of everything is clear to Celan – the rough stubble of the walls, the lights flickering in their sconces like little stars, the smoothness of her sandals sliding over the floor. The world is beautiful; every step, every breath, every beat of her heart is sacred and holy. Every speck of dust is perfect and shining. On impulse, she spins forward a few steps, twirling out her new skirt. Her foot catches on a loose tile and she teeters for a second until Taegh reaches over and gives her a steadying hand.

"Are you sure you're OK?" Cyrinda says again.

"Rin, please. I'm fine. You guys do this all the time."

Cyrinda steps out in front of her. "Really? And how do you know that?"

"I have amazing powers of observation."

Cyrinda frowns. "Did Taegh – "

"No," Celan says flatly, "it's not his fault."

"Then *who*?"

"Mira," Taegh says, smoothly inserting himself between them. "I don't know how she figured it out. But what happened happened and there's nothing we can do about it. So let's stop the interrogation. Just let her enjoy it."

"She's *eleven*," Cyrinda says acidly. "She has to be back in 'scuela on Monday."

"Back in – seriously? You're going to worry about that *now*? The biggest show we've ever played and all you can think about is 'scuela?" He shakes his head. "Why does it even matter? Kids around here grow up fine without it."

"But she's not a kid from around here. She's a ranchita. She could be an elegida someday."

Taegh's brow tilts wryly. "She might as well be one now."

"Really?" Celan says.

Taegh gives a short laugh. "Really. What do you think the elegidos learn anyway? The elders?" He spreads his arms wide. "This!"

"Taegh!" Cyrinda says, stamping her foot in frustration. "She's not supposed to know – "

"No one's supposed to know." He sneers. "Except for the chosen ones and they'll never tell. I think she should know she's not doing anything they don't do. She's not doing anything wrong."

He crosses arms in front of his chest and Cyrinda follows suit – a face-off in full glower. Celan ignores them, leaning in to examine the pattern on Cyrinda's scarf. Her sister jerks it away.

"Really, Rin," she says, "you need to relax."

Cyrinda looks from her to Taegh and back again for a long moment, her expression unreadable.

"Fine," she snaps. "Guess it doesn't matter now." She turns to Taegh. "Give me the pinche transfer."

Taegh removes it from his pocket and brandishes it with a flourish, but Cyrinda just snatches it out of his hand and stomps off toward the courtyard. He watches her go with a patient sigh.

"She'll be in a much better mood when she gets back."

He takes Celan's hand, leading her through a doorway into the communal band room, jam-packed with hangers-on and wishers-well. Tomás is slouched against the wall inside, chatting up a short girl with bright blue hair. He turns to greet them and immediately does a double take. He gestures to the girl to wait a moment and approaches with a low whistle of astonishment.

"She took the transfer when we weren't looking," Taegh explains. "We don't know how she knew."

Tomás bows and mock-solemnly shakes Celan's hand, eyes shimmering like Taegh's.

"Aviadita!" he addresses her. She dips her head in

humble acknowledgment.

"How are you feeling?"

"The most beautiful I've ever felt."

"And are you going to sing for us too?"

"I don't think so," she says, as if she's considered it very seriously. "I think I'm just going to dance."

Tomás chuckles, then cuts his eyes to Taegh. "Where's la reina?"

"Well, ah, she's not too happy about this, as you can probably imagine."

"Oh, I can."

"But she took off with the transfer so things should be improving."

Tomás smirks. "Yale just started so we've still got a while." He jerks a thumb toward the far end of the room, where people crowd a long table. "You should check out the spread. They really did it up."

"You hungry?" Taegh asks Celan.

She shakes her head no. "I'm really thirsty, though."

"So'm I."

They beeline for the food and drink as Tomás refocuses on the girl, Celan sticking close to Taegh's side. The scene isn't intimidating though, just kind of hyperreal, tiny details taking on momentous momentary proportions. Here and there pairs of eyes glitter, jewel-like.

So many fusers!

And she never would have known; she's smirking

over her coup as Taegh hands her a cup of apple juice.

"Better stay away from the hard stuff tonight," he says, although he has a beer in his own hand. "What's so funny?"

"People's eyes," Celan says, gleeful. "It's like a secret club."

Taegh chuckles. "Uh, something like that." Then he clears his throat and raises his drink, intoning, "That was quite a trick/You pulled today/Just don't tell the folks at home, OK?"

Celan dissolves in a giggle fit, but manages to clink glasses with him as Cap materializes with a bottle of wine.

"Well, *someone's* having fun over here," he says pointedly, but his eyes are calm and placid and Celan remembers that he doesn't fuse. Best not to mention it to anyone who can't already tell. Taegh apparently agrees.

"You ready?" he says, throwing an arm around Cap's shoulders, shaking him as if to loosen him up.

"Fuck yeah! Asses will be kicked tonight, my friend."

Taegh grins, swigging his drink. "Think you can help us out a little? Keep an eye on this one?" He juts his chin in Celan's direction. "Don't want her getting into any trouble." She barely catches his wink.

"No problemo." Cap turns to Celan, jocular. "Wanna go catch the openers?"

"Sure," she says, her disappointment fleeting. She'd

rather hang out with Taegh, but Cap has always been nice and besides, the way she's feeling right now anything and anyone would be fun. She downs the rest of her juice and plunks the cup on the table.

She and Cap turn to go as a buzz jumps through the room and Cyrinda sweeps through the door in a blaze of stunning perfection, eyes bright as fire. The crowd parts respectfully as she sails toward them beaming and alights next to Taegh, pulling him in for a kiss amidst scattered whistles.

"See you guys later," Cap says, but they don't seem to hear, so he and Celan retreat out into the corridor, slipping swiftly into the wings of the stage and squinting past the lights at the vast audience arrayed in Arlo's main hall.

Celan sucks in a breath at the sheer numbers, all rapt with the hushed enchantment of the music. There's a skinny blonde guy at the mic, singing and strumming a guitar in front of a rawboned guy with a cello and an auburn-haired girl with a harp. His raspy drawl blends with the girl's high lonesome cry and the music wends its way into Celan's soul as she takes it all in, awed by the amplification of the notes through the speakers. It's like she's *inside* the music and the moon and stars are dancing a joyful, hopeful reel.

She blinks, and the stage lights fizz and flash like sparklers across her vision.

"Wow," she says.

"Pretty good, huh?"

Dimly, she makes out some uniformed figures in the front row. "There are a lot of techs here."

"Oh yeah," Cap says, sotto voce. "They love this stuff. You wouldn't believe it – out here celebrating Arlo's thirtieth like anybody. Pretty funny when you think about it."

"Yeah?"

"Oh yeah. Definitely," Cap cocks his head to the side. "You know about the history of the wayverns, don't you?"

"No," she admits.

"It's pretty interesting." He gulps some wine, flipping straw-colored bangs out of his eyes, and motions her back out into the hall as he warms to his subject.

"Y'see, when the expros first came here the techs weren't sure what to do with 'em all. Didn't want to let 'em live right in the city, what with them transing and all, so they helped them build these...bunks, they called 'em. Grouped the rooms around a main hall, where everybody ate and they could hold meetings. Discuss things. Educate us."

He hesitates like he might be boring her, but Celan motions for him to go on. He passes her the wine and she takes a quick swig.

"Well, over time, y'see, we started getting bored – only so many lectures a person can stand."

Celan giggles.

"And so we got to entertaining ourselves. Playing music, skits and stuff, art and all that. And the techs, they started to get into it. Started wanting to come out and watch. So we took back our halls and started making 'em pay for the pleasure. And that's what we've been doing ever since."

He shoves hands in pockets and grins, gloating. "Think they thought they'd get us all to come live in their city. Give up all our ways. But no, even those that work for 'em, soon as they're outta that gate it's out with the transfers and off to the wayverns. And the techs? They can't help but follow."

Celan tucks the bottle neatly under her arm and gives his speech a tiny round of applause. Cap beams.

"Can we go out front and watch?" she says, washing the question down with another draught of wine.

"Sure," he says, motioning for the bottle. "You heard Taegh though. Don't want you getting in any trouble."

"Don't worry. I can handle it."

Cap raises an eyebrow. Then he laughs. "Yeah," he says, "knowing your sisters, I bet you can."

WHY DID I EVER WORRY? Cyrinda thinks, smiling so wide her cheeks hurt as she basks in the glow of the room. Everyone who's anyone on Transway is here tonight and they're all looking at her and Taegh, throwing beams of pure bright energy and love their way. Her father would have been so proud. She squeezes Taegh's hand and accepts the glass of wine he offers.

"Better?" he says, and she nods.

"See? It all worked out. I got Cap watching Celan. She'll be fine. We're gonna have a great night."

Cyrinda takes a sip and gazes into his eyes. Those beautiful violet eyes! How could she ever have been angry with him? She laughs at the thought, dismissing it forever. He's the most wonderful thing she's ever known, no matter what his failings.

So he's a fuser, so what? So is she, occasionally. If he gets sick, she'll cure him. She'll never refuse him a single thing ever again. Dipping a finger into a miniature pocket in the bodice of her dress she extracts the transfer and presses it into his palm.

"Here," she says, "all you."

Taegh smirks, tucking it away. "Knew you'd come around."

She throws her arms around his neck, pulling him close for another delicious kiss. She could live on kisses forever. Kisses and wine.

"Look at you two lovebirds," comes a voice, and they part to see Aleta, arm around a happily disheveled Zita, watching them with amusement.

"Looks like we're not the only ones," says Taegh.

Zita sighs, squeezing Aleta's hand. "She's amazing."

"Best drummer we've ever had," Cyrinda affirms.

"Oh, she's talented alright."

"Looks like you got your fuse on too," Aleta says, looking Cyrinda hard in the eyes.

She waves an airy hand. "Things happened."

"Yeah," Aleta cracks. "Things do. So where's the kid?"

"Cap's on it," Taegh says quickly.

"Nice."

There's a small commotion near the front of the room as Tomás, Jenner, and Stino duck out into the hall amid scattered cheers.

Aleta cocks her head towards the door. "Looks like Fused Up!'s about to roll."

"Then vámanos aviadoras," Taegh says with exaggerated charm.

The girls laugh and Cyrinda pecks him on the cheek. "Let's go check them out."

But he starts to roll a smoke, like he's got time. Aleta rolls her eyes and turns, towing Zita out of the band room and into the corridor. Taegh leans over and brushes a strand of hair off Cyrinda's neck with a long finger. She shivers.

"What?" he says.

She leans in, breath against his ear, heart hammering. "I want you," she says.

And she does, badly. The fuse doesn't hit her same the way it hits him, not all the time. Sometimes it makes her so revved up she doesn't know what to do. One touch and it's like a chain reaction. She wants everything, all at once. Right now, all she wants is the crush of his body on hers.

"Oh yeah? Where?" he says teasingly.

"Anywhere."

Taegh purrs low in his throat and pushes her against the wall, kissing her slow and deep. When they finally part they're both breathing hard.

"Outside," he says. "*Now.*"

A ROAR GOES UP AS Fused Up! rips furiously into their set – Tomás, blue-black hair sculpted to outrageous heights, grips the neck of his guitar like he wants to throttle it while Jenner beats the crap out of his old drumkit and Stino, eyes shut tight, bangs the bass for all its worth.

Down in front with Cap, the sound hits Celan like a wall, completely enveloping her like another wave of fuse. Tall bodies start to jump and leap, suddenly huge and dangerously close. For a moment she feels herself compacting, shrinking, and she's afraid she'll be crushed – until strong hands lift her under the armpits and she finds herself perched atop Cap's broad shoulders. She yells her thanks into his ear and he squeezes her calf, big-brotherly.

From up here she can see the whole writhing crush, tan uniforms among them, faces shiny with drink and sweat, obviously having the time of their lives. Then, out of nowhere, Zita and Aleta are right beside them, laughing and jumping and screaming along with the words that erupt out of Tomás' throat like a volcano.

Baby's first inoculation starts the virus' mutation
Doctor says she'll be fine, she'll be fine
Baby's first alleviation and you'll call it recreation
Doctor says she'll be fine, she'll be fine

You'll be fine, you'll be fine
It's all in your twisted mind
You'll be fine, you'll be fine
It's all in your twisted, so complicit
In your twisted mind

Baby's first indoctrination and you'll call it education
Teacher says he'll be fine, he'll be fine
From that first incarceration you'll feel such a liberation
Teacher says he'll be fine, he'll be fine

You'll be fine, you'll be fine
It's all in your twisted mind
You'll be fine, you'll be fine
It's all in your twisted, so complicit
In your twisted mind

And it's such a fine romance now
When you don't stand half a chance now
Face the music and you'll dance
They wanna see, they wanna see

ATRAVESAR - TO GET ACROSS

All of that proverbial incongruity

By the second chorus Celan is screaming along with everyone else like she's heard these words a million times before.

TWELVE ANGRY SCREEDS AND BUCKETS of sweat later, bows are taken and the applause begins to die down. The cacaphony in the hall recedes into a steady thrum as the curtains close and stagehands converge, changing out gear in preparation for the headliners.

Out front, in the far corner of the stage near the left wing, Taegh stands with an arm around Cyrinda, looking out over the packed house like a king surveying his court. He takes a drag off his smoke and passes it to her as they step aside to allow a burly man carrying a snare drum and cymbals to pass. With the motion, a group in front spies them and a whoop goes up. Cyrinda waves.

"They couldn't even fit everyone," she marvels. "They had to open all the windows. There's a bunch of people outside listening from the street."

"Not bad for an expro bastard, huh?"

Cyrinda slaps lightly at his chest. "Silly," she says, "you're perfect." She gazes out over the crowd, eyes dreamy. "Maybe your real mother's here. Maybe she'll see you and she'll just know."

"I doubt it. She probably died years ago."

Cyrinda wheels on him. "That's awful! How can you say that?"

"Because it's probably true," he says calmly. "Or not. Maybe not. Maybe my real parents are aliens. From another planet."

Cyrinda laughs, thinking he's playing. "That would explain a lot."

Taegh's eyes search her face like he's looking for something vitally important, but failing to find it he sighs, resigned.

"C'mon," he says. "Let's go find Cap and Aleta and do this already."

He grabs her hand, squeezing a bit tighter than necessary, and brusquely tugs her through the throngs in the hallway. When they reach the band room Cyrinda snatches her hand away, annoyed, and hastily smoothes her hair. The Fused Up! crew is chugging water and beer and slapping each other on the back while Cap perches on the edge of a beat-up sofa doing card tricks for a mesmerized Celan. No one looks her way.

"Nice work," Taegh says, going over and punching Tomás in the arm.

Tomás grins broadly. "Hate to have to follow that, *ese*."

Cyrinda steps up beside Taegh, fixing Tomás with a haughty stare. "Follow nothing. From now on we're going to be leading, *ese*."

Tomás laughs, but there's an edge to it. He looks at Taegh, who shrugs.

"You heard what the girl said."

"Claro que sí."

Suddenly alert to a snideness in their tone, Cyrinda stiffens, face falling into sullen lines. "What the fuck do you mean by that?"

"What?" Tomás says, feigning innocence.

"Yeah, Rin, what?" Taegh echoes. "We were *agreeing* with you."

"Fuck you, Taegh."

"Again?" He mimes exhaustion.

She whirls, snatching a mug off the table and flinging the contents into his face.

"Give me that transfer, you fucking asshole fuser!"

Tomás guffaws, enjoying the show.

"What the fuck, Rin?" Taegh says, mopping his brow with his sleeve and backing away from her furious form. "Don't be giving me any more of this shit, OK? Your eyes are brighter than the sun right now."

"So?" she counters. "I haven't fused in two weeks. You can barely go two hours."

Taegh's face reddens as people begin to whisper and stare. "That's not true," he says tightly. "And this isn't the time for this."

"So when is the time? When you're so sick you can barely stand up, barely get out of bed?"

"When have you ever seen me like that?"

"I've heard about the coming attractions."

"Great. Then you've heard about the leaving

225

attractions too." He turns swiftly on his heel and pushes through the crowd to the door.

"What is *that* supposed to mean?" Cyrinda says.

He halts for a moment, but doesn't turn around.

"Right now, it means we've got a show to play. In case you forgot," he says, and marches out into the hall.

Cyrinda glares at Tomás, who's grinning unctuously, and then around the room at the rest of the faces regarding her not with shock, but with a certain decorous curiosity – like they're used to this kind of scene by now but it's still somewhat embarrassing to have to witness. Even Celan shrugs, picking another card from a bemused Cap.

Humiliation crawls up Cyrinda's spine, settles in her stomach, and curls into a tight ball that threatens to explode into another angry outburst until she gathers herself up, stares down every last one of them, and marches purposefully after Taegh, spine straight.

I'll show them. I'll show them all.

She'll be queen again before the night is out.

THERE'S A MOMENT OF SILENCE in her wake and Cap lays the cards down with a sigh.

"Better get going."

"Yeah," Celan says. "Let's get it rolling."

Out in the corridor she spies a ribbon of purple on the floor – one of Cyrinda's scarves. She bends to retrieve it, looping it around her own neck.

"Matches your skirt," Cap says, and they share a quick grin.

Backstage, they pause to take in the scene behind the curtain – Taegh tuning his guitar, studiously ignoring a primping Cyrinda, while Aleta drills out nonchalant drumrolls. Then Tomás comes up behind them, jovial and reeking of beer.

"Ven aquí, aviadita," he says, laying a hand on Celan's shoulder. "You're not in the band yet. Let's go out front."

With a 'good luck' and a hug for Cap, she follows Tomás into the main hall. The crowd parts respectfully for them until they're front and center, joined by Jenner and Stino, who's beaming from ear to ear with the success of his recent debut. The curtain opens to cheers and whistles.

Cap starts off by plunking at his bass, conferring wordlessly with Aleta, who smiles and smooths her staccato beats out into a hypnotic roll. Taegh strikes the first jarring chord on his guitar. Celan recognizes the song as one they played on the radio the other day, described by Cyrinda as a paean to the plight of the expros. But now, with one last glare at Taegh, she grabs the mike and howls:

It's the groove of a grave of a grind
That never skips a beat in your mind
It's the tourniquet of a vise

Between two extremes of a life
And every day you pay, but every day you stay
And you say and you say and you say and you say
It's what now? Enough now
It's what now? Too much now
It's what now? Enough now
Enough now
Enough!

The crowd stomps and hollers as Cyrinda rages, possessed. Celan feels the same rush come over her as she did with Fused Up!, but something new, something more. Something like a spell being cast, weaving her seamlessly together with everyone else in the room, like they're all one being with different heads. The thought makes her giggle until she stops thinking and just moves – dancing, jumping, totally free – holding down her own space in the crowd.

One song chases another at a hectic pace, Cyrinda strutting and fretting and spinning like a purple whirlwind while Taegh dives deeper and deeper into his guitar until he's almost submarinal, wrenching sound out of it like it hurts his bones. Behind them, Cap and Aleta keep the beat driving like it's a celebration, like no one has a care in the world. The tension is incredible, as if the whole thing could fall apart at any moment but by some unholy miracle it doesn't.

Until the last song, when a spotlight finds Cyrinda

and she starts, a cappella, eyes closed:

> *She is like the shadow of a white rose*
> *in a silver glass*
> *It's not strong, but it's built to last*
> *She gets her way and it doesn't matter*
> *Whose head is on the platter*
>
> *No, she don't know her own strength*
> *But she needs to learn*
> *Hit the remote control and watch the scene again*
> *See where the tide begins to turn*

Then the beat kicks in and Taegh's guitar rings out as she rips into the next verse.

> *Do you wanna start a revolution*
> *or do you wanna dance?*
> *Spin away without another glance*
> *You got the moves, but do you got a plan?*
> *There's more than one way to kill a man*

She tries to kick into the chorus.

> *No, she don't know –*

But Taegh lets loose with squall of noise that rails against the vocals.

– her own strength

He strikes again and she fixes him with a stare of such fury that even Cap and Aleta skip a beat. Taegh meets her eyes calmly though and, stone-faced, falls into a parody of the chords, letting her know he's playing her tune but he doesn't really mean it.

– she needs to learn
Hit the remote control and watch the scene again
See where the tide begins to turn

Now is the time for his usual solo but Taegh defaults, forcing Cyrinda into the next verse.

She is flying colors like a sweetheart
for a wasted class
It's not strong, but it's built to last
She knows the way, and she doesn't care
Whatever fate awaits her there

No, she don't know her own strength
But she needs to learn
Hit the remote control and watch the scene again
See where the tide begins to turn

A quick bass and drum coda and that's it – the room explodes into a screaming, frenzied ovation as Celan stands open-mouthed, thunderstruck.

CENTER STAGE, ARMS RAISED, CYRINDA bathes in the adoration. She's not looking at Taegh or Cap or Aleta, but straight out into the crowd. She's done it again. Made them love her. She knew she would. She's been doing it since she was a kid and it's the most extraordinary feeling – like pure bright sunlight shining just for her. The first time she felt it she was three years old. She ran onto the stage during one of her father's songs and started dancing behind him and the whole room roared and cheered. Maybe their mom loved Nola better but her dad loved her and she was a star.

And I still am.

She turns joyfully to the wings as the curtain closes; ready to forgive, ready for her and Taegh to embrace, to share this moment of triumph like they always do.

Ready for her encore.

But he's gone. She eyes Cap questioningly. He shrugs, lifting the bass strap over his head and setting the instrument down.

"Looks like the show's over."

I TOTALLY GET IT NOW, Celan thinks, pulled along in the crush with Tomás and Aleta and the rest of them, eager to get backstage and revel in reflected glory. *This is why they need to live here and not in the ranchos. They could never make this kind of music there – the elders would never allow it.*

She's not sure why she thinks that, but she's positive that she's right.

There's some muttering behind her about the lack of an encore and Celan shakes her head. Can't they see it was perfect the way it was? Anything more would have been too much. Anyone could see that Cyrinda and Taegh were ready to kill each other.

She frowns. Cyrinda doesn't understand him, not really. He doesn't like to fight like she does. She explodes on you and then ten minutes later she's sorry and it's forgotten. He's different though, he can't do that. That's why he fuses so much. So he can forget too.

Suddenly it hits her, the perfect idea to cheer him up: She'll tell him about this morning, about how she saw him fusing with Tomás and how happy she is that she did it too. He'll be happy knowing that someone understands.

They surge through the band room door and merge into the crush; Celan peers through the crowd but there are too many tall heads surrounding her. On instinct, she trails Aleta to a corner near the picked-over spread to find Taegh hunched in a chair, nursing a beer and ignoring the glad-handers flocking thickly around him.

She tugs at his sleeve. She knows he'll understand. She has to tell him her secret. She's bursting with it. She knows now that he'll be proud. He'll be proud that it was him after all.

"Hey Taegh?" she says, circling around in front of him.

He drags at a smoke, a half-smile curling on his lips, eyes sad.

"Hey Celan," he drawls. "So what'd'ya think?"

"You were amazing. I loved it!"

"Figured you would." He tousles her hair affectionately.

It's now or never.

"I saw you, you know," she says, with a shy smile. "That's how I knew."

"Huh? Saw what?"

"You and Tomás this morning. Fusing. I was there. In the closet. I was looking for stuff to read and then you came in and I hid. But don't worry, I won't ever tell."

The world stops, everything hushed. Taegh gapes at her. She's waiting for him to burst out laughing – anticipating their shared mirth, their little secret. Instead, his face falls like a dying star. An awful feeling settles in the pit of her stomach.

"I – I just wanted to know," she stammers. "What was going on."

"Well," he says, "guess you found out, didn't you?"

He gets to his feet and stalks away into the crowd. Her heart sinks.

"Taegh! Taegh, wait! I'm sorry. I didn't mean – "

But a mass of warm bodies presses in, cutting her off, and he is gone. Furious, embarrassed, hot tears in her eyes, she shoves fiercely through the crowd until she reaches the door. She cranes her neck – there's no sign of him in the hall.

Maybe he went back to the house.

She tears off down the corridor and out into the night, feet pounding the ground like pistons. She wants to talk to him, to tell him that it wasn't his fault, to stop that hollow look in his eyes. The one she caused.

She's almost across the courtyard when it happens – a tremendous roar, followed by a shockwave that lifts Celan off her feet and slams her forcefully to the ground. When she staggers up, stunned and bruised, heat engulfs her. Arlo's is a wall of flame.

She blinks for a moment, uncomprehending. Then she screams, an animal sound from deep within that sounds alien even to her own ears, as chaos erupts around her. Other screams break out and people run back and forth, hands hastily grabbing possessions from apartments, shouldering friends who are too stunned or intoxicated to mobilize themselves. Everyone is barreling in the direction of the rear alley near the latrine, the only way out now that the ones in front are choked with smoke and fire.

Celan hurtles toward Cyrinda and Taegh's apartment. The fire hasn't reached it yet. They'll be safe. They'll be OK. Hammering on the door she shouts their names. No answer. It occurs to her to try the knob and to her surprise it turns easily. She hurries inside.

No one's in the front room. Bedroom – no one in

there either.

Dread creeps into her chest, making her tremble, but she pulls herself together and darts out the door. They'll be out front. On Transway. They have to be. She heads for the rear alley, thinking she can use the next one over to get out onto the street in front of Arlo's.

They'll be out there, they'll be out there. I know they'll be out there. Her heart beats with the rhythm of this litany like she can will it to be true just by repeating it.

Others apparently have the same idea about circling around and she's carried along by the crowd out onto Transway and into complete pandemonium. Wild with adrenaline, immune to fear, she runs straight for Arlo's, where flames blast out of every door and window and thick smoke roils up into the sky. People are lying in the street, being dragged by friends, making mad dashes toward the building only to be repelled again by the inferno. Frantic, Celan searches faces for someone, anyone, she knows.

They'll be out here, they'll be out here. I know they'll be out here.

Suddenly she sees one.

"Tomás!"

He turns, eyes watery and unfocused.

She grabs desperately at the front of his shirt. "Cyrinda! Taegh! Where are they?"

"Aviadita," he says through parched lips. His face is rough, blackened, blistered in spots. He must have barely made it out alive.

"Where are they?"

He looks down and shakes his head.

"No! They can't be!" she yells, releasing him.

She tears off again, questioning anyone and everyone. But there's no sign of them anywhere; no one who's seen them, no sign they got out in time.

Finally, she just runs blindly through the streets and alleys until she collapses, spent, in the garden of some nameless wayvern – where she sobs into the soft earth for a long time until blessed unconsciousness descends.

☐► 13 ◄☐

A pleasant warmth presses against Celan's face and a strong, safe wall against her back. Curled on her side under a canopy of bean trellis she feels full of the sweetness of life and growing things. She sighs contentedly and stretches, opening her eyes to a moment of blinking confusion – *Why am I in a garden?* – before the events of the past night rush in, burying her peace under an avalanche of fear.

Cyrinda and Taegh...gone.

But maybe it's not really real. Maybe it was all a bad dream; something caused by the fuse, by the wine. Maybe she'll go back to Arlo's and it'll still be standing like nothing happened. Cyrinda will be worried sick. But a look down at her sooty clothes tells a different story.

It happened.

But just because nobody saw them that doesn't mean they're both dead. Tomás was so fucked up he probably had no idea what was really going on.

She sits up, squaring her shoulders. She's not giving up. She'll go to Arlo's and ask around. Maybe some of the apartments are still intact. If they are, people will be there trying to salvage what they can. Someone must know something.

Getting to her feet, she rubs her eyes and picks her way through the alleys until she finds the one that leads to the courtyard of Arlo's. As she thought, not all of the apartments burned, but Arlo's itself is a heap of charred remains. Her stomach twists at the sight and she retches into the dust.

"You OK, chiqui?"

A comforting hand rests on her shoulder and she turns her face up mutely, wiping her mouth on her sleeve. It's Zita, looking about as bad as she feels – even her fiery red hair looks exhausted.

Celan's eyes fill with tears. "Cyrinda? Taegh?"

Like Tomás last night, Zita shakes her head.

"Are Cap and Aleta – ?" Celan starts, but the look on Zita's face says it all.

"Sorry," Celan says.

"Mira," says Zita, "I gotta go get cleaned up now. Gotta work in a few hours. Come find me later. Over by Maddy's. We'll figure something out, OK?"

For lack of anything else to say she nods and Zita offers her a hurried half-hug before staggering off to whatever it is she does.

Celan stares after her for a long moment before wandering around to the front of Arlo's, kicking up dust and stones. Already, the offerings are being left – little trinkets and bunches of flowers among the still-smoldering ruins. She ambles along the periphery until she spies the incongruous sight of a roller and a trim, neat figure in blue. She squints. The tech seems to be trying to talk to people, asking questions about the fire, but they shy away as quickly as possible. Celan, however, has no such qualms. Maybe this man knows what happened. Cold hard facts.

Swiftly, she advances.

"Hey," she says, and he turns: It's the man she talked to the other day, the man from the market. The tall one. He seems surprised to see her, but oddly pleased as well.

"You're the little girl who asked about the scanners… the one with the sister, Cyrinda."

Celan swallows hard, not trusting her voice at the mention of the name.

"Celan, was it? Right?" the man says, mistaking her reluctance for shyness. "Está bien. You can talk to me. Do you live with your sister? Your mother?"

At this last, she bursts into tears. The man looks around helplessly, then carefully pats her on the shoulder.

"I'm sorry. I didn't mean to upset you. I'm guessing they are – gone?"

Through her sobs, she nods yes.

"In the fire?"

Another nod, but she amends it chokingly, "My sister. My m–mother passed a year ago."

Another stiff pat. "Well, I'm very sorry to hear that." But somehow this awkward gesture from a stranger manages to take the hard edge off her grief. Her sobs fade to a sniffle and she drags a hand across her eyes, feeling foolish. Crying in front of a tech. What would Cyrinda say?

The man gazes down at her, his expression puzzled and slightly pained, but still friendly. "I have a theory I'd like to explore a bit, Celan. That is, if you don't mind."

She sniffs again. "OK," she says, relieved to be talking about anything safe, neutral, and unrelated to the horrors of last night.

"Excellent." He reaches into his breast pocket and produces a flat, rectangular object about the length and width of his hand, which he taps and swipes at the face of with a forefinger.

"What's that?" she says, curiosity piqued in spite of everything.

"My server. Ah, there we go." He detaches a tiny pencil-like thing from the base of the object. This he holds out to Celan, who takes it gingerly.

"Now, I want you to touch the end of this stylus to

240

the inside of your cheek. Then, carefully, hand it over to me. And whatever you do, do not touch that end with your fingers."

She does as instructed.

"Bueno," he says, shifting his weight to one hip. He's about to touch the end of the stylus to the server when he pauses. "Maybe you'd like to watch this, eh?"

"Sure," she says, though she has no idea what he is doing.

He crouches so she can see over his shoulder. A quick tap with the stylus and there on the face of the small screen is a stylized colorful rendition of two ropes twisting and spinning, exactly parallel to each other and connected by short bars at regular intervals. Celan recognizes the image immediately.

"The spiral ladder!"

He looks up sharply. "What?"

"The spiral ladder. The elders used to have us climb it sometimes, in the astral, when we were fixing things. We could make ourselves real tiny. There are millions of little ladders like that, in our bodies, everywhere, they said."

"Interesting," he mutters, and then addresses her in an instructional tone. "The correct name of the 'ladder' is D-N-A, deoxyribonucleic acid, and yes, it is everywhere. In fact, it is the very building block of life."

Celan beams at the twisting ropes, happy that she knew something he hadn't expected, until abruptly they stop spinning and are replaced by two sequences of odd dashes.

"What is *that*?" she asks.

"That," he says, tucking away the server and getting to his feet, "is proof that my theory was correct. You are, unquestionably, my daughter."

She gapes at him.

"Your mother was named Mair Tyras, was she not?"

"Y-yes."

"An elegida, as you call them, originally of Rancho Pescados, who ran off to Transway with her man Arlo Bonitas soon after her induction into the order. Together they ran the wayvern known until yesterday as Arlo's for many years, during which time they bore two daughters, one of whom was named Cyrinda. Then Arlo died. An accident, I don't recall the details. Sometime later, your mother and I met and began a relationship. We had planned to marry. She was going to come live with me in Albakirk and raise her girls there. When I returned from my trip Winnipeg."

He frowns. "But when I got back she had gone. Vanished back to the ranchos I assumed. No one claimed to know where."

Celan's eyes are as wide as saucers.

"Apparently," he says, "she was pregnant with you when she left."

She blinks.

"And neither she, nor anyone else, ever mentioned it

to me." He crosses arms in front of his chest, looking extremely put out.

"But," Celan starts, "why did you think – ?"

He clears his throat, scratching at his short beard. "Cyrinda Mairs made quite a name for herself around here. It was obvious she was the same girl I once knew; she was always very distinctive-looking, even in her youth. When I saw the both of you at the market I started to wonder. You were just about the right age. I wasn't sure if I should interfere, but – "

"But who *are* you?"

The man smiles. "Aside from your father, I am Theodore Timanti, one of three Lead SocEns for the City of Albakirk."

"So-shen?"

"Social Engineer. It is the highest engineering rank, encompassing all other disciplines."

Celan looks suitably impressed.

"So you're like a tech elder...kind of?"

Theodore laughs. "You'll find our social structure a bit more advanced than the deluded hierarchy of your farcical theocracy."

"I will?" She has no idea what he means.

"Oh yes," he says firmly. "I am, apparently, your sole surviving parent, Celan. And, as such, it is my intent that you should come live with me in Albakirk and be educated properly. You have far too inquisitive a mind to let it be wasted on 'climbing spiral ladders' and other such nonsense."

Her head starts to swim. "But Jillyanne – "

"Who?"

"My tia. I was living with her, back in the ranchos." But the image of the cottage at the springs already seems hazy, indistinct, like someplace she remembers from years ago. "I was only visiting here," she finishes lamely.

"Well of course we will inform Jillyanne of the change in plans," Theodore says. "We wouldn't want her to worry. You can write her a letter and I will see that she gets it." A delicate pause. "You can read and write, I hope?"

"The elders taught us."

"At least they managed *something* useful."

He turns and walks briskly in the direction of the roller. Celan stares after him, too stunned by the speed of events for it to occur to her to follow. But as he gets into the driver's seat, he motions her forward. So, putting one foot carefully in front of the other, she crosses the distance between them, climbing in next to him with a tentative smile as he reaches into the rear seat and fishes around until he finds an oversize hooded jacket. This he hands to her, motioning for her to put it on. She does, and he starts the engine.

Nothing more is said and Celan is content to watch Transway roll by around her, too exhausted to care about leaving it for good. After all, she was only here for a week – it's not like it was her home. But as the imposing girth of the city gate looms up ahead, her heart starts to pound as she remembers the transfusion, the scanners.

Has it been twelve hours yet? What will he do if –

Theodore, however, turns the roller to the right, heading out into scrubland, hugging the edge of a dun-colored wall.

"Where are we going?"

"We're not going through the gate."

"Oh," she says, feigning disappointment.

"We're going in a different way," he says. "I have an idea."

Her father's brows draw down very seriously. "I'm not sure you realize this, Celan, but there are certain... attitudes towards transers in Albakirk. You can't help where you came from, but that's all in the past. You're here and you're my daughter and as far as I'm concerned you are perfect. But not everyone has such liberal ideas about transers and I want you to have every possible social advantage."

She eyes him suspiciously. "So?"

"So. I have recently had a visit from some of my contemporaries from Winnipeg – "

"What's that?"

"A city northeast of here."

"And people still live there?"

"Yes, of course."

Strange. The elders never mentioned a city called Winnipeg. But maybe there wasn't anything too bad to clean up there, so they never bothered to go.

"Is it far?"

He sighs impatiently. "Far enough that we don't travel there very often. Anyway, the point is that, as I told you, I spent some time in Winnipeg right around the time you were conceived. And so it is conceiv*able* that you could be the child of a woman from there as well. That is what I am going to tell people."

"That your friends brought me here from there?"

"Exactly."

"But I don't know anything about Winnipeg!"

"Neither do most people in Albakirk. Only the highest level Ens have traveled there in person."

Celan digests this, scrutinizing his face until he looks away nervously.

"Are you ashamed of me?" she says, her voice very small.

"Absolutely not." He strikes the palm of his hand against the steering wheel for emphasis. "Like I told you, you're my daughter and you're perfect."

Reaching out that same hand he pats her shoulder again, with something approaching affection. "But I want everyone else to see that too. Which is why I think it best we do it this way. It will explain any discrepancies in your deportment and knowledge and allow you the necessary time to catch up with your peers." He smiles reassuringly. "Which I am fully confident you will."

Celan contemplates this. Another lie. Just like Jillyanne lied about her mother. But maybe this is the way all adults are. At least this time she's in on it, instead of the one being lied to.

"OK," she finally says.

Her father looks relieved.

"Of course, you'll need some time to prepare before being formally introduced. And so," he continues, raising his eyebrows almost mischievously, "we're going to sneak you in the back door for now."

With that, he stops the roller in front of a small, nondescript door in the wall. There's a strange symbol painted on it, kind of like an arrow with a cap on one end. It looks like –

"A transfer," Theodore confirms. "This is the transer lab. Where our volunteers come to help us with some of our experiments. Sometimes it is necessary that they be transing when they do so, so obviously they can't go through the scanners. This makes it easier for everyone."

He pulls out his server again and performs a complex-seeming series of swipes and pecks. Then, stretching long legs, he disembarks from the vehicle and taps at a silver pad set into the door where a knob would normally be. There's a subtle click-and-release.

"Key code," he says, pulling the door open as Celan scrambles out of the roller. "Changes once a day. We use readers for everything else, but again, in this circumstance it's just easier."

A light flickers on above their heads as they climb a

short flight of stairs to another door, apparently unlocked since he yanks it open.

"Stay here."

The door closes behind him and Celan sits down on the top step to wait. The floor and walls are made of a grey, stone-like substance that's cool to the touch. Staring at her grimy sandals she's aware all at once of how dirty she is, how she must look after the events of last night. There's a big tear along the hem of her new skirt, and a dark, ugly stain down by her right knee. The skirt Trina made, she'd loved it so much. Now she can't wait to get it off.

Get rid of it. Burn it. I don't care.

Then the door swings open and, startled, she jumps to her feet.

"The coast is clear," Theodore whispers conspiratorially, and she slips inside, pushing off the hood of the jacket and craning her neck, eager to get a good first look inside the tech city.

But the room is disappointingly barren, more of that smooth grey stone with the only furnishings being benches, chairs, and tables and some big screens set into the walls. Part of the opposite wall is mirrored and she catches her reflection looking as disheveled as she'd imagined.

Maybe even worse.

"In there," her father says, motioning to another door on the right. "You can wash up in there. Just push the button on the wall in the shower. We don't have readers in here, only a fixed timer. You can throw your old clothes out when you're done."

Fine with me, Celan thinks but says, "What am I going to wear then?"

He reaches for his server. "I'll print you out a uniform while you wash. Stand still, arms out like this." He demonstrates a t-shape with his own. "Bueno."

He passes the server briefly over the outline of her body. "OK, got it."

She lowers her arms, skeptically eyeing the device in his hand.

"Your server's going to make me new clothes?"

"My server's going to pass your measurements to the Bank and your new clothes will print out over there." He gestures to a small, recessed square in the far wall.

"They come out of the wall?"

"They come out of the printer," Theodore corrects, tucking his server away with a look of satisfaction.

She considers asking how the printer works, but the sudden pressing need to be clean wins out over curiosity.

"Huh," is all she says in reply.

THE SHOWER IS NICE AND steamy hot and Celan stands under it for a long time, hitting the button again when the water stops, lathering up and letting the grime of last night disappear down the drain. Finally satisfied, she grabs a thick towel off the shelf and rubs until her skin fairly glows. Tucking it around her, she tiptoes to the door and cracks it open.

"Hey," she whispers. "I'm good now. Are my clothes all ready?"

There's a quick shuffle of feet as her father pulls the door open the rest of the way. He's holding a small bundle topped by a pair of boots in his free hand.

"There's a Sanichute and a Sterichute in the wall by the sink," he says, pointing out the two openings. "Steri's for the towel. Sani's for your old clothes. That box to the left will dry your hair. Just stand under it. It's automatic."

"OK." She lets the door close again. After a brief blast from the hair dryer, Celan dons the tan uniform and socks and shoes, silently marveling at the perfect fit and the fact that they feel surprisingly real for items that appeared out of a wall. She catches her reflection again and this time she grins.

I look just like them.

She gathers up the wet towel and dirty clothes to dispose of them in the proper places. The clothes are about to get dumped when a glimpse of something bright catches her eye – Cyrinda's scarf. She tugs it out and balls it up, thrusting it into her pocket. Then she tosses the rest and turns, hurrying out into the main room.

Theodore gives her the once-over and grunts, satisfied. "We're going to go to my bunk, my personal rooms. There are some things we will need to go over and we will need privacy. Most people are at Rec at the moment so we shouldn't run into to too many of them, but if we do it is very important that you do not say a word. Understood?"

She nods silently, practicing.

Her father smiles. "Good. Now watch this door, it's different than the others." He presses a panel on the wall and instead of swinging open, the door slides with a whoosh to one side, revealing a long empty corridor. He strides forward and Celan, taking a deep breath, follows.

Her first glimpse of the inside of Albakirk proper is not much more interesting than the lab – a series of hallways and a little room that moves called an elevator, which zips them up several floors until they reach another hallway and another door that also slides open at a touch.

"My bunk," her father says by way of explanation, and Celan eyes with interest what must be his living quarters. The front room isn't much more elaborate than the one in Cyrinda and Taegh's apartment, just a small sink and hot plate and a simple table and chairs. This surprises her.

Isn't he supposed to be the boss?

"Doesn't look like much from here, does it?" Theodore says, like he can read her mind. "Come on."

A hallway veers off from the left side of the

kitchenette and it quickly becomes apparent that this place is much larger than she first thought. There are two doors on the right side of the hall and another at the far end. Theodore whooshes open the nearest one.

"You can sleep here."

It's empty save for a small bed, but she's impressed by the large, floor-to-ceiling window that covers one entire wall. She can see outside. Somehow, that's a huge relief.

He passes the next door with a brief, "My room," and stops before the last one, grinning almost impishly.

"And now," he says grandly, "the best room of all. The library."

The final door opens to reveal a heavy, old-world desk, overstuffed chairs, ornate lamps, and, most bizarrely of all, books – ancient books stacked on dark wooden shelves that cover all available wall space. It's such an incongruous sight inside this high-tech city that Celan bursts out laughing.

Her father frowns. "You don't like it?"

"No," she says. "I love it! It's so...different."

His grin returns. "I know. The fruits of my many labors in the interest of old-word studies. Not a very popular subject, I'll admit, but one that I enjoy immensely."

"And they let you have all this space for it all to yourself?"

"Being a Lead has its advantages."

They both stand silently for a moment, lost in thought. Then Theodore sighs. "You must be exhausted, Celan.

Why don't you go take a nap and I'll go down to the caf and get you something to eat. Do you like tamales?"

"Sure." The mention of food makes her realize she's starving, but she's eager to follow instructions. She returns to her room and lies dutifully on the bed. The door slides shut, leaving her to womblike silence and the sun shining through the big window, bright on her face like it did this morning. The familiar warmth reassures her; she's still got the same face, even though every single other thing has changed.

SMOKE AND FIRE. SEARING HEAT. Screaming. Running and running, desperately scanning faces. *They have to be alive. They have to!* An earth-shaking explosion drops her to her knees. A rain of ash falls as she struggles to breathe.

Wake up! It's just a dream. Wake up!

Celan kicks against the currents of terror toward the shimmering surface of consciousness. There. She's safe in a dark, quiet room on a soft, clean bed.

She raises a shaking hand to her still-hammering heart. *Breathe*, she tells herself, *in and out, slowly, like the elders do.* A thin sheen of moisture coats her brow and she wipes it away with her other hand. Shivers a little. It was only a bad dream. It's over now.

To soothe herself, she gazes up and out through the window at the vast night sky, silently naming constellations. It's peaceful under the stars. Maybe

Cyrinda and Taegh are up there somewhere, watching over her. Would they be mad that she's in the tech city? Cyrinda might be but it's too bad. Her father said she had to stay with him now.

As the fight-or-flight response begins to recede her stomach grumbles loudly. *Food.* Did he get some for her? He must not have wanted to wake her. Maybe he left it in the kitchen.

Carefully, Celan sits up, letting a wave of dizziness pass. She licks her dry lips.

Water first, then food.

Padding over to the door she runs a hand along the wall where she remembers seeing that push panel earlier. *There.* She presses, momentarily fearing it might be locked, but it slides open with a whoosh.

There's a faint glow from the kitchenette and she stumbles in that direction. A plate covered in some kind of wrapping sits on the table. She lifts a corner and peeps underneath. Tamales.

She takes a cup from a low shelf and holds it under the faucet, looking for a lever to twist like the one on Cyrinda's sink. There's nothing except for a black box next to the spout. Frustrated, she pokes at it.

"Trouble with the reader?" comes her father's voice from the hall, and she nearly drops the glass she jumps so hard.

"Sorry, I didn't mean to scare you."

"No, it's OK," she says quickly. "How do you work

this thing?"

He steps closer and takes the glass from her, casually flipping the top of the box open with his thumb nail and pressing the pad of it against the silvery surface inside. A gush of water releases and he fills the cup, removing his thumb when he's done and flicking the box closed.

"The reader," he says, "reads the pattern of your thumbprint. That way we can record how much water people use so we can make sure we always have enough."

"Huh," she says, examining the whorls of her own thumb.

"When you get your bots your prints will go into the Bank. We use readers to keep track of almost everything, so you'll have to get used to them."

Celan shrugs. *Doesn't sound too hard.* She takes the cup from him and automatically wraps her hands around it, closing her eyes and stilling her breath.

Theodore's voice cuts across her concentration. "You don't need to trans it."

Her eyes fly open. "But we always – "

"The water is perfectly clean. What do you think all this is for?" He gestures around at the sink, the walls, and by extension, the whole city. "We filter it. There are no impurities."

"But I'm not using transferon to do it," she says. "Kids don't need it."

"It doesn't matter. If our plan is going to work,

you'll need to get out of the habit entirely."

She clutches the glass nervously but manages to tip back a few swallows. It's oddly flat, but other than that there's nothing off about it. It tastes like water.

After a moment she ventures, "Theodore?"

"Yes?"

"Why is transing so bad? I thought it was only transferon that you didn't like."

"Kind of late for this tonight." Her father drags a hand over his eyes and Celan realizes all at once how tired he looks. Has he even been to bed or was he up working in his library?

"The short answer is that the process known as 'transfiguration' is a dangerous manipulation of the electromagnetic energy surrounding living things. Very hard to control or direct properly. It caused a lot of problems at the end of the old world. There are better ways of accomplishing things."

"But the elders say – "

"From what we can tell, your elders are nothing more than a rule of charlatans, encouraging people to believe in all manner of bizarre fantasies that merely serve the purpose of maintaining their mental and emotional hold over the populace. People living on air? Preposterous! The body needs to take in food and drink to sustain and nourish it, to help it grow. If it weren't for our generosity, many of your kin would not have survived the famine."

"You mean the expros?"

He clears his throat. "Yes. They recognized the blatant stupidity of the theocracy's ways and came and asked for our help, which we gave in exchange for their cooperation with our work. Perhaps one day they can be fully integrated into society."

"If they stop transing?"

"Exactly. So far they have been most unwilling to give up their naive superstitions and their reliance upon the drug that serves to maintain them. But I, for one, hold out hope that eventually they will. In the meantime, we continue to work with them, within certain bounds, of course."

"That's why you have the scanners?"

"Yes. We do not permit certain practices among those who wish to work within our city. With the exception of the test subjects in my lab."

"And that's why you have the special door."

"Precisely." He stifles a yawn. "I think it's gotten a bit past my bedtime."

Celan takes another sip of water. "Me too," she says quickly, "but I slept a long time. Is it OK if I eat these and then go back to bed?"

"Claro," he says. Then, "I have meetings in the morning but I'll be back around 13:00. Stay here until I return. I'll leave you breakfast and some games to play on the screen in the library – they will help you to adjust. I'll leave instructions on how to access them. You've got a lot to learn and the quicker it goes the better."

"OK," she says, sliding into a chair and tearing the wrapper off the plate of tamales. She looks up to thank him, but he's already gone.

"Good night," she says softly.

14

It's going to take a month or two at least, he figures, to get her ready for even limited socializing, let alone Ed. But that's alright – he's got the time and unlimited resources. It'll all work out.

I hope.

Theodore guns the roller, tearing through dust and scrub in the direction of Transway. His investigation of the fire at Arlo's had been, of necessity, cut short yesterday, so now he's got to get in another round before his ten hundred with Martinez and Balor. Balor's completely up in arms about this – seventy-nine techs killed, which is tragic. But it's not like she gives a shit about the other lives lost. As far as she's concerned, transers are nothing but sub-mental parasites.

He shakes his head, thinking once again what a

travesty it is that an otherwise brilliant person continues to let irrational prejudice blind her to so much possible potential – to say nothing of the necessity of the expros' current (and extremely useful) experimental niche. She blames what she patronizingly calls 'Theodore's liberal tendencies' on his relative youth. He grimaces. Ariana Balor is only ten years older than he is, but acts like it's a century and a half.

At thirty-six, he is the youngest Lead SocEn ever selected, as is protocol, by a convocation of emeriti. Only a year into a fifteen-year term and he's already getting a reputation as an iconoclast. But that's fine. He's confident of the correctness of his stance on the expro question and, luckily, Martinez usually backs him. When it comes to the Leads' Transway policy, Balor is definitely the odd one out.

His mentor, Francis Campana, had been the one to originally nurture the seedlings of this mindset. An old man now, almost ninety, he'd been there at the start – a brand new Lead SocEn himself when the first expros came to Albakirk looking for relief from the famine. His arguments were crucial in creating the policy that allowed them to stay and settle on what became known as Transway.

But Transway was only supposed to be a temporary home until the refugees could be successfully reintegrated into the larger tech community. That process, however, had taken some unexpected detours; the transers showed remarkable tenacity in clinging to their ways and beliefs.

Many techs who had been ready to welcome them as equals (of a sort) fifty years ago are now convinced that they really are inferior and will always remain incapable of true integration.

What's been lacking is a shining example, a transer who made the leap effortlessly. Unfortunately, those have been in extremely short (which is to say, *nonexistent*) supply. Until yesterday, that is.

My daughter.

He can hardly believe his luck. Obviously, he can't tell anyone where she came from right now, that would spoil everything. But he's willing to play the long game. When she's eighteen and gets her post, or twenty-two if she makes En level, a revelation like that (with her permission, of course) would really blow some minds.

And hopefully change them.

Of course, the success of such a venture is entirely contingent upon the success of Celan herself. If she can't hack it in Ed... He shudders. Though she does seem very bright; he'll see what the tests say and proceed from there.

He swings the roller out onto the broad avenue, narrowly dodging a staggering girl with what looks like last night's makeup smeared all over her face. Probably one of Maddy's girls. He chuckles, indulgent.

The 'games' he set up for Celan are basic intelligence tests, geared for a younger child but guaranteed to accurately assess her mental competence. He'd made sure to leave very detailed instructions about how to turn on the screen in the library and how to operate the software. Even so, it's an entirely new experience for her and he doesn't want to get his hopes up too high.

A thrill of fear goes through him. What if she's not as intelligent as he suspects? What if she can barely turn the screen on? What will he do with her if she can't ever go to Ed? What will he tell people?

But it's too late. He already called in a few favors to Winnipeg. Late last night he'd sent a message to his old friend Alan Fielding by encrypted drone. The Winnipeg Ens owed Theodore for the beta bots he'd sent, and the many hours of counseling he'd provided on strategies to get people to accept them. His assistance had been crucial to the success of their program.

So of course they'd "remembered" his youthful romance with "Katrina" – and now he's got a predated official statement about the whole affair in his pocket to show anyone who might question Celan's origins. And a record of his official reply: So sad that Katrina's passed on. A sweet woman, though she never told him she was pregnant. But her daughter – his daughter – was welcome to live with him in Albakirk if that had been her mother's final wish.

His real wish is that his daughter will stop transing everything in sight and learn to conduct herself properly as soon as humanly possible. She can't stay holed up in the bunk forever and the longer she does the stranger it will look when she's finally introduced to her (and his) peers. The faster Celan can learn, the smoother things will go – but he won't know how fast until he sees the test scores.

He glances up at the sky, silently pleading for a higher intelligence to intervene on his behalf. He knows it's silly and dramatic, like a character in one of the old world books he loves. Still, he hedges his bets.

Over one thirty, that's all I ask.

The higher the better, but as long as his daughter's IQ is over one hundred thirty it will give him something to work with.

With this request logged, he jerks the roller to a halt in front of the blackened bones of Arlo's and turns it off with a sigh, digging in his breast pocket for his server. An hour is all the time he's got to work on this today. Better make it count.

FROM HER BEDROOM, CELAN HEARS the main bunk door whoosh open and the sharp clip of her father's boots as he enters, muttering to himself. She's sprawled on the bed, engrossed in a book she found in his library. It's great, all about talking animals that take over a farm. They kick out the farmer and celebrate being free of his rules. But then they start making rules too.

Theodore's shadow falls across the page.

"So how were the games?"

She shrugs. "OK. A little boring." She had guessed

pretty quickly that they were some kind of test.

"Really?"

"Yeah, but I did them anyway."

"And you had no problem following the instructions?"

"No, it's pretty easy once you figure it out."

Theodore smiles. "Well let's go and see."

Reluctantly, Celan puts the book down and trails him into the library, dawdling along the shelves wondering what she should read next as her father pokes at the screen on his desk. Suddenly, he utters a startled sound that makes her jump in her skin.

"What?"

"Nada." He waves a hand reassuringly. "A message from a colleague that surprised me."

Good, she thinks, turning back to the stacks, *nothing that I did wrong.*

THEODORE BLINKS AT THE SCREEN in disbelief at the number before his eyes: One sixty-two. He wants to jump up and down, dance for joy, but he tamps down the impulses. Still, his heart races, exultant. This folly of his may end well after all. More than well.

Brilliant.

"So I wrote my letter to Jillyanne," Celan says from across the room.

He forces his face into a neutral expression and meets her eyes. "Really? Well let's see it then."

"It's on the screen somewhere. In one of those little

white squares. When I got done with the games I was looking around and I opened some up and saw they had words in them. So I made a new one and wrote in it with the letters on the pad and then it asked me if I wanted to save it so I did."

"Did you now? Clever."

His daughter beams, but it quickly fades. "I'm not sure how we'll get the letter out though, to give it to her."

"Don't worry, we can print it later."

"OK." A pause. "Theodore?"

"Yes?"

"Am I going to go to tech school? I was talking to some kids the other day and they said that's where they go."

He shakes his head no. "The 'tech school' is a remedial school, for expro children. You are extremely intelligent. As soon as you are ready, you are going to be in regular Ed with your peers."

"When will that be?"

"Well," he says, "that all depends on you. The faster you can learn enough to catch up, the quicker you can begin."

"Next week?"

Theodore chuckles. "Maybe not quite that soon. There's quite a bit of material to cover."

"But do I have to stay in here until then? Can't I at least go out and see the city?"

"Eventually. You still need time to adjust. I'll let you

know as soon as you're ready."

She sighs, shoulders slumped. "Alright."

"You can see the city on the screen for now. Every last bit. It'll help you to get as familiar with it as possible. Winnipeg too."

"OK."

"And I've got something else we can do together that might help pass the time."

"What?"

He reaches into a cupboard behind the desk and pulls out a flat square board, the face of which is checked in small squares of brown and gold. Tucking it under his arm, he then extracts a mesh bag filled with sculpted figurines. He places the board on the desk, shaking out the figures in a pile.

"Chess!" Celan says.

Theodore raises a brow. "Do you play?"

"A little. People play at the casagrand. My friend's brother showed me some."

"Well," he says. "Ready to learn for real?"

"Claro," she says, all business.

Theodore drags a plush chair around the side of the desk and motions for Celan to sit. She does and immediately starts arranging pieces on the board, lips fixed in a determined line. He pats her shoulder with pride before settling down himself and shooting his cuffs, with the air of a man who's ready for the game to begin.

15

Celan peruses the board for a long moment before jumping a knight out close to the center, taking her father's rook. She's figured out that the best way to win is to get her pieces in the middle. Then they can move the most. Sacrifice the pawns, protect the king. Let the others do the real work. That is, until the queen comes out. But it'll be hours before Theodore returns and makes his next move.

She yawns, peering around the library. It's nice in here, but it's starting to get boring.

What's the point of being in Albakirk if I can't see anything other than these rooms? And the shower room.

She's allowed in there only on off hours when everyone else is in bed. Her father waits for her outside, standing sentry. It's getting ridiculous; she can pretend to be from Winnipeg for five minutes at this point. She's not going to trans her tamales and embarrass him. It's been three weeks.

What is he waiting for?

Frustrated, she turns to poke the screen to life. She likes the way it looks so flat and black when it's not in use, but once she turns it on she can see straight into another world of objects and information. She can reach in and touch things, move them around. After a while, her body feels like it's barely there anymore – like she's on the tech version of the astral. She smiles to herself, thinking how grouchy her father would be if she ever said that out loud.

But it's true. Like the way the techs use the sun to disinfect water – it's filtered very cunningly through tubes and flats in the pyramids, a process which also naturally heats it for cooking and showers. How is that different from transing it though, when you really think about it? It's all the same prana.

She sighs.

It's been constant tests and lessons lately, but at least most of it is interesting. She especially likes learning about the vegetative surfaces – walls made of plants that clean the air and provide aesthetics. Some of them even grow food. Apparently, there are also vast greenhouse gardens in the city. She wants to see them live and in person though, not only on the screen. Time on the astral needs time in the earth.

Maybe once she starts Ed she can learn to be an AgTech, it seems like they get to actually touch the plants. There are a lot of different kinds of tech you can be – SanTech, CompTech, MedTech, EdTech, SocTech – mentally she checks off a few examples. And then there's the En Level. That's a whole other thing. If you're really smart and the committee picks you, then you can be an En and tell everyone else what to do.

Do AgEns get to touch the real plants too, Celan wonders, *or do they spend all their time on the astral bossing people around?*

She stretches, raising arms high above her head, then starts, jolted out of her thoughts, as the door slides open to reveal Theodore, all smiles. He strides across the room and consults the board, taking out a pawn with his remaining rook. Then he clasps his hands behind his back and leans forward, scrutinizing her.

"So are you ready," he says finally, "to go out?"

She jumps to her feet. "Yes!"

"Bueno. Today's the day then. We're going to go to a MedLab. You need to get your bots installed."

Celan cringes. This isn't the grand tour she was expecting.

"But aren't those just so you can go outside the city? I mean, I've lived outside for years already, so…" She traces a finger along the edge of the chessboard. That rook's right in the path of her bishop. She could take it. But there's a pawn protecting it.

Grrr.

Her father tsks, annoyed. "Don't be silly. The bots do far more than protect us from contamination outside the city. They monitor our nutrition and caloric needs, repair cell damage, and rectify any epigenetic fluctuations. They are nanoscale, composed of completely non-toxic materials, and are perfectly safe." He frowns. "But you know all this. You've been studying it for weeks."

"I know. But – "

"But what?"

"Just..."

Oh, I can get that pawn with a knight.

She glances around the board. Nothing else looks threatening.

"Mírame, Celan."

She meets his gaze, jutting her chin out defiantly. "It's just not natural to have those things in your brain."

There. She said it. She braces herself for anger and is taken by surprise when he bursts out laughing.

"What?" she demands. "What's so funny?"

He rounds the desk, putting an arm around her and pulling her close. She's even more taken aback by this gesture than she was by the laughter and is further shocked when, seconds later, he plants a kiss on the top of her head.

"Your mother," he says, "said the exact same thing."

And this decides her. Mair rejected all this and returned to the ranchos instead, only to lose control over her transing and end up dead.

That is never going to happen to me.

So if bots are what it takes then bots are what she'll get. She only wants to know one more thing.

"Will it hurt?"

"Of course not," he says, looking almost offended. "The MedTechs know what they're doing. A quick DNA scan and they'll fit them right to you. It only takes a few minutes. Once they're in you won't even know they're there."

That doesn't sound too bad, but the mention of a scan gives her pause. There obviously wasn't anything amiss with the first one. Why does she need another?

"Didn't you already scan me when we first met?"

Theodore looks a bit chagrined "Well, yes of course. But that was just the paternity scan. This is more comprehensive."

That makes sense. "Well, OK then."

"Oh, and one more thing. Just to be one hundred percent certain no one can ever trace you to Transway, you will officially be known as Lana Timanti from now on."

"Lana?" Her stomach pings uncomfortably.

"Yes, similar enough to your real name but different enough to be safe. Like a little nickname."

Lana. It's pretty at least.

"OK."

"Excellent." He turns for the door.

Celan surveys the chessboard one more time, deftly takes out the pawn, and follows him through the bunk and out into the corridor.

As the elevator sinks, her pulse begins to rise. She knows that she looks perfectly normal in her close-fitting uniform and neat hair, but as the little room drops, so does her stomach. *Remember everything*, she instructs herself, then winces at the absurdity of that directive. Instinctively, she grabs her father's hand. He gives it a quick squeeze and releases it. Down and down they go until they finally stop at what must be ground level. She finds that she's holding her breath as the door slides open and they step out onto an enormous plaza.

The interior of a massive, translucent pyramid rises hundreds of feet in the air above their heads. Through its panes, the sun bathes every surface in a heavenly glow. The blue sky arches above – they could almost be outside. She swears she even feels a breeze. Around the base, the smooth walls stretch out in soothing shades of pearly white and soft beige interspersed with patches of green where living plants and flowers carpet them – neatly tended and so artfully designed they could almost be paintings.

At the heart of the plaza, a fountain gushes water that falls to trickle gently over rocks before collecting in a small pool, ringed by more plants that sway gently in the spray. Benches are arranged in a graceful arc around it, occupied by people sitting and talking, eating, tapping at their servers. Celan ticks her eyes back and forth, taking it all in.

"So?" says Theodore. "What do you think? Does it pass muster?"

"It's amazing. I mean, I've seen the pictures on the screen but in person..." She trails off.

"It's pretty impressive," he finishes.

They advance across the polished floor, moving counter-clockwise and passing the mouths of several corridors, which disgorge uniformed figures that all look like they have very important things to do. The ones in tan acknowledge her father with serious looks that say, 'Yes, sir, getting the job done.'

Finally, Theodore makes a decisive turn down one brightly lit hallway and she has to scurry to catch up. He's busy checking the numbers on the doors, so he doesn't notice the red-haired woman approaching until she's almost right in front of them. She's dressed in blue, like him, but her uniform hugs her in a way that, to Celan, is decidedly un-tech-like. She almost reminds her of –

Amanzita.

Celan smothers a laugh.

"Theodore," the woman says, crisp blue eyes crinkling in the corners. "Babysitting? I didn't think you were the type." Her tone is light but there's a whiff of critique behind it. "You and Martinez – honestly! Am I the only Lead who has time for a family?"

A brief flash of panic skitters across her father's face, but it quickly vanishes. He smiles.

"I may yet surprise you on that count. I certainly was surprised myself."

"Oh really?"

"Yes. You see, this child is my daughter." He rests a firm hand on Celan's shoulder.

Celan takes a deep breath and in her most clear and careful voice says, "Nice to meet you."

The woman's eyes widen momentarily, but then she laughs. "Really, Theodore! You almost had me going there for a second."

"No, I'm completely serious. Fielding brought her down from Winnipeg on their last visit."

"But why – how – did that happen?" the woman stammers, clearly unaccustomed to being at a loss for words and not taking well to the experience.

"I think we both know how it happens, Ariana."

"Very funny. I mean, how did you not know about her before? All this time she was in Winnipeg and you never knew?"

"I spent quite a bit of time in Winnipeg back in the day, while they were adopting bot technology. I had a few…encounters there, but was never informed that one of them had borne fruit."

"But – "

"Her mother passed away six months ago. She told Fielding her secret before she died. He was skeptical at first, but DNA doesn't lie." A shrug. "We've been having a very nice time getting to know each other, though, haven't we, Lana?"

Celan nods and addresses Ariana again, choosing her words with care. "I really like your city. It's beautiful and a very interesting place. I'm especially intrigued by your water purification system and vegetative surfaces. I'm sure I'm going to like it here."

Ariana clears her throat, recovering her poise. "Yes, well. Nice to meet you, too. Lana was it? Lovely name." She extends her hand and Celan gives it a neat little shake. Then her teasing tone returns. "Well, I've always said you needed a woman in your life, Theodore, but I never dreamt she'd be ten years old."

"Eleven," Celan corrects politely.

"The same age as my daughter." Ariana looks to Theodore. "We'll have to get them together soon."

"Yes, fine," he says hurriedly. "But if you'll excuse us, we've got an appointment for some bot work. Don't want to be late."

"Oh, of course," Ariana says, stepping aside to let them pass. "See you at the social?"

"Wouldn't miss it." He strides past her, gently nudging Celan forward, and presses the panel for room number ML625.

As they step inside Celan registers her father's small sigh of relief.

SHAKING HER HEAD FROM SIDE to side, Celan tests again to see if she can feel anything rattling around in there.

Nada.

She's still amazed that she can't tell at all. The bot installation had been fast and it hadn't hurt, just as her father promised. It was actually kind of dull. They went into the MedLab, gave the tech at the desk their names, and were quickly ushered into a pristine room where a MedTech in a white coat took her fingerprints and image and gave her another test like the one Theodore did outside Arlo's.

She'd been a little nervous about the results – *What if there's something abnormal? What if they can tell?* – so she'd tried some surreptitious transing. *Make it look like a normal tech's,* she thought, letting her prana leak into the stylus as she touched it to the inside of her cheek.

It must have worked, because when the results appeared on the screen the tech merely skimmed them, grunted affirmatively, and reached into a chilled cabinet where he removed a silver cylinder and brushed her hair aside, touching one end to the side of her neck. Before she could ask what was going to happen she'd felt a puff of cool air and a strange shimmery sensation that reminded her uneasily of the fuse. That was it though – her father thanked the tech and they were free to go.

Anti-climactic, she thinks, testing out a word from her latest library book.

But the rest of the city, even the limited amount she'd gotten to see (including the plaza and, at her request, one of the indoor gardens), was fascinating. All those hours spent transing water and pulling weeds, where here they grew the plants in long troughs of water or soil that was always clean and contamination- and pest-free. Theodore said there were even insect bots that did the pollinating like they did in nature, but even better because they'd never spread disease or die off when they were needed.

On the way home they'd stopped at a caf, where with her bots installed and prints in the Bank she was finally able to get her own lunch. Proudly, she'd thumbed the reader just like her father. Theodore explained she could have anything she wanted, it was all carefully nutritionally calibrated. The bots would help keep her weight stable, but she shouldn't be greedy. 'Only take what you know you're going to eat – waste too much and you'll be put on Notice and that's embarrassing.'

Briefly, she'd glanced at the Notice board, where all techs' infractions were displayed along with their images. If you screwed up, everyone would know. She'd shuddered.

Don't want that to ever be me.

Tomorrow, Theodore said he would show her the fitness area. All techs are required to exercise a certain minimum number of hours per week to maintain overall health and muscle tone. The bots can't do everything.

Apparently, there's a big room somewhere where you can choose any program – running, swimming, bicycling, anything you like – and it'll feel like you're doing it outside. You can even swim in the ocean.

It all sounds great to Celan; they make everything so simple here. She doesn't understand why the elders thought this was all so bad. In many ways, it's so much better.

She stretches out on the bed, folding the book face down next to her. She can't concentrate on made-up worlds right now, not when the real one is finally getting interesting. How anyone could have thought this city was boring is utterly beyond her. It's magic.

She sighs in satisfaction, but it catches on a sharp pang of guilt. Cyrinda was the one who said it was boring. But her sister didn't understand; she never even went inside. She didn't know what she was missing. And now she never will. She and Taegh are dead and they'll never know about this wonderful place. And deep down, Celan knows it's all her fault.

Because only she knows the terrible truth about that night at Arlo's – that if she hadn't fused, then her sister wouldn't have either and Cyrinda and Taegh wouldn't have been fighting. And she never would've upset Taegh by telling him about seeing him and Tomás fusing. They all would have been together and they all would've gotten out OK. She'd be home right now, curled up next to Tanny and Max with Oso licking her face, telling Jillyanne that she was right about Transway – that she was really sorry and she'd never run away again.

Celan swallows against the lump in her throat and rolls over on her stomach, fumbling for the book and forcing her eyes to the words on the page until the made-up world takes over and the real one recedes.

"MARTINEZ." THEODORE NODS TO THE shorter man as he enters the caf, converted for the night into the barest approximation of a wayvern, with a feeble bar along one wall and a small heap of snacks wilting in the corner. Several algalamps cast a wan glow over the long tables.

The two men share a despairing look, having agreed long ago that the monthly Soc socials would be better held (and attended) at the real thing. But Ariana wouldn't be caught dead at a wayvern and the young SocTechs who organize these events all know it, so here they are. Blue and tan uniforms mill around somewhat haplessly, far more adept at society-building than actual socializing.

"Bet they'd look a lot more lively at Maddy's," Theodore says.

"What? And corrupt our young techs' delicate sensibilities in that den of iniquity?" Martinez presses the cold glass of his drink against his forehead, as if to ward off a faint.

Theodore's lips twist with amusement. "A wretched hive of scum and villainy," he intones solemnly, quoting an old world screener.

"We must be cautious," Martinez finishes, and they both cackle. Martinez pauses for a quick pull on his drink, then arranges his face more seriously. "So, I hear you have exciting news, Theodore."

"Word travels fast."

"But a child? Su hija? Looks like your profligacy finally caught up with you!" He takes another pull, chases it with a merry wink. "Better you than me."

"Oh, I don't know," Theodore says, sidling past him and over to the tables to procure a drink of his own. "I'm actually kind of enjoying it."

Martinez laughs, incredulous. "Really? Never took you for a family man, Theodore."

"It has its advantages." He takes a quick swig of whiskey and looks past the other man, out to the panoramic view of the Sandias silhouetted in the moonlight.

I hope, he silently amends.

"I'm sure it does, but it all seems rather *inconvenient*. I mean, they brought her here from Winnipeg and just dropped her off? Didn't give you any warning?"

Theodore starts to repeat the same story he's been telling everyone (complete with a ritual server-based display of his ersatz exchange with Fielding) when they're interrupted by the arrival of Ariana Balor, tugging a waifish woman in tan along by the arm.

"Bettina, you've got a son about the same age as Lana and Shariah, don't you?" she's saying.

"Yes," Bettina says, somewhat shy in the presence of all three Lead SocEns. "Liam's in Ed with your daughter."

"Perfect. I think it is absolutely necessary to get Lana into the same class. It's never too early to start thinking about pods, after all."

Theodore pretends to ponder this. "That's a great idea. As soon as she's ready, I'll arrange it."

"Ready?" Ariana trills a laugh. "Of course she's ready. She seemed like very bright girl from what I saw."

"Yes, she is. Very much so. But the educational system in Winnipeg, while improving, is still lacking certain refinements that we take for granted. So I'm tutoring her myself until such time as I feel she'll be comfortable in our more rigorous system."

Bettina beams at him, tucking straw-colored hair behind her ears. "That's so generous of you. With all you have on your plate. You're obviously a wonderful father!"

Theodore casts his gaze down modestly. "I'm doing the best I can, but I'm still learning. I'm sure that you and Ariana will be invaluable in your guidance."

"Oh, yes! Anything you need."

Ariana raises her glass. "To our children," she says, and they all toast, Martinez giving Theodore a rather long and significant side-eye.

"Well," Martinez says after a quick swig. "I'll leave you all to argue the finer points of child rearing. Got to have a quick word with Nigel." He struts off smugly.

Theodore glares after him. *That damned GISH proposal.* So stupid to want to waste resources sending personnel out to the ocean. They've already seen the drone reports on the contamination levels; it's far too pointlessly dangerous. The planet is hopelessly broken and if they should be exploring anything, it is a way to get off it for good. He was hoping to get to Nigel first – he's got the inside track with the MedEns – and bend his ear about Mars.

Ariana waves an airy hand at Martinez's departing form. "Men and their politics. This is supposed to be a social evening!"

Bettina nods vigorously but Theodore can barely suppress a groan. No one is more political than Ariana. This must be a new game of hers – induct him into her anti-Transway coterie, have them pepper him with earnestly-voiced concerns about 'the children.' Before Lana she never bothered, knowing that he and Martinez were a solid block to any plans of hers to dismantle it.

'It's a built-in experimental group,' they'd argue, 'and an outlet for any sensation-seeking tendencies. The bots can repair any internal damages incurred. Give people a little freedom and gain a world of acquiescence.' Their logic was psycho-sociologically sound and she knew it, but she also knew they were no strangers to the occasional outlet themselves. And so it rankled, but she tolerated it. Barely. With the destruction of Arlo's, however, her arguments have gained momentum among certain factions. Bots can't resurrect the dead. Yet.

"So, Theodore," Ariana says, a wicked glint in her eye. "It must be quite a challenge to have been thrust into fatherhood so abruptly."

"It's hardly an uncommon experience."

"Yes, but it must be a whole new perspective now that you've got your child's future to think about. I'm sure you must be concerned about what sorts of influences she might be exposed to. I mean, growing up in Winnipeg and all...she's never had to deal with the issues we face here."

"Oh yes," Bettina chimes in earnestly, cheeks aglow. "With the recent tragedy we really need to start steering our young people away from Transway. Give them better things to do. If the transers don't want to integrate, we should cut them loose once and for all. It's been fifty years. They can't be allowed to put our children in jeopardy."

Down with Transway! Theodore thinks sourly. *I totally called it.*

"Well, you certainly are passionate about the issue," he says.

"Oh yes! I am. I mean, there's just no reason why they should all be running around like that, doing whatever they like. It's not like they contribute anything useful."

"Really?"

Theodore pauses, running his thumb along the edge of his glass. "What about the bot tests?" Out of the corner of his eye he sees Ariana frown.

"Well, uh – " stammers Bettina.

"I mean, surely you're too young to remember the bot lottery. We all are. But I assure you I've heard plenty of stories and it wasn't at all enjoyable for those who got chosen, before the expros arrived and took their place.

"Imagine," he says, scratching thoughtfully at his short beard, "raising a child all those years, only to have their number come up? Or yours? Or your husband's? Never knew what would happen. Most of the tests were successful of course, and everyone went on to live normal lives. Those that weren't...well, at least you got leave to have a second child if things didn't work out."

Bettina looks chilled. "I – I – didn't think – "

"Of course you didn't. Like I said," he continues, "you're too young to remember that. And I fervently hope, now that I have a child of my own, that we will never have to relive those times again. If we need to tough out the occasional incident on Transway, I think it's a small price to pay for the assurance that our children will have better, safer lives overall."

Theodore hoists his glass. "To our children," he intones and they all clink – Bettina now contrite, Ariana looking like she wants to strangle him.

Ha, he thinks, *beat you at your own game.*

Maybe this nascent fatherhood will prove to be advantageous in more ways than he ever could have imagined.

NUZZLED DEEP INTO A THICK bathrobe, Celan smiles shyly at the old woman drying her hair across the room. The woman smiles back, grandmotherly, and she feels a curl of warmth around her heart. People are so nice here, not weird machines at all but regular people like everyone in the ranchos.

It's nice to finally be able to use the showers during the normal day, without supervision. She'd needed one after her run in the fitness area – through forest trails that looked exactly like the ones in the East Mountains. Being out in nature had eased her homesickness, even though she knew it wasn't really real. But the holos felt and smelled and looked and even sounded genuine. The crunch of dirt under her feet. The chirps of birds. Even the angle of the sun was right for the time she was supposed to be out. The first time she'd had to wave an insect away from her face she'd laughed out loud. She was running on a track the whole time.

The women's shower isn't far from her bunk; there are communal bathrooms on every residential floor. Briefly, Celan wonders why her father has a whole library to himself but still has to shower with everyone else. It probably has to do with the Five Social Precedents, the tech civil foundations that she's drilled in every time she touches the screen: Unity, Clarity, Curiosity, Diligence and Nonviolence. The bathroom thing must be something to do with the first one. Make everyone shower together and they'll all feel more equal or something.

Stuffing her feet into slippers she pads down the hall and pushes the door panel. Expecting the kitchenette to be empty, she's surprised when the whoosh of the door reveals Theodore laughing heartily over a drink of amber liquid with another man who seems vaguely familiar. He's got roughly the same coloring as her father, but with rounder features and a moustache sans attendant beard. Even seated she can tell he is shorter. Then, with a horrific shock, she remembers – *The market!* He was at the Saturday market; the man with her father when she asked about the scanners that day.

Celan ducks her head and tries to slip past them quickly, but Theodore is in a jovial mood and he stops her as she tries to pass.

"Lana, mijita! Come and meet my third, and mercifully my last, fellow Lead SocEn. Frank Martinez." He gestures toward his friend with more exaggeration than necessary.

"Uh, hello," she says, eyes lowered, pulling the robe tight around her as if in modesty, though it's so thick and long that any impropriety is impossible.

"Mucho gusto," Martinez thunders slushily and she realizes that the stuff they're drinking is the same kind of stuff they drink on Transway.

She's drunk it too, and it made her fuzzy in the brain. From the looks of things, they're both pretty fuzzed at the moment. *Good.* That can only help her.

"Mucho gusto," she says politely, still keeping her head down.

"Wonderful!" says Martinez. "Adorable girl, Theodore, I can see why you're so taken with her."

"Well I – "

"Must have gotten all your genes, too. She's the spitting image! No doubt she's gotten your intelligence as well."

Her father beams, taking another sip and rattling the ice in his glass. "She most certainly has. She's brilliant."

Celan isn't sure if a response is required, so she settles for a brief nod and escapes. In the hall, she pauses before pressing the panel at her bedroom door.

"Lovely girl," Martinez is saying. "Lovely girl." She hears the faint scrape of chair legs against the floor.

"Well, vámanos then," he continues. "No lovely girls in Albakirk for us. Better try our luck on Transway."

Her father gives a short laugh. "It's getting about that time, isn't it?"

"Now that's the Theodore I know and love."

There's a thunk of glasses on the table and the whoosh of the door as it opens and closes.

Celan retreats to her room, strips off the robe, and pulls on her sleepware. She climbs into bed and takes a few deep breaths to still her nerves.

I don't like that guy. He's creepy. But I think I'm safe. It doesn't seem like he remembered me.

But what if he did? What would happen if they found out who she really was – would her father send her back to the ranchos? The thought makes her shudder. She can't go back, not now. Not when everything is finally starting to get interesting.

And she has nowhere to go anymore anyway. Theodore said he'd brought her letter to Jillyanne personally, and that her tia had told him congratulations and that she wished Celan well. Jillyanne has enough people to take care of – good people, the kind who don't run away – that she doesn't need some disobedient brat reappearing on her doorstep like a bad chit.

Nothing will happen, Celan tells herself. *I'm here, and I'm his daughter, and I'm perfect. I'm one of them now. No one can tell.*

She squeezes her eyes shut tight and burrows deep into the pillows, as if by the sheer force of belief she can will it all to be true.

⊐▸ 16 ◂⊏

Celan's stomach flutters and she pushes the bowl of quinoa and fruit away. Notice or no Notice she can't finish breakfast this morning. Because today's the day: After sixteen weeks of intensive study she's finally been deemed ready to join her first Ed class.

The class will have no more than twenty students, which is how they are grouped until age twelve. After that, they break into learning pods of six that will be their permanent study groups until they get their posts at eighteen. Unless they're tapped to be Ens – then it's four more years of Ed.

I only want to be an AgTech, she thinks. *It can't be that hard. If the plants don't grow right I can just trans them and no one will ever know.*

She'd asked her father to come with her today, but

he said that that isn't how it's done. No one her age will have their parents with them. It would be strange.

She glances around the caf. Maybe there's someone else here who is her age – someone to walk with. But no one catches her eye, so she picks up her server and tucks it in her pocket, slides her half-full bowl into the San window, and trudges resolutely off to the Ed wing.

At the end of a maze of corridors it emerges – Room EC540. Students stream inside, trading greetings with a pleasant-looking EdTech, a woman of middle years with dark hair gathered in a soft bun at the nape of her neck. She looks nice enough, but Celan hesitates, waiting until the last few students have entered before taking a deep breath and stepping forward.

"Hi. I'm Lana Timanti. It's my first day in class here."

"Oh, *hello*, Lana!" the woman enthuses. "I was informed last week that you would be in my class and I've been looking forward to having you join us."

"Thanks," she says.

"I'm Mrs. Allet."

"Nice to meet you."

The woman looks up and down the hallway as if searching for stragglers. Seeing none, she places a warm hand on Celan's shoulder.

"Well," she says, steering her through the door, "let's get you settled in. The class is so excited to meet you."

Nineteen faces already seated at their work stations stare as she enters the room, but Mrs. Allet's comforting touch keeps her steady as they pause at the front.

They can't tell, Celan counsels herself, *you look just like them.*

Still, she wonders if she'll make some mistake, some slip, and they'll start to wonder. 'You'll be fine,' her father's words ring in her ears. 'If you do anything strange they'll chalk it up to Winnipeg.'

Mrs. Allet clears her throat.

"I am immensely pleased to introduce Lana Timanti to you all today. You've all heard the news about her recent arrival from Winnipeg to live with her father, Theodore Timanti, here in Albakirk. It is wonderful that another of our Lead SocEns has a daughter who will now be part of our class. Please give Lana your warmest welcome."

Celan smiles tentatively and scans the faces. They seem friendly enough for the most part, benignly curious. But one in particular catches her eye – a slender girl with almost-black eyes and long, brilliant white-blonde hair, who is peering at her intently.

I should definitely stay away from that one, Celan thinks, and is relieved when Mrs. Allet escorts her to a station on the opposite side of the room.

The lesson itself is a blur – words and images flying by simultaneously on her personal screen, server, and the large screen at the front of the room. The pace is fast and the students eager to answer questions, to demonstrate their knowledge, to be the best. Celan is called on several times – for all her niceness Mrs. Allet isn't about to let her slide, even on her first day – but she acquits herself well enough, giving poised and accurate answers. Once she gets into it, surrenders fully to the ebb and flow of information, it really isn't that hard. She's good at this, and it makes her happy. It's almost a letdown when she finally hears the words, 'Lunch break.'

Her head is abuzz with joy and relief as she tucks away her server; she'll grab lunch from the caf and eat by the fountain in the plaza. She needs some time alone to process everything. But as she turns to go, someone's blocking her path: The white-blonde girl, grinning wolfishly. Celan shrinks back a fraction, but the girl smiles even wider and offers a slim hand. She shakes it dutifully.

"Shariah Balor," the girl says briskly. "My mother's a Lead SocEn like your father – Ariana Balor."

"Oh," Celan says, recalling the woman with the bright red hair. "I met her. She looks really different from you."

Shariah rolls her eyes. "Well, of course. I mean, we were styled differently."

"What?"

"Styled," Shariah pronounces precisely. "What, you don't style in Winnipeg?"

Celan feels a surge of panic. This was not something her father's prep had covered.

"Um, not usually," she mutters.

"Well, that's ridiculous!" Shariah says, looking

alarmed. "I mean, who wants to take a chance on something like that? An ugly kid? You never know what genes will do on their own."

She narrows her eyes, scrutinizing Celan's face. "I mean, *you* turned out alright, luckily, but the natural thing is just so risky. Take a look out on Transway sometime. They're all natural and it's frightening." She shudders. "It's *much* safer to style. When I grow up and have my kid, he's going to be a boy with hair like mine and eyes like my mother's. Nice and tall, too. He'll be perfect."

"Great," Celan says weakly.

"Anyway," Shariah continues, cocking one hip and crossing arms in front of her chest. "You seem bright enough. It'll be nice to have some more competition. Most of this class is tech-tracked to the max."

"Huh."

"But it'll be different next year, when we get into our pods."

"Aren't the pods selected randomly?"

Another eye roll. "Please. That's in name only. If a Lead SocEn wants their kid in a certain pod, it happens, believe me, like that." She snaps her fingers in Celan's face for emphasis.

"Wow."

"It's true. And the better pod you have the more you learn, and the better chance you have at En."

"That's, uh, good to know," Celan says, fingers

itching for her server. Maybe she can pretend there's a message to meet her father for lunch. But what if this girl follows her to the caf and he's not there? Or already eating with a colleague? Things are awkward enough.

Shariah continues, undaunted. "So, do you have transers in Winnipeg?"

"Not really," Celan says. "Not like here."

"You're so lucky. We have tons of them. They live outside the city and mooch off of us. They're *so* gross."

Celan says nothing.

"They all take this stuff called transferon," Shariah continues, "and it makes them crazy." She leans forward conspiratorially. "They even give themselves shots of it!"

"We get shots, too, though," Celan points out, trying to steer the conversation onto another track. "I had to get some when I first got here."

Shariah crinkles her perfect nose. "Ew, how can you say that? We don't get shots, we get in-o-cu-la-tions." She enunciates each syllable like she's talking to an exceptionally slow five-year-old.

"The basic mechanics are similar," says a new voice and Celan turns, relieved, to see a sandy-haired, dark-skinned boy with wide, friendly blue eyes.

"Bryan Patten," he says, then continues, addressing Shariah. "I mean, the basic mechanics of a jet injection are the same in both cases."

Shariah shakes her head. "Honestly, Bryan, you are *such* an idiot."

He shrugs, and turns to enligthen the new girl. "My mom says the transers aren't that different from us, even though their genes may have mutated a little from living outside for so long. Some SocEns even say," and here he pauses and looks pointedly at Shariah, "that they could still be reintegrated into society if they gave up the transferon."

"Which they won't," she retorts. "And besides, why would we even want them? They are totally useless."

"They do a lot of work for us. They test the bots."

"Only so they can sit around and take their stupid drug. They don't care about science; they don't care about *learning* anything."

"They're necessary to the social order," Bryan counters. "Do *you* want to be a bot tester?"

"I would if it meant getting rid of them!" Shariah says passionately. "I trust our bots. I trust our SocEns. Do *you*?"

"Of course. I'm just saying that – "

"You're an idiot? We're already aware."

With that she wheels around, hooking her arm proprietarily through Celan's and steering her toward the door. "Come on, Lana, " she says loudly enough for everyone to hear. "Let's go do something *interesting*."

Unsure how to disengage, Celan lets herself be led.

Shariah tucks her head in close. "Have you seen the gardens yet?" she says, giving Celan's arm a friendly squeeze.

"A little."

"Well let's get lunch and then go look. Have you ever seen a bee-bot? They're so cute! Much better than talking to dumb old boys."

THE CONFERENCE ROOM IS CHILLY and bare and Theodore shifts in his seat, pausing to glance at his server again. *Nada*. No new messages. Two solid weeks of endlessly cajoling every En he can corner with every argument he can think of and his progress is still nil. There is overwhelming support for GISH and barely any for his Martian proposal.

Sure, he's got the Comp and MechEns on his side, but that's to be expected. They'd jump at any opportunity to build a spacecraft. But everyone else, from GenEns to SanEns, is in favor of GISH. If he'd gotten to Nigel first maybe he could have locked in the support of the MedEns, and everyone knows the GenEns vote with the MedEns. With both of them on board, he could have had a chance. Now he's pretty sure he's dead in the water.

Theodore sighs, staring out the window. Way out on the mesa, a lone coyote lopes across barren rock.

Probably has an extra tail or three ears, he thinks sullenly, *not like it cares. It just goes on living, generation after mutant generation, like nothing ever happened. Just like us. Oh sure, we have our little fortress here, but what's the point of it all?*

But he knows that's not entirely true. After a century

296

of enclosure with the main focus on survival, the last fifty years have brought an amazing amount of progress. They've made great leaps in bot technology, eliminated the constant low-grade fear of the bot lottery, and established varying degrees of contact with other city-states. People can go outside now, move around more. The storms have lessened; the climate is beginning to stabilize, as is the magnetosphere. There's a new feeling of buoyancy in the air. Of hope.

So why waste this new enthusiasm on some half-crocked scheme to clean the ocean? It's complete toxic soup. Do the GISHers really think they can fix it? Even using quantum processes, it's a stretch. Statistically speaking, there are plenty of nice, new habitable worlds out there. Why are people so attached to this one? They could go to Mars at least. Start terraforming.

The whoosh of the door whisks these thoughts from his head as Ariana strides into the room, an angry scowl creasing her brow.

Great, now I have to mop up her excess bullshit too.

But as she stalks toward his chair, it's obvious that this is no simple bad mood. She's angry at him, specifically.

"What?" he says mildly. Whatever she's mad about is ridiculous. He hasn't done anything wrong.

She slams her server down on the table. "Some example you're setting these days!"

"Example of what? What are you talking about?"

"Deliberately encouraging our young people to put themselves in harm's way."

He dismisses this with a faint sneer. "I did nothing of the kind."

"Oh really? Then what do you call *this*?" She points her server at the screen, jabs it viciously, and there he is with Martinez – larger than life and laughing uproariously at something the scantily clad girl sitting next to them is saying. They are obviously at Maddy's. None too sober either, by the look of things.

"This," Ariana hisses, "has been making the rounds of the SocTechs this morning. Everyone getting a good laugh at the Leads. Out on Transway, having a high old time. Letting everyone know that it's perfectly fine, perfectly safe, perfectly acceptable."

Theodore takes a deep breath. He is not going to rise to the bait. "So? It *is* perfectly acceptable. We've been over this a hundred times. Transway is a psychological outlet – "

"Outlet, my ass! Look at you two. You're as useless as fusers! Would you want your daughter to see this?"

My daughter, he thinks, *has likely seen worse.* He stifles a laugh, but not quickly enough. Ariana gives him a look that could stop a clock.

"You think this is funny?" she says, her voice like dry ice. "You think it's funny when eighty techs end up dead in a fire because of those idiots out there? So brain dead with transferon that they can't even manage to run what's basically a caf without destroying everything in their path."

This returns him to gravitas. "No, no, of course not," he says hurriedly. "But we can't prepare for every last contingency, Ariana. It's impossible. Accidents happen and there are dangers inherent in everything. I should know. If you recall, I lost both parents to the Luna Sigma project."

She opens her mouth to interject, but he holds up a hand and pushes on. "And if we're going to continue to go outside these walls, whether to attempt to clean up the oceans or to explore extraterrestrial options we're going to have to deal with accidents. With the unexpected. Better that people are psychologically prepared for it beforehand. That they understand *risk*."

Crisp blue eyes appraise him coolly. "Nice logic," she says, with a heavy dollop of sarcasm. "A mission to Mars is hardly the same thing as a night on the – "

A whoosh and a click of boots announce Martinez's arrival. He's pink in the face and panting slightly.

"Sorry I'm late."

"Late and winded," snaps Ariana. "I suggest you start spending more time in the fitness area and less on Transway. I'm surprised you haven't been put on Notice."

Martinez ignores this. He takes a quick glance at the image on the screen and grins. "Quite an evening," he says, with a shameless wink.

Theodore chuckles and Ariana makes a moue of disgust. He and Martinez share a brief look of triumph at shutting her down, but this fleeting joy is soured as his fellow Lead takes a seat and rather fussily removes his server from his breast pocket.

Back to GISH. Theodore's stomach sinks.

"Well, as I'm sure you both know," Martinez starts, "I now have full endorsement from seven of nine of the En groups. If that's not a mandate, I don't know what is." He points his sever at the screen, replacing the current image with the vote results. It's official.

But Theodore has yet to make his final appeal. Two out of the three Lead SocEns must approve a measure before it is adopted, no matter what the other Lead Ens endorse. Ariana's got the final vote. And she's mad right now, but at both of them. Maybe he can still convince her. He gets up and begins to pace the room, delivering the argument he'd prepared:

"It is my opinion that we should be applying our resources towards exploring other habitable worlds rather than wasting them on this one. We already know what's out there." He pauses for a dramatic gesture out the window. "Pollutants. Radiation. The earth will be poisoned for millennia. This whole thing is pointless! Sure, we can purify our city – a relatively small, contained area. But the rest? Forget it. If the old world had one saving grace it was its ability and desire to explore space, and that is where we should be directing our resources.

Find another planet – a fresh, new one – and resettle there. A chance to start over. Not make the same mistakes twice."

Martinez sighs patiently. "That is nothing but a pipe dream, Theodore. You know it and I know it. The Earth has been our home for millennia and it will continue to be so. The GISH proposal concentrates on cleaning up the world we already have. And it can be done. The bots have been proven time and again to be effective in neutralizing small-scale contamination within each of our own bodies every time we make contact with the outside world. It's time we started expanding them for use on larger-scale areas. Our MechEns have identified quantum processes that might be useful and they want to test them."

He shrugs, continuing, "It's perfectly feasible. The western ocean is an easily manageable journey once the transports have been refitted to accommodate a stay of several weeks. It's far more economical to try and clean up what we have, rather than wasting resources on some space venture that may never pan out. We don't even have a viable fuel source. We don't have a warp drive. Even if we got out there, we wouldn't get very far."

"But there's Mars," Theodore contends. "That's only a six-month trip. Three, if we get the timing right. They made it there before, in the old world."

"Once. And it was incredibly difficult just to get

a few people from here to there. We're talking about a massive amount of equipment and personnel. The scope of the resources needed to create a habitable environment on Mars are simply beyond our reach at the present time."

"But you said they're experimenting with quantum processes – "

"And I suggest we apply them closer to home."

Ariana breaks in, holding up her hands like a referee. "OK. Enough. I am now officially sick of listening to this argument. I've heard it for the thousandth time and it's giving me a headache. I say it's time to vote."

"Fine," says Theodore, not wanting to aggravate her further.

"Let the recs show I cast my vote in favor of GISH," Martinez says.

"Opposed," Theodore counters.

Ariana smiles sweetly. "I'm afraid I'm going to have to go with Martinez on this one. The scope of the resources is simply too great for a space venture right now. I vote in favor. Let the recs show that the GISH proposal was approved by the Lead SocEns, two to one."

Theodore shakes his head; this is what he gets for being early – an argument and a downvote. Ariana may be mad at Martinez too, but he was the initial target and the one she snapped at. And he, unwisely, snapped back. And now this proposal will go forward, all because of a stupid image from Transway.

Ridiculous.

He snatches his server off the table and stalks out of the room without another word. Fleetingly, he wishes for an old world door, one that would slam behind him.

A whoosh just isn't the same.

⊏▶ 17 ◀⊐

A dozen or so colorfully-dressed figures sprawl on benches along the wall; some indifferent, others nervous, and a few obviously ill. Tan uniforms tend to them, poking and prodding. Celan stares fixedly through the thick glass, knowing they can't see her but still worried.

Do I know any of them?

None look familiar, but her gut churns anyway; this was a really bad idea. She'd let the first flush of success at Ed trump sense and begged her father to take her along and show her some of his work. She thought she'd get to see him arguing impressively, making decisions, designing new bots or something. She hadn't bargained for the transer lab.

Theodore's voice cuts across her thoughts. He's

been explaining what is known about the scientific properties of transferon.

"…extremely psychoactive, but very unstable under laboratory conditions. It appears to be a product of the interaction between water and the crystalline structure of the minerals that compose the 'vial' portion of the transfer. These are usually held in stasis, but they are somehow released during the application of a form of electromagnetic energy by the subject, commonly known as transfiguration or 'transing,' that turns ordinary water into something much more potent."

He pauses, frowning. "Are you listening, Lana?"

"Yes, uh…crystalline structure?" She looks down at the server in her hand, as if she's been taking notes.

He squints suspiciously, but continues. "As I was saying, once the vial has been transed by the subject, the resulting product is highly psychoactive. That is, it interacts with certain parts of the brain and produces a variety of different effects."

This earns her full attention. Maybe she'll get an official explanation of what happened to her when she transfused.

"These effects seem to be concentrated into one of three general classes – the dopamine, endorphin, or serotonin systems."

She stares at him blankly. Those terms haven't been covered in Ed.

"They are all types of brain chemicals," he says.

"In transers' brains?"

"In everyone's. Techs and transers. They are all perfectly normal and help to regulate our moods, our responses to pleasure and pain, and our perceptions of time and space."

"And transferon changes them?"

"Transferon appears to stimulate or inhibit their production – with the extraordinary part being that the class of chemicals it affects tends to follow the wishes and needs of the subject. For example, let's take Class D, the dopamine group. What these subjects seem to seek most is the feeling that is produced by a flood of dopamine rushing to their nucleus accumbens."

"Their what?" she interrupts.

"It's a part of the brain," he says, and grunts like something's just occurred to him. He types a few commands into his server, points it into the air, and a three-dimensional model of a human brain springs to life, hovering above them.

Celan inspects it curiously.

"Behold! The brain," Theodore says, with another swipe at his server. A tiny light begins to blink somewhere in the lower left portion of the image. "That is the location of the nucleus accumbens, the bundle of neurons that processes pleasurable sensations and reward."

"And we've all got one?"

He nods, affirmative.

"A flood of dopamine to this area produces a highly stimulating sensation in the Class D subject, a rush of energy and purpose that they greatly enjoy."

Celan recalls the first few moments of the fuse; she knows exactly what sensation he means. It had been intense, nearly overwhelming, but not exactly what she'd call enjoyable.

"What about the other two groups?" she says, eager now.

Her father smiles, pleased. "Class E is the endorphin group. Endorphins are produced by the pituitary gland and the hypothalamic neurons."

Additional sections light up and begin to flash in different colors.

"They bind to receptors in our brains, like a key fitting into a lock, and help to produce feelings of pain relief and euphoria."

"You-foria?"

"Bliss, joy."

Taegh, she thinks, *was definitely Class E*. She starts to smile, but one glance out the window and it dies on her lips. She can't picture him waiting in that cold room – no matter how much he wanted to fuse.

"Please pay attention." Theodore's voice snaps her into the present and she swings her eyes back to the blinking brain.

"Class S refers to serotonin, which is primarily manufactured in the raphe nuclei of the brain stem, but also in the pineal gland." Two more lights come on. "And some in the enterochromaffin cells, but those are in your gut. When serotonin receptors are affected it can cause changes to perception, a distortion of time and space and even hallucinations. Class S subjects seem to enjoy getting lost in fantasy, seeing things that aren't really there."

She remembers the flower lady and the shimmering lights: They were interesting, but not something she'd want to see every day.

"Most subjects report some activity in all three areas, especially when they first try transferon. But with repeated exposure, one particular class of response tends to dominate their experience."

Celan gazes up at the brain, attempting to process all this information.

"So," she says finally, "if these feelings all come from chemicals normally in our brains, why is there anything wrong with them?"

Her father gives her a stern look. "There's nothing wrong with them when they occur naturally. They serve evolutionary purposes – to help us avoid pain and increase pleasure. If you touch a flame, it hurts, right?"

"Yes."

"So you learn not to do it again. But if you're hungry and you eat something, you feel good. So you learn to enjoy food, which helps you to grow and thrive."

She considers this. "But transing helps people, too. It helps them live outside. And heal."

Her father shifts his weight impatiently. "They may *think* it's helping them. In the long run though, it is actually doing them some very serious harm."

She must still look doubtful because he presses on aggressively. "When feelings like excitement or euphoria occur due to normal stimuli they serve to help us make sense out of life – to qualify experience. But repeated exposure to them through unnatural stimuli like transferon can create a state of mental and emotional weakness and imbalance. Eventually, the brain can even become reliant upon these unnatural stimuli for enjoyment. And that can be dangerous.

"That can lead," he says darkly, "to an intoxic state."

"Intoxic," Celan repeats, tasting the word on her tongue. "And that's what the transers are?"

"The majority of them, yes."

Images of elders rise up in her head – flowing white robes, calm and peaceful, guiding them through their lessons. She sees Jillyanne and Lena making dinner, carving beads, traipsing with Tanny and Max through the fiesta on Liberation Day. None of them seemed weak or unbalanced, they all seemed perfectly normal.

"But what about the ones in the ranchos? Are they intoxic, too?" she asks.

"Well, we don't really have much contact with them, do we?"

"Not in person. But you have drones. You can watch them and see."

Theodore clears his throat uncomfortably. "The drones have an unfortunate tendency to malfunction in ranchos airspace."

This makes her a tiny bit exultant. The elders must know about the drones, must be shorting them out somehow.

Ha, she thinks, *you don't know everything*.

But her father doesn't seem to notice her giddy dissent. He continues briskly, "However, extrapolating from the transers we do see, many of whom, like Mair Tyras, came here from the ranchos, it is highly likely that they are as intoxic as their compatriots on Transway."

The mention of her mother sobers her immediately.

"But they don't really transfuse over there," she mutters lamely, "most of them."

"It's not the method of administration that matters so much as the repeated exposure to the intoxic substance. Admittedly, the 'fusers' are in the extreme, but they are just most drastic example of the harm that occurs to all long-term consumers of transferon, whether they are aware of it or not."

Celan says nothing, avoiding his gaze as he clicks off the brain and steps up next to her at the observation window.

"Watch them," Theodore says, "and you'll see what I mean. Look at that one, she's obviously suffering from CERS - Class E Reaction Syndrome."

He points out through the window and Celan reluctantly directs her attention to where a thin, nervous woman stands with shaking hands smoothing a shabby dress. She looks ill and exhausted. A short, blonde tech directs the woman to an odd silver chair in the corner of the room. She sits and it reclines backward slightly as she places her palms on the hand rests.

Another tech hands her a transfer, which she cups lovingly as she closes her eyes, concentrating. After a minute, she opens them and hesitantly passes him the vial. He unscrews the cap and squeezes the bulb so that a few drops of transferon fall on the face of his server. Then he returns the dropper to the woman's trembling hands.

She rolls up her sleeve and Celan finds she has to look away. When she plucks up her nerve and looks back it is as if a storm has passed. The woman's eyes are placid and she's stopped shaking, but there's a funny expression on her face like someone hit her on the head with something heavy.

The tech says something to the woman, but she doesn't seem to hear him. He repeats it – once, twice. He must be telling her to get up, because finally she struggles to her feet and staggers over to a bench where she collapses, head lolling vacantly to one side.

A sliver of shame pierces Celan's gut.

Is that what I looked like?

Watching this grotesquerie play out makes her want to run out of the room, but she finds that she's transfixed. Suddenly, the transer's head snaps up and her eyes grope along the one-way mirrored wall until they come to rest on Celan's. It's like the woman can somehow see through the glass and straight into her soul. Celan shudders, feigning absorption in her server.

I'm not like that, she thinks, tapping feverishly at the screen. *I'm Lana Timanti. My father's a Lead SocEn. I'm not a transer, not an expro.*

She's a tech.

I'm not like them. And I never will be.